MW01104637

# DON'T LOOK BACK
## The Kluskus Trail

### By
### Faye Cyr

PRESS

*Don't Look Back*
*The Kluskus Trail*
by Faye Cyr

Printed in the United States of America

ISBN 978-1-60477-118-3

Edited by Don Cyr and Darcy Nybo.
Thanks to Hugh Cyr, Wendy Letwinetz, Neil Elder and Mark Leiman for their expertise and advice.

Unless otherwise indicated, Bible quotations are taken from the New Living Translation, New Life Study Bible, Copyright © 1996 by Tyndale House Publishers, Inc., Wheaton, Illinois, and The Holy Bible, the New International Version, Copyright © 1985 by Holman Bible Publishers, Nashville, Tennessee.

The story, characters and names used in this book are fictitious.

www.xulonpress.com

I would like to dedicate this book to my mother. Her faith, courage and wisdom have guided the paths of five children, thirteen grandchildren and six great-grandchildren. God bless you, mom.

For Kalem

# FORWARD

Little has been published about the unprecedented appre-
hensions of seventy-two children in Quesnel, BC the
fall of 1997. The bustling community of 25,000 was more
preoccupied by the business of supplying two world-class
pulp mills and seven sawmills with timber, the U.S. softwood
tariff dispute, and confirming reports that a beetle infestation
was posed to destroy staggering numbers of the spruce and
pine trees in the region.

The office of Family and Children Services was facing
its own crisis. Pleas for help from single teenage mothers,
the disabled and unemployed with families who couldn't
afford nutritious food, rent, and electricity were unrelenting.
Serving the unique needs of the Nazko First Nations People
transitioning into the city was equally daunting.

Supervision, follow-up and reporting were inadequate.
Communication on several planes suffered. Finally, when
communication with Aboriginal Family Support Worker,
Roberta Headrick broke down, she complained to the Chief.
This voice would be heard.

Within days, the B.C. government ordered an audit of
the office, its procedures and the clients. Approximately two
dozen social workers from around the province were sent

to reestablish communication and screen each family for children at risk. When they were finished, twenty-three First Nations and forty-nine other children were placed in foster care.

The supply of local foster homes was quickly exhausted. Foster homes in the neighboring cities of Prince George, Williams Lake and Vanderhoof were also filled. Hotels were used to temporarily shelter children. Siblings were separated and many parents didn't have a clue where their children were.

It took months to teach the new staff how to handle the special needs of the community. Eventually, all but five children were returned to their families, according to Headrick. Their whereabouts is still unknown. They may have eloped from the system.

New initiatives were gradually implemented to deal with some of the city's most pressing social problems. A government-sponsored daycare program was started to help teenage mothers return to school. A satellite college/university campus brought post-secondary education closer to home. Career counselors were hired to assist confused high school graduates with career choices and help the unemployed to find jobs.

In 2007, Quesnel Family Services is again under tremendous strain. Budget restraints and social evolution have created an almost unbearable workload.

---

One of the finest examples of human kindness I've ever observed was the three elderly women from Nazko who visited their First Nations family and friends in the Quesnel hospital. They came many times during the twenty years I lived in Quesnel. This story would not have been written without their inspiration.

# CHAPTER ONE

# THE ROCKING CHAIR

It was a sight they would never forget; their seventy- year old grandmother rocking in her rocking chair beside the antique woodstove, contently humming and twisting brightly colored yarn about her twisted fingers, her floral print dress and buttoned navy cardigan stretched across her rounded waist with baggy woolen grey socks down at her swollen ankles.

Pausing to nudge the drugstore spectacles back above the bridge of her flattish nose, she would take a long delicious slurp from her dainty porcelain teacup, unaware that their obese orange tabby cat was wagging his tail beneath her rocking chair.

From the loft bedroom of their grandmother's log house, fourteen-year old Tyler Chantyman and his thirteen-year old brother, Chester, lay on their stomachs peering at her through cracks in the plank floor, giggling in hysterics. How they longed to witness the marvelous consequences of a missed rhythm: the blood-curdling "Yeowl" of the cat, the teacup and its contents, two knitting needles and miles of unraveling yarn, all in mid-air. In their estimation, no academy performance could compare to it and if it were left to them, they would lay awake all night waiting for it.

Their grandmother, however, had her own ideas. Every night, at nine thirty, when she had had enough of the two boisterous teenagers, Tilda Chantyman would send them upstairs to bed so she could enjoy a few minutes of peace and quiet by herself. Yes, she expected them to pound each other a while longer, laugh and cry. When it dragged on past ten, she would bellow up at them in her crossest Carrier voice, "Go to sleep, stupid kids!"

If that didn't stop the shenanigans, she would hobble to the round, lace-covered table in the centre of the kitchen and dim the oil lamp sitting on it so they couldn't see her. But it never worked; they couldn't go to sleep until she did.

Tonight, as she headed for the lamp, she appeared unsteady, as though her legs would barely hold her up. The past few months she had become weaker. They had noticed her limping, occasionally using a stick to steady herself along the dirt path around the house, but nothing like this. After she had dimmed the lamp, and started wobbling back to her chair, she suddenly gave a muffled cry and collapsed on the wooden floor with a sickening thud.

Scrambling to the loft railing, they strained to see what had happened. In the flickering glow of the woodstove, all they could make out was two still moccasined feet directly below them. They mounted the banister and rode it to the bottom, though their grandmother had scolded them about it nearly every day of the five years they had lived with her. "You'll break your necks or get burned on that stove," she would holler at them, shaking her finger. And they had come close to proving her right many times.

As they knelt beside her, her face and lips were an ashen color. A stream of bright red blood, from a tiny cut on her left temple, trickled onto the steel-gray braid coiled beneath her head. Air puffed from the drooping corner of her mouth.

The vacant bewildered expression in her eyes questioned whether she was truly seeing at all.

"Let's see if we can roll her onto her back, maybe sit her up," suggested Tyler.

When they lifted her shoulders, her floppy legs untwisted and thudded to the floor. She cried out in pain and feebly swung at them with her left arm. The right one hung lifelessly from the shoulder. Guessing a broken arm was the problem, they gently repositioned it next to her body, expecting her to wince or cry out. But there was no response.

"Something is wrong," said Tyler. "I mean seriously wrong. We need help."

"I'll get a pillow for her head," said Chester, dashing up the stairs. A minute later, he returned with not only his pillow but all the bedding from their double bed. "Nothin' but the best for our atsoo," he said clumsily lifting and rolling her head from side to side, positioning the pillow under it. Atsoo was what most Carrier children called their grandmothers.

Before they lived with their grandmother, they had lived with their mother, Lizzie, in a faded blue one-bedroom house next to Tilda's on the Nazko First Nations Reserve, a hundred kilometers west of Quesnel, BC. Their father, Tilda's son, had tragically died in a car accident on the Nazko highway on his way home from town a few months after Chester was born. From the tracks, the RCMP suspected he had fallen asleep at the wheel. Tyler vaguely recalled his tall slender form but neither boy really had any memories of him. All they had been told about him was that he had been a very kind, handsome man who had left a hole in their mother's heart that could never be filled by anyone else.

Five years later when her agony and depression began to lift, she started to complain about life on the reserve. She said there was nothing to do on the reserve except watch videos and kids. She and Tilda would argue about her moving to Quesnel with the kids so she could find a job and start a new life. Tilda's side of it was Quesnel was no place for two young Carrier boys. "They'll forget the traditional ways," she'd say. "End up on drugs, and in trouble with the police."

Then one night, after Lizzie had had too much to drink, they got into it again. She ran out the door screaming and crying that she couldn't take it anymore - said she'd be back for the kids. That was five years ago. Now the only time they saw their mother was when Tilda took them to town with her to buy groceries - once a month.

Tilda, like many First Nations women over thirty, became the mother and single parent to her grandchildren. In her modest stable home, she provided an ample supply of hugs and scolding, clothing and spending money. She sat with them at night when they were sick or afraid, wrote notes and discussed learning problems with their teachers, watched their softball games and school concerts. She was everything to them and there wasn't a thing they wouldn't do for her.

"What's wrong with her?" Chester shivered with fright.

"I once saw this in a movie," replied Tyler. "An old man was mowing the lawn. Suddenly, he keeled over and passed out on this huge pile of leaves. When he came to, he was staring up at the sky. He couldn't talk or move one side of his body. When the ambulance came, the paramedics said he had had a strike or something. Whatever it was, it must have been pretty bad because when they left, they were in an awful hurry. The lights were on and the sirens blaring."

"How are we going to get an ambulance to come way out here?" asked Chester. "It's ten o'clock Sunday night in the middle of a January snowstorm. There's got to be ten inches of snow on the road. Who in his right mind is going to come all the way out here for one sick old lady? Maybe if it was for a big accident and there were four or five people they would come."

"Don't be stupid, Chester. They pick up only one person all the time. Besides, we have a much bigger problem than getting her to the hospital right now. Yesterday, when I was at Jenz's store, I overheard a woman telling Mr. Jenz that the government had sent twenty social workers to Quesnel to take kids away from their parents if they couldn't afford to look after them. She said one woman lost five kids. If we take her to the hospital they might take us away too."

Jenz Supermarket was considered downtown Nazko. You could mail a parcel, fill up your gas tank, buy a few basic groceries, rent a new release video, or sit down at one of the two tables and have a cup of coffee - catch up on the latest news about Quesnel and the other two hundred residents of Nazko.

"What are we going to do then?"

"I don't know. But I know someone who might. You stay here and watch Atsoo while I run to Tonya's. Maybe she can help. I sure wished we had a phone."

Everyone in the Nazko Valley longed for the day when the government would run the telephone and cable lines. The region had been serviced with electricity and running water for twenty years, but still waited for telephone and cablevision. "Any day now," they kept promising. In the meantime, appointments, business and personal information could only be exchanged in one of two ways, on the radio twice a day, or by word of mouth.

Fourteen-year-old Tonya Clement was Tyler's best friend. She lived with her parents and ten-year old brother in a house next to the reserve dispensary. Her father was one of two RCMP officers in the village and her mother ran the dispensary: a two-room cabin with a doctor's office and a waiting room. Once a month, when the doctor from Quesnel held a clinic, she reminded people about their appointments and assisted him. Sometimes she weighed newborn babies or changed bandages. The people who usually came were mothers who had young children with sore throats or elderly people that needed their blood pressure checked and prescriptions reordered. Though she wasn't an actual nurse, Tonya's mother had looked after lots of sick people in their homes. In her dining room was a cabinet full of thick medical books and health magazines.

Not wasting time for a toque and winter boots, Tyler pulled on his light ski jacket, leaving it unzipped, and sprint the two fields with its cross-pole fences, between his place and Tonya's. He had flown over those fences so many times he was sure he could do it in his sleep.

When he reached the Clements he was shaking and out of breath. Frantically, he banged on the back door, hoping to calm himself and catch his breath, in case one of her parents answered.

"Tyler!" startled Mrs. Clement, flipping on the porch light and opening the door. "What are you doing out this late?"

"Please, could I speak to Tonya, Mrs. Clement?" he puffed. "It's urgent. I forgot my science textbook at school and we're having a big test tomorrow." Tyler felt badly about lying. His grandmother had taught him that God didn't like it when we lied. But he hoped God would understand and forgive him this once.

In a few seconds, Tonya came to the door. "Hey, Tyler that test isn't until next Monday."

"Shhhh! I know, I know," he whispered forcefully, waving his bare hands to get her to be quiet. "I had to tell her that so I could talk to you. I didn't think she would let me unless I had a good reason. Something's wrong with Tilda. I think she's had a strike. She can't speak or move one of her arms."

"She's had a what?"

"Shhhh! A strike! It might be serious and I don't want anyone to find out or they might take us away."

"What in the world are you talking about, Tyler Chantyman?"

"Let me in and I'll tell you. If we can find out what's wrong, maybe we can figure out what to do and look after her ourselves."

"Okay! Okay! Come in. Take off your," she said, suddenly noticing his feet. "Tyler, where are your boots? There must be a foot of new snow out there. Aren't you cold?"

He shook the fluffy snow from his damp moccasins and placed them neatly inside the house then tiptoed into the living room after Tonya. "Mom," called Tonya, "Can I borrow one of your medical books?"

"Just make sure you put it back in the right spot this time. And remember to put the key in the drawer where you're finished."

"Yes, Momma."

They unlocked the glass bookcase where the prized books had been meticulously arranged. Gingerly, they retrieved the volume with the S-T letters embossed on its spine and lay it, ever-so-carefully, on Tonya's mother's favorite piece of furniture; the Lemon-Pledged-to-death red mahogany dining room table. When half of the massive text accidentally fell open, slamming the table, everyone gasped. Tonya's father looked up from his newspaper, over his reading glasses and cleared his throat. Her mother warned, "Take it easy."

They flipped through the pages until they reached the STRs, then, line by line; they combed the rest of the page. They could find *stroke*, but not strike.

"This is it," Tyler whispered excitedly. "No speech, one-sided weakness. It's called a stroke."

Positioning the book between them so they could both see it, Tonya read, "A stroke occurs when blood flow to the brain is interrupted by a clot or hemorrhage. Symptoms may include facial drooping, difficulty swallowing, one-sided weakness. Immediate medical intervention may prevent permanent damage and possibly death."

"This is it. This is what the ambulance guys in the movie called it, a stroke. I was afraid of this." Tyler said. "She's had a stroke and needs to go to a hospital."

"What's so bad about that?"

"When I was in Jenz store yesterday I overheard a woman telling old man Jenz that the government had sent twenty new social workers to Quesnel to take kids away from their parents. If they didn't have enough food in the house or couldn't look after their kids properly, a social worker and the RCMP would come to the house and take the kids away. Kids are getting dumped into foster homes with strangers all over the place. I don't want that to happen to us."

Just then, Tonya's mother peered over their shoulders.

"What are you looking for?" she asked.

"Nothing in particular; just looking up something for an assignment at school," replied Tonya.

"Sure is nice to see you two taking such an interest in your school work."

Tonya shoved the heavy book back into its slot, then locked the cabinet, and returned the key to the drawer before she and Tyler scurried to the backdoor.

"We're really scared, Tonya. What should we do?"

"Don't worry. I'll think of something and see you in the morning. In the meantime, turn her on her side and keep her warm."

When Tyler got back to the house, all the lights were on and Chester was kneeling over Tilda, wiping the blood and sweat off her face with a damp facecloth. Somehow, he had managed to swaddle her with the quilt off their bed so that she looked like an Egyptian mummy.

"She still can't speak," he said, "and she chokes on water. I don't think she can swallow properly."

Wanting to see for himself, Tyler lifted her head and cautiously trickled a teaspoon of water into her parted lips. She coughed and sputtered until her face turned purple. "You're right," he said. "She can't swallow. This isn't good. She can't drink and we have no way of getting fluids into her. Animals die when they get like this. People can't be that much different. This is going to be tougher than I thought."

Then Chester thought of another problem: "What are we going to do if she has to go to the bathroom? What if she goes – you know? How are we going to clean her? She'd kill us if we saw her; if we changed her clothes."

"Don't be stupid, Chester. If she goes, we'll have to change her. There's nobody else. Besides, she may not have to. She didn't drink all of her tea and that's probably all she's had since supper. Help me turn her onto her side. Tonya said we're supposed to keep her on her side. I'm not sure why, but if she says so, it must be right. We'll leave her here tonight and in the morning, when Tonya comes over, we'll lift her into bed."

They rolled her onto her side, supporting her back with pillows and padding her behind with bath towels. Then they hauled the bedding from her bed to the living room so they could build beds on the floor next to her to keep her warm.

Tilda's quilt, like many others she had sewn, was a work of art. Shortly after moving to her place, she began to work on one for their bed. For weeks, she tediously stitched hundreds of multi-colored print triangles into a collage of pinwheels, stars, diamonds and birds. Every spare minute she had went into the project, until her fingers were raw and bleeding. Even then, she hated to put it down. She said winter was coming and they would need their quilt when the temperature dropped to forty below.

Satisfied that she was comfortable, Tyler zigzagged across the bedding to the light switch by the back door and turned it off. Tilda had always preferred the tranquility of a dimly lit room. "Electricity is one of the greatest blessings to the Nazko Valley," they had often heard her say. "Lights, refrigerators, electric stoves, washing machines and radios make life on the reserve so much easier." But in the evening, after the sun had set, she loved to turn off the electric lights and light the tiny oil lamp on the table. She said its soft glow reminded her of when she was a girl and times were simpler, when people took time for one another and families spent time together.

She loved to tell them about the salmon runs in the summertime when her aunts and uncles, cousins and grand-parents camped in tents in the open field across the Fraser River from the village of Quesnel. "Everyone worked hard," she would say. "In the daytime, the men and older boys speared and netted countless numbers of fish. Then the women cleaned, filleted, salted and dried the catch on raised wooden racks or in moss-covered stick smokehouses."

"The children had chores too. The older children were supposed to mind the younger ones. Girls were responsible for picking and preparing berries. Soapberries had to be mashed into ointments. Wild strawberries, raspberries and blueberries had to be dried in the sun so they could be stored for winter. The boys had to collect enough firewood to keep the fires burning day and night so the meals could be cooked on time and predators like black bears and cougars kept away from the camp."

"In the evening, when the day's work was done, as the lowering sun painted a kaleidoscope of mauves and oranges on the western sky, everyone sat around the campfire for a feast of savory roast salmon, golden cornmeal cakes and juicy sweet berries. After dinner, while the women put away the leftovers and older children fed the dogs, they would sing hymns to the Creator and songs of the trail. Laughing children and barking river-soaked dogs chased through the crowd until they collapsed."

"Later, when it was quieter, after the little ones had been tucked into bed, the older children would sit patiently by the crackling fire, with their chins in their hands and flames dancing in their wide eyes. They were waiting for the thrilling details of the latest pursuit and capture of some trap-robbing varmint."

Tyler lay on his back with his arms crossed under his head, staring up at the rafters of the sixty-year old log house. He wondered what they'd say if they could speak. Would they say his grandparents had been happy here? He had never met his grandfather though he felt he knew him to some degree because Tilda talked about him all the time. "Thomas liked his potatoes fried this way or Thomas wore his belt that way." He guessed he had been a kind man, a good husband and father. His grandmother certainly thought so.

Then he thought about his own father. Had he been happy? Had he been a good son, obedient to his parents? Did he love fishing and hunting? Did he have a dog? Did he ever have a crush on the girl next door?

From the ceiling, his gaze turned to the living room window where the snow was twirling and tumbling in the blue white glow of the streetlight. On a snowy night, it was his favorite pass time. He loved to slip downstairs after everyone was asleep, lie on the couch, nestled in a blanket, and watch the falling snow. He wondered if his father had enjoyed this too, or if there was even a streetlight when he lived here. He wondered what his father would have done tonight. Would he have risked the life of his mother? His thoughts seemed to be swirling faster than the snowflakes outside.

"You okay, Ches?" he called. "Do you have enough blankets?"

"Oh yeah; this is kind of cool actually." Then it was quiet. Tyler thought Chester had fallen asleep. Suddenly he mumbled, "How long do you think she's going to be sick?

What if she's still sick in the morning when we have to go to school?"

"We might have to miss a day or two of school. Hopefully, she'll be better in the morning," he replied then fell asleep.

The next day, Tyler was awakened by Tilda humming in his ear. At first, he couldn't figure out why she sounded so close then he remembered where he was and why he was there. He rolled over to see her, crunching his elbows and hips on the wooden floor. She lay on her back, smiling with a crooked mouth, at the snowflakes dancing by the window. There wasn't a hint of pain or worry on her round flushed face.

"Atsoo," Tyler whispered, trying not to wake Chester. "How do you feel?"

Like the question had been spoken in a foreign language, she didn't respond. The same puzzled look came over her face as it had the night before. A few seconds later, she managed a "Gggg."

"We think you've had a stroke. That's why you can't speak or move your right arm."

Despite the whispering, Chester awoke. "I thought I was having a bad dream," he yawned. Rubbing his eyes, he saw her lying there between them and groaned. "I wished I was asleep. Then he reluctantly asked, "Are you still sick, Atsoo?"

"I'm afraid she is," Tyler replied. "But she does seem a bit better."

With that, she wiggled the toes of her right foot, which she wasn't able to do the night before. "Did you see that?" beamed Chester. "She couldn't do that last night. She could move her left arm and leg but not the right ones. Now, she can move the right foot. Can you move your right arm, Atsoo?" he urged her excitedly. But the command went unheeded. "That's okay, Atsoo. Maybe in a few hours it'll start to work again."

"We've got to put her into her bed," Tyler said.

"Maybe we could lay her on the couch so she can watch TV."

"No, Ches. If somebody comes to the door, they'll see how sick she is and we'll have a lot of explaining to do. We'll cover the mattress with plastic bags, pull her over to the bed on a blanket and lift her in."

"How on earth are we going to do that? She must weigh as much as a horse," Chester kipped.

"Chester!"

Just then, there was an impatient rapping on the front door. Through the two frosted windowpanes in the upper half of the door, Tyler recognized Tonya's hooded winter parka. It startled them because she usually came to the back door. She was dressed for school with a lunch bag and textbook in her gloved hands. When he flung open the door, he heaved a huge sigh of relief, "Whew it's you!"

"Who'd you think it was, silly, the police?"

"I don't know. We just can't afford to take any chances. What are you doing coming to the front door anyway?"

To repay him for his irritable greeting, she ignored him. "How's your atsoo this morning?" she asked, kicking her boots off and laying her coat and books on the couch next to the door. Then she knelt on the floor beside the elderly woman. Combing loose strands of hair to the side of her face, Tonya laid the back of her hand against the warm cheek.

"Wow, she's hot. I think she might have a temperature. Have you got a thermometer?"

Chester ran to the kitchen cupboard where the medicines were kept and brought back a glass thermometer. Tonya put it under Tilda's arm then watched the clock for three minutes. When the time was up, she lifted the thermometer to the light and scanned the slender glass tube for the end of the silver line.

"Hmm," she squinted. It looks like 38 degrees. That's up a little - nothing serious, yet. Mom says people sometimes get temperatures when they get a little dry - when they haven't had enough to drink. When did she last have something to drink?"

Over tired and defensive, Chester lashed out, "We tried to get her to drink last night, but she nearly choked to death. So we gave up!"

"Chester," snapped Tyler, "she's just trying to help. You don't have to rip her head off."

"Well she acts like we don't know anything."

The expression on Tonya's face suddenly changed from concern to hurt. Tears welling up in her eyes, she turned away and sniffled.

"Don't worry about him, Tonya," said Tyler, wrapping an arm around her shoulder and glaring at Chester. "He doesn't mean anything by it. It's just that he's really scared and he hasn't had his beating yet today. We think she's had about half a cup of tea since supper last night."

"Has she gone to the bathroom yet?"

"Luckily, not yet," Tyler replied. "We hope she does that while you're here."

Having said that, Tilda began to, "g..gg.ggg." and fidget on the floor. Repeatedly, she twisted the good leg from side to side. "I wonder if she's got to go to the bathroom, now." "Do you have to go to the bathroom, Tilda?"

Tilda whimpered then started to weep.

"Bring me some newspapers and old towels, right away," ordered Tonya.

"There are towels under her," replied Chester, trying harder not to offend her.

"Then, bring me some newspapers!" she demanded. "And hurry!"

He bolted to the wooden bin beside the stove where the firewood and discarded newspapers were kept. Tilda always had lots of store flyers in the house. She loved to study them at great length and tweak her monthly shopping list which could include anything from a mousetrap to the usual five hundred dollars worth of groceries. She insisted the time to do your shopping was *before* you went to the store.

Jabbering away, Tonya casually removed the dampened towel the boys had padded her with the night before then she spread the new towel and some newspaper on the floor and they rolled Tilda onto them. "We'll have to wash the towels. But the newspaper can be burned. That's what we did when our dog, Twister got too old to go outside," she said. "Of course that only happened a few times before my dad shot him."

Tyler and Chester began to giggle. "What's so funny about that?" she asked.

Tyler led her a few feet away and whispered, "You should be more careful when you talk about shooting things when they get old," he said nodding towards his grandmother. All of a sudden, it registered and her face turned beet red.

"Are you going to school today, Tonya?" inquired Tyler, "because if you are, you're walking. The school bus just drove by."

"In that case, I guess I'm staying here."

"How's that going to look if all of us are away from school?" said Chester.

"They'll probably just think there's a bad flu going around school again and that we have it," replied Tyler. "Forget about it. Let's get her into bed."

They lined the mattress with a layer of black plastic garbage bags they found under the kitchen sink and a layer of newspaper. Then they covered them with some freshly laundered flannelette sheets Tyler found in the bathroom cupboard and Tilda's exquisite tan and peach floral quilt. When it was made, the bed looked comfortable and inviting. The rest of the room tidied, they prepared for the transfer.

They rolled Tilda onto a blanket and the boys pulled her to the side of the bed.

"Okay," said Tyler. "It's time. Chester, you take her feet. I'll take her head and Tonya; you support her in the middle. When I count to three, we'll lift. Is everyone ready? One... Two...Three... LIFT!" It went off without a hitch.

# CHAPTER TWO

# SCHEMING

With their grandmother safely in bed, they started the morning chores. Tyler threw on his grey fleece hoodie and hiking boots and headed outside to restock the firewood box while Chester lugged the bedding back upstairs, made the bed and tidied their room. Each week they alternated chores because the one who made the bed also had to do supper dishes.

Tilda was very strict about chores - particularly the morning chores. If soiled clothing was found in the closet or under the bed instead of being put into the hamper, or the firewood box wasn't full, they weren't allowed to come to the table for breakfast, which usually included their favorite food - toasted homemade white bread and raspberry jam. As much as they loved toast and jam, it seemed neither of them was accustomed to doing chores without at least two prompts. It was a little unsettling this morning to find they were doing their chores without being nagged. It was as if they had instantly grown up and missed the rest of their childhood.

She certainly badgered them all right - about everything from belching out loud to sniffling instead of blowing their noses. But she was very proud of them too. Despite her guarded infrequent praise, they often overheard her telling her friends at Jenz or Safeway, how good the boys were. She gushed about their schoolteachers' glowing accolades of how polite they were. Her eyes beamed as she boasted about how much firewood they could carry up the back steps, and how handsome they were becoming.

Her comments about his looks embarrassed Chester. He felt anything but good-looking. His tightly cropped charcoal black hair was too wavy to brush the way he liked. Instead of lying neatly across his brow, his bangs invariably curled up like a snow shovel waiting for the next blizzard. Equally frustrating was his height. He was half a head shorter than Tyler and he could stare his atsoo straight in the eye. He, like her, needed a stool to reach the second shelf of the kitchen cupboards. Whenever he bought a new pair of jeans, at least six inches had to be lopped off the legs and they were always uncomfortably tight around his waist and seat. He didn't hide it; he loved Pepsi, chocolate bars and Cheezies.

Tyler and Tonya were the same height, five foot five inches, wore pencil thin blue jeans and were enviably attractive. His raven black jaw length hair swept about his tan face and almond shaped dark brown eyes. His well-developed shoulders and long muscular arms looked almost too mature for a fourteen year old.

Tonya's sweaters and jeans clung to her slender curvy body, capturing the attention of the older boys in the school. Her biggest beef with her appearance, despite her captivating light brown eyes, ivory skin and lustrous, ebony shoulder length hair, were her glasses. When she looked in the mirror, the only thing she saw was those two ugly brass rings around her eyes.

Along with the glasses, came the vexation of poor reading comprehension. To unravel the meaning of a sentence with three and four syllable words generally required numerous readings. Many a time, she had to stop mid-sentence, put down the blasted textbook and hunt through her pocket dictionary for the meaning of a word. Man how she hated that. She could read well, if she wanted to - if she slowed down and thought about what she was reading. But she was always in a hurry to get through her schoolwork so she could hang out with her friends outside and her impatience cost her dearly. No matter how hard she crammed the night before, the best she could muster on an exam was seventy-six percent. She could outrun anyone in school but the top mark in the class was never on her test paper.

Tyler and Chester also struggled in school. It was difficult for them to sit quietly and listen for longer than five minutes. After that, a picture on the classroom wall or a bird sitting on a branch outside the window distracted them and they often missed half the lesson or the home assignment. They read poorly too, but for a different reason than Tonya.

A few months after Tyler and Chester came to live with Tilda, a pretty lady with blonde curly hair and long purple fingernails met with them in the school library. At first, she talked to them individually, asking them a lot of strange questions like; "Did they know much about their parents, had anyone ever touched them inappropriately, did they like school, to which they both emphatically replied, "NO!" Then they wrote a test which seemed to take hours.

The next day, while they waited on a bench in the hall outside the principal's office, they overheard the lady tell their teachers and Tilda that they had mild forms of Fetal Alcohol Syndrome. Along with short attention span and hyperactivity, she explained, they might, one day, display more serious behavior problems such as impulsiveness, violent outbursts of temper, irresponsibility with money and a preoccupation with girls. The part about the girls didn't sound so bad.

While the boys finished their chores, Tonya set the table for breakfast with three bowls and three spoons and an unopened box of Cocoa Puffs she spotted at the back of a crowded shelf in the cupboard. Reaching for the milk in the fridge, she noticed a calendar pinned to the wall with the approaching Wednesday and Friday circled by a red highlighter.

"Why are these days circled on the calendar, Tyler?" called Tonya as he disappeared through the back door for the fourth armful of firewood.

"I don't know. I'll be right back."

When he returned, he stomped the snow from his boots, crossed the kitchen floor to pile the last of the firewood onto the already brimming wood box. He pulled off his snowy sawdust-covered work gloves, lifted the calendar from the wall and studied the dates and the mini-messages scribbled around the perimeter. For a minute, he stared at it blankly. Then he gasped.

"Oh no! The doctor is coming on Wednesday. Atsoo always goes to the clinic so he can check her blood pressure. What's he going to think when she doesn't show up?"

"Maybe she'll be better by then," said Tonya.

"What if she's not?" Tyler looked worried.

"Maybe we should get him to come and see her."

"I don't think we can risk it," said Tyler. "I'm sure he'd tell Social Services."

"What if she dies - can we risk that? You'd get taken away from her anyway."

"You're right, Tonya. She needs help - just not here. We've got to take her somewhere where she can be looked after and we won't be discovered."

Catching bits of the conversation from the loft, Chester thundered excitedly down the hollow wooden stairs and slid sideways across the glossy plank floor to within inches of them. With a mischievous gleam in his eyes he breathlessly blurted out, "I know what we can do!"

"I definitely don't like the look on your face, Chester Chantyman," said Tonya.

"What day does the doctor fly into Kluskus?" asked Chester.

Kluskus was another Carrier reserve located about fifty kilometers west of Nazko. Many of the Nazko Carriers were related to those in Kluskus but because the road was so unpredictable, they seldom visited. A few kilometers past Nazko, the paved highway dwindled to one of the most notorious bush roads in the northern BC interior called the Kluskus Trail. Passable only to 4x4s, ATVs or snowmobiles, in January when the ground was frozen, the trip could take as little as eight hours. In the spring and summer, when the rivers and marshes were flooding, it wasn't uncommon to hear a crossing had taken days or a week. It was said the people of Kluskus wanted it that way because the reserve was situated on the famous Alexander Mackenzie Trail and they were afraid an influx of tourists might spoil their tranquil lifestyle.

"You're not actually considering taking Tilda to Kluskus are you?" asked Tonya.

"Tilda's sister lives there," said Chester. "Maybe she can look after her until she gets better. The social workers will never find us out there. Their wimpy new vehicles would never make it."

The three sat around the table crunching on Coco Puffs, staring into his or her own bowl, silently brainstorming a way to sneak Tilda off the reserve.

"We could ride your horse Tonya, and drag her behind on a sled," suggested Chester.

"If we do that, my parents will wonder where my horse went."

"We'll have to pull her on a toboggan ourselves," stated Tyler.

"That's a stupid idea. With all the new snow, it'll take forever. Do you know how far that is?" protested Chester.

"Why don't you shut-up, Chester! It's not a stupid idea." With lightning reaction, he pounded Chester's right upper arm, sending a paralyzing pain from his shoulder to his hand. He hated Chester second-guessing him, especially in front of Tonya.

Chester clutched his arm above the elbow, unsuccessfully squelching a whimper and flow of tears. He felt like such a fool crying in front of Tonya. He had a huge crush on her. He knew he didn't have a chance as long as Tyler was around but he lived with the hope that one day he might somehow impress her and win her. Crying would not advance his cause.

Now he was mad. All he could think about was getting even. He grabbed Tyler by the hair and smashed the side of his face onto the table. In a desperate attempt to free himself, Tyler swung blindly, knocking the cereal bowls and their contents off the table and all over the floor.

"STOP IT! Stop it, right now!" yelled Tonya, jumping to her feet, hands on her hips. "If you two don't grow up, I'm going home and you'll be doing this on your own."

She stomped to the back door, grabbed the broom and thrust it at Tyler. Then she yanked the dripping dishcloth from the sink and plastered it to Chester's face.

They were shocked. Chester wiped his face with his shirtsleeve, quickly got down on his knees and started corralling the soggy cereal into a bowl. Never at a loss for words for too long, under his breath he muttered, "You're right, Tonya. He's not worth the trouble."

Hearing the crack, Tyler shaved the top of his brother's head with a glancing blow of the broom and retorted, "We've got more important things to think about right now you moron, than how much we hate each other."

"Will you two, be quiet! We're never going to pull this thing off if we don't work together," barked Tonya. Their fights infuriated her so much. Every time the three of them were together, it came to this. Why did she even bother?

After the mess had been cleaned up, the three of them sat around the table, chins on folded arms, silently nursing their grudges for what felt like hours. Finally, Tonya sat up straight.

"First of all, we have to consider how far it is. My dad says it takes seven to eight hours to drive it in the winter. I doubt we could walk it in a day - that means it will take us at least two days and a sleep over. We're going to need enough supplies for two to three days and a place to sleep. Is there a warm dry place to spend the night between here and Kluskus?"

"I've heard there's an abandoned cabin near Fishpot Lake," said Tyler. "That's nearly halfway. It's probably not in the greatest shape, though. If I can find Atsoo's forestry map, it might be marked on it. Information like that is really important to her."

Tyler tore off into Tilda's bedroom where she was curled into a fetal position, snoring peacefully. He tiptoed around her bed to the antique cedar dresser and gently slid open the top drawer. It was stuffed with countless bills stamped, PAID, expired guarantees, letters from relatives, and dozens of birthday cards dating back twenty years.

He sifted through the pile of rubble until he found not only the map, but a peculiar faded black book with a zipper all the way around it. Cradling it with one hand, he unzipped it and it fell open. The pages were thin like onionskin and as delicate as silk. Darkened from years of handling, particularly along the edges, they crinkled as he turned them. Words had been underlined and notes written down the sides with red, blue and green ink. Yellowed photos and documents popped into view, including his and Chester's birth certificates.

Excited, he quietly closed the drawer and hurried back to the table. "Look what I found," he said. "It's a really neat old book with a zipper."

"That's a Bible," said Tonya. "I got one of those two years ago when I went to a church camp at Chubb Lake. It talks about God and a whole bunch of stuff. It's kind of cool, actually."

"Look at all the old letters," marveled Chester. "And here's a picture of us when we were babies with our mom."

Each of them seemed to be interested in a different aspect of the book. "Can I see it?" asked Tonya. As if it was one of her mother's cherished antique porcelain teacups, she gingerly opened it to the inside front cover. An inscription with meticulous brown handwriting, somewhat blurred by water and time read:

Congratulations Tilda,
For memorizing one hundred Bible verses.
Love your teacher and friend,
Miss. Penelope Edmunds
St. Anne's School, Dec. 1937."

"Wow, this book is seventy years old," gasped Tonya. "St. Anne's must have been the school she went to."

"Actually, it's only sixty, Tonya," interjected Tyler. "Math never was your strength."

"Yes, nor anything else at school, except maybe lunchtime and final bell," giggled Chester.

"You guys can talk. What are we going to do about school anyway? How are we going to miss school for three days without somebody getting suspicious?"

"We'll get to that," said Tyler. "First of all, we've got to figure out how we can go to Kluskus without being seen and start making the list of supplies. Then we can think up excuses for our teachers and your parents."

Tonya closed the living room curtains, so no one could see them huddled at the table. Their mission would be a covert operation, unlike any Nazko had ever seen. They turned on the kitchen lights and Tyler carefully unfurled the limp tattered map. To their amazement, the trip between Nazko and Kluskus had been outlined with blue ink. Two X's, divided the trip into thirds. The first was at Fishpot Lake, where a tiny house was drawn, and the other was between the two arms of the Coglistiko River where there was a picture of a tent. Fish of various sizes had also been drawn on rivers and lakes; the places with the better fishing, they assumed, were represented by larger fish.

Tyler was ecstatic. "It looks like there's a cabin and a campsite, if we need it."

"This should be a piece of cake," said Chester. We can camp and fish. Maybe do some ice fishing; my favorite kind of fishing."

"I'm afraid there's not going to be time for fishing this trip, Ches. We have to pack our food and get back here before anyone notices."

"There's a point. What happens when we get back? How long will it take before somebody realizes your atsoo isn't here?" asked Tonya.

"We'll figure that out when the time comes," replied Tyler. "Right now we've got to concentrate on getting her to Kluskus."

The plan seemed a bit short sighted to Tonya: Where would she tell her parents she was going for three days, or more, if there were problems? What if there was a delay caused by a snowstorm or they were attacked by starving wolves, a cougar or a grizzly? And how were they going to keep Tilda's disappearance a secret for a month or longer?

She must be out of her mind to even consider it, especially with these two. Tyler was right about one thing – Tilda did need to be looked after and not in her own house where she might be discovered. And right now, Kluskus was the only option they could think of.

Tyler took a piece of notepaper and a pencil from a pad on the kitchen counter and handed it to her. "Here, start making a list."

"Toboggan," piped up Chester.

"Wool blankets for your atsoo, sleeping bags for us," said Tonya.

"Hatchet, matches, newspaper for fires and for under atsoo," said Tyler.

"Packaged food; like miniature boxes of cereal, crackers, noodles. Oh, and dried food like beef jerky, pepperoni sticks and then apples, bananas, licorice, jujubes, chocolate bars," said Chester.

"I knew you'd do a good job with the food, Ches," said Tyler.

"Yes," agreed Tonya.

"Just remember," said Tyler. "All we have is one backpack each. Everything we need has to fit into three backpacks. That's not a lot of space."

"Just remember - all we have is one backpack each. Everything we need has to fit into three backpacks," mimicked Chester.

"C.h.e.s.t.e.r," warned Tonya. "Quit it! Don't start anything." Tyler shut his eyes and shook his head. "Let's each pack food for four days," she continued. "That should be enough for three days for the four of us and any delay. At Kluskus, we can get supplies for the trip home."

"Wow, that's a great idea, Tonya," amazed Chester and Tyler.

"Thought I couldn't do math, hey? Now all we have to do is figure out what to tell the grown-ups," said Tonya.

Again, there was a long silence around the table. Tyler picked up the calendar and studied it. "Today is Monday. The doctor comes to the dispensary on Wednesday," he said running his fingers through his hair. "Does our class have a field trip this Friday, Tonya?"

"I don't think so. I think we're watching a boring forestry film – something about the spruce and pine beetles and how they eat trees."

"Could we use the field trip as an excuse to leave for the weekend? Could we be back by Monday morning if we left on Friday morning?"

"You're crazy!" sneered Chester. "There's no way we can pull Atsoo up the Kluskus Mountain on a toboggan and be back by Monday. We'd have to walk non-stop."

"That's right, non-stop. Think about it. If we didn't sleep over anywhere, we wouldn't have to bring sleeping bags. We wouldn't have to pack food for three days. We could pack lighter and walk faster," said Tyler.

Chester and Tonya grew silent.

"It's pretty risky," said Tonya. "What happens if she gets worse or one of us gets hurt? There's no room for an error. And what am I going to tell my parents? My parents can spot a lie a mile away."

As an R.C.M.P. officer, Tonya's father, Richard Clement was trained to read facial expressions for lies. His Carrier background had also given him exceptional perception of people's character. He was always saying how much his native upbringing helped him in his work. "It's in their eyes," he'd say. "The eye is the window to the soul. If they can look you in the eye and not turn away, ninety-nine percent of the time they're telling the truth."

Natalie, her mother, had a French background. Though she couldn't speak a word of the language, she was obviously proud of her roots. French paintings and fleur-de-lis wallpaper decorated the dining room and her favorite dinner was Chicken Cordon Blue, mashed potatoes, broccoli and cheese sauce with chocolate éclairs for dessert. She too despised dishonesty. She told Tonya that while she was growing up her harshest punishment had been for lying. When she was thirteen, she told her parents she was going to a mid-week band practice at school. When they found out she had gone skating on a lake with thin ice and one of her friends nearly drowned, she was grounded for a month. She missed her first date, the Christmas Dance and her best friend's birthday party and sleepover. She was so mad at her parents she didn't speak to them for three days. But she never lied to them again.

"I don't know how I can possibly pull this off," said Tonya. "I'll have to be asleep or dead when I tell them. My eyes and my big mouth always give me away."

All was quiet until Chester blurted out, "I've got an idea." Chester wasn't good at many things, except maybe eating, but when it came to getting out of ticklish situations, he was a master. The solution, though frequently a bit shady, always made you pay attention.

"Why don't you tell them the truth? Why don't you tell them we are going to visit Tilda's sister in Kluskus for a few days and we would like you to come with us? We could tell our teachers the same thing and ask for a few days of home-work so it looks like we really care about our schoolwork."

"You know, I think it could work," admitted Tyler. "That way we're not limited to being back on a certain day."

"What if they ask us who's taking us?" said Tonya. "And what about the clinic on Wednesday?"

"I'll take her pill bottle to the doctor and show him that it's getting low and say she wants a new prescription," said Tyler. "As for the ride, tell them, Atsoo's friend, old Bill, is taking us. Ask them if you can stay at our house Wednesday night because we're going to leave early Thursday morning. It'll give us time to see the doctor, pack our supplies and leave after dark on Wednesday."

"Now, go to school and act normal. Tell the teachers everyone at our house has the flu. Say you're late because you stopped to check on us. Ask for homework – to make it look good. Then come tomorrow morning, before school, to help us with her. We should be able to manage her the rest of the day on our own."

With a generous hug of gratitude, they embraced her and she left.

# CHAPTER THREE

# THE OLD TRADING POST

The rest of Monday went smoothly. Tilda briskly opened her eyes when they spoke to her, albeit with a blank stare at first, but before she faded back into her sleepy healing world she would smile with a crooked smile. She wasn't able to roll over on her own because the right arm was still paralyzed. And they soon discovered if they changed her position more often, she moaned less. An hourly routine of leaning her forward and trickling juice or water into the normal corner of her mouth, changing the newspaper, if it needed it, then rolling her onto the other side kept her sleeping most of the time.

The night had gone equally well. At eleven o'clock, after they had watched Batman, for the second time since renting it from Jenz', they turned out the lights and went to bed. There wasn't a sound in the house until Tonya tapped on the back door about eight o'clock Tuesday morning.

She stomped the compact snow from her black leather knee-highs on the mat at the back door and let herself in. Before she could hang up her burgundy ski jacket and matching toque on one of the wooden pegs by the door, Tyler and Chester were standing in front of her. Her nose, cheeks and chin were rosy pink and her lips so numb she could barely articulate words. "Brrr... it's cold out there. It must be ten below. Woe, you guys should put some clothes on. How's your atsoo today?"

Without T-shirts, rubbing the sleep out of their eyes and shivering, they tried to hide their flannel boxers. "We don't know. We just woke up. She didn't make a sound all night," yawned Chester.

"Did you talk to your parents last night?" Tyler said stretching.

"No, I didn't have the nerve. I'll do it tonight, *for sure.*"

"Tonya, you've got to tell them!"

"I know. I know. I will tonight - I hope," she added under her breath.

The boys tore upstairs and threw on yesterday's wrinkled blue jeans and T-shirts, reeking of perspiration, and then everyone shoved into the Tilda's bedroom and stood around her bed. "Good morning, Mrs. Chantyman," called Tonya from the foot of the bed. But there was no response. Previously, bumping the bed or their noisy chatter had stimulated the flicker of an eyelid or a brief change in her breathing. This morning there was nothing but rapid shallow rattled respirations.

Tonya leaned forward and touched her forehead with the back of her chilled hand. It was incredibly warm. She knew her condition had deteriorated but she didn't have a clue what was wrong or what to do about it. The expression on her face made the others uneasy. Glancing between the boy's faces and Tilda, she tried to remember some of the things her mother said to the anxious parents of children with high fevers.

"Has she had anything to drink or gone to the bathroom since I was here?"

"She's had about a glass of apple juice and wet the newspaper once since yesterday," they replied.

"I guess that's alright. Just don't give her anything to drink until she's awake. And make sure you sit her up or it can go into her lungs - I saw that once on TV."

"I can't believe how bad she is today - sounds like there's fluid in her lungs," said Chester nervously. "I'm getting really worried." Tyler's expression reflected the same feelings. "Is there anything else we can do?"

"I'm not sure there's more anyone can do for her, but I'll look in my mom's medical books tonight when I'm doing my homework. She'll think I'm working on our science project, Tyler. I'll come better prepared tomorrow. And I will talk to my parents." A few minutes later they walked her to the back door and she left for school.

Watching Tilda and repositioning her every hour, as well as doing chores and making breakfast, made the morning disappear. By noon, they were exhausted. If something didn't change they would be burnt out by the end of the day, and there was still one more day before they left for Kluskus. A two-hour vigil, they agreed, would be more manageable. In between, they would take turns going outside, watching TV or napping so they could rest.

At two o'clock, it was Tyler's turn for a break. The pressure of the ordeal and the confinement was taking a toll. If he didn't get out of the house, he was going to snap. He put on his hooded parka and hiking boots, foregoing the gloves, and stepped onto the backdoor porch. The air was fresh - he felt alive again. It was as if he had been underwater, struggling to surface and finally made it.

He nervously scanned the neighborhood for eyes peering from behind curtains or people strolling in the fresh snow like they usually did when the sun finally came out after a winter storm. The carport roof, which ran the length of the house and a sparse grove of immature spruce and pine trees, hid him well from view.

He couldn't remember a more beautiful day. There wasn't a cloud in the sky and the dazzling snow hurt his eyes. Hoar frost lined the branches of the barren bushes. Shafts of sunlight streamed through the boughs of the snow-laden spruce trees that encircled the half-acre back yard. Off in the distance a couple of dogs bantered, no doubt about the moose bone one of them had found. It seemed like weeks since he was outside.

Beyond the grove, in the five-acre field next to Tilda's property, was the favorite hang out of every teenager on the reserve. Nestled in the stiff pale yellow billowing grasses, was a hundred meter wide circular pond. Around it was string of half-buried logs. After school and on weekends, they went there to catch up on everybody's business: who had a crush, who failed a test, who had a fight with whom. In the winter, they skated on it. In the summer, they swam in it. When nobody was around, they went there to reflect and cry. As Tyler carved a path towards it, in the foot-deep snow, he wondered if he'd ever be able to join his friends there again, the way he used to, if Tilda didn't get well.

But there was another place in the field of special interest to Tyler. Backed against the spruce and brush hillside, not far from the pond, was a weather-beaten abandoned two story log structure with a tin roof that could be seen from anywhere on the reserve – the old trading post. Tales about it had always intrigued him.

According to Tilda, it was built in the early 1800s, and had been the hub for a lucrative fur trade. Carrier and Caucasian men, alike, brought their trap line catches to the trading post in exchange for supplies. Beaver, rabbit, muskrat and fox pelts were traded then shipped to Europe, eastern Canada and the United States, where they were crafted into hats and coats for the very rich. With their credit, men bought the latest guns and hunting knives, fishing line, saws, axes, shovels, tobacco, pipes and whiskey. Women bought imported tea, sugar, salt, flour, fabric, sewing notions, kitchen utensils, furniture and some medicines.

It was said the Carrier women of Nazko did considerable business at the trading post with the clothing they made. Taught by their mothers that animal hides provided the best protection against the minus forty temperatures of winter and the horseflies of summer, they tirelessly fashioned deer, caribou and moose skins into coats, dresses, trousers, moccasins and blankets, each beautifully decorated with ornate beaded animals, trees, wildflowers, the sun or moon. The curved knives for skinning the hides and the needles for the beadwork had to be brought in from Europe, by special order. The proprietors didn't mind though, because the beautiful clothing generated so much revenue for them.

Now all that remained of the trading post was the faded grey timber shell with its two half-inch thick 2' x 2' cobweb-covered window panes. Everyone, and especially the children, was supposed to stay out of there to ensure its preservation. This was because two foolish young boys nearly burned it down and themselves four years ago while they were experimenting with cigarettes. The elders were angry for weeks. Tyler still felt bad about it.

He kicked the three-foot snowdrift away from the entrance and shouldered the creaking door open. The structure seemed to heave and sigh eerily with blustery arctic gusts. Inside, his breath disappeared in the chilled musty-smelling air. The faded brown forty-year old floral couch, with it's burnt off armrests, frowned at him from the centre of the empty room. The memory of a willowed-hot behind and hours of lecturing in the Carrier language, none of which he understood, had kept his curiosity in check until now. Today, there was a longing in his soul for comfort that was stronger than the painful past.

His eyes surveyed the rugged timber ceiling and walls for an ancient feathered or leather Carrier artifact, but all there was, was a blackened knotted old bridle tangled in a corner. What he really wanted was a sign, some direction or better - someone to talk to about his fears.

When he and Chester's first came to live with Tilda and they couldn't fall asleep at night, she would sit on the side of their bed, listen to their fears, and then pray for them. Afterwards, they always felt better, reassured. If there was ever a time when Tyler needed reassurance, it was now. In the reverent stillness of the old trading post, he sensed that prayer would help and this was the ideal place for it.

It was awkward at first. How do you talk to the Creator? He closed his eyes and thought about how immense he must be – a sovereign powerful enough to call solar systems and atoms into existence. Surely, the God of the universe, as Tilda referred to him, would notice that he had lied to Tonya's mother about the stroke, and that he had pounded his brother countless times. He wondered if the Creator would even listen to the prayer of one so undeserving.

Then he recalled how, on numerous occasions, when Tilda got angry and called Chester and him, "Stupid kids," she would later, usually in the evening while she was knitting in her rocking chair, ask God to forgive her. A couple minutes later, she felt better. A peaceful smile would come over her face and she would begin to hum.

If she could do it, why couldn't he? He thought it best to start by apologizing for the obvious - the lie and Chester's many beatings. An image of Chester's pouting face, wimpy crying and the way he mimicked him came to mind, and it made him snicker. But he decided if he was going to get anywhere with the Almighty, he'd better start by feeling some remorse for the way he treated Chester. He was having a little trouble with it until he remembered the time Terry Black, a loudmouth bully from the tenth grade, stole his lunch and pushed him into a muddy ditch on their way to school a couple of years ago. He certainly didn't enjoy being bullied. He imagined Chester felt the same.

"God, I'm sorry for lying to Tonya's mother on Sunday night. And I'm really sorry for treating Chester so badly." With that out of the way, he felt better. He continued, "I would appreciate you showing me if I should take Atsoo to Kluskus or not. If it's your will for us to go, help me look after her and Chester. If it's not, help me to look after them here. But, *please*, don't let the social worker take us away from her! Thanks."

When he opened his eyes, he felt led to climb the rickety stairs to the loft. In the corner, partially hidden by a tan-colored hide tarp were two pairs of perfectly preserved snowshoes. It was as though a spot light was illuminating them, telling him the trip to Kluskus was not only the right decision but would receive providential care. Bathed in the glory of a timeless moment, he had a vision of towing his atsoo, on a toboggan, over the Kluskus Mountain in the rosy hues of first morning light.

When he returned to the house, he could hardly wait to share his encounter with Chester and show him the snow-shoes. Chester was riding his own emotional roller coaster. He was livid. Before Tyler could close the door, he attacked him, "Where have you been? Do you have any idea what time it is?"

Tyler rolled back the sleeve of his parka to look at his watch. He couldn't believe it, it was 4:45. Where had the time gone? He turned and glared outside - the full moon was just peering over hills in the east. He hadn't even noticed it or how dark it was.

"Where were you?" fumed Chester.

"I'm sorry, Ches. I walked to the pond then went to the old trading post."

"You're not supposed to go in there. You know what Atsoo told us."

"I know. I know. I thought I could find something that would help us on the trip and I did. Look at these!" he said, holding up the snowshoes and leather tarp."

From Tilda's room a harsh croupy cough could be heard, so persistent that it sounded like she could barely catch her breath. Tyler tore off his parka and toque and pitched them towards the coat peg, missing it by three feet.

"Chester, how long has she been doing this?"

"Ever since I gave her the last drink of juice about four o'clock."

"Did you do something different?"

"Did you do something different? Of course I did something different, you moron! I fed her by myself because you weren't here. I could barely lift her and when she took a drink, she must have taken too much and she choked. She hasn't stop coughing since. I think some of it might have gone into her lungs."

"Do' you think?"

"Look, Bozo, this wouldn't have...."

"Look you fat little creep. Quit calling me a bozo, okay!" Before Chester knew what hit him he was sitting on the floor, legs spread, trying to wrestle free from the strangle hold Tyler had around his throat. With a move of his own, he managed to reach over his head and pull Tyler's head and shoulders over him on to the floor in front of him. Tyler lay on his back staring at the ceiling in disbelief.

"That was good, Ches. When did you learn how to do that?"

Chester wasn't impressed by the compliment. All he could think about, was when he needed Tyler most he was off on some treasure hunt.

"I thought Atsoo was going to die. She was choking and gasping and her face was purple." All he wanted to do was punch Tyler in the face until he begged for mercy. Swinging wildly, he managed to plant a knuckle into Tyler's upper lip, splitting it. Bright red blood instantly filled his mouth and smeared across his cheeks and nose.

In their P.E. classes, their teacher Mr.Roonie, a black belt in Tae Kwan Do had been teaching them some basic holds. He insisted they know the proper use of force – to protect the innocent and never as an expression of frustration or anger. Calmness and reason, he explained, were always to be employed first to work out conflicts. The students were expected to spend time on the mats and practice what he had shown them. Chester and Tyler frequently had to be untangled when their tempers flared. "You two just don't get it, do you," Roonie would growl, as he steered them by the ear to separate benches on the sideline.

The come back was swift. Before Chester knew what hit him, he was face down on the floor. A sharp pain ripped through his nose and blood spurted all over his hand as he reached up to touch it. "Tyler, you're going to die for this!"

Stunned by a rage they hadn't experienced before they crawled to their knees. Panting and dazed, they watched as a steady stream of bright red blood trickled to the floor beneath them. Suddenly, there was a *swoosh* between them, followed by a bigger *SWOOSH*. Scratching and pawing for traction, the cat was chasing a light brown mouse under the table and through the legs of the chairs into Tilda's bedroom.

Tyler and Chester stared at each other with a puzzled half-smile then scrambled to their feet, wiping their bloodied faces on their shirtsleeves as they darted towards the bedroom.

"Crackers, you had better not…"

But before the words were out, the obese tabby and his sidekick had made the first of three laps up the foot of the bed, along Tilda's side, and over her pillow. When the racers sped past her face, she turned and stared. Her violent cough suddenly disappeared.

On the final lap, the cat and the mouse crouched motionlessly on the foot of the bed - panting and staring at one another. Then, as quickly as it had turned into the bedroom, the race was diverted; back to the kitchen, through the chair legs and down the steps to the crawl space. Tyler and Chester howled.

As they stood there, wondering what in the world had gotten into the cat, two bruised, bloodied faces with hair spiked by dried blood materialized in the mirror on the bedroom wall.

"Wow, is that us?" marveled Chester. "We look cool, eh?"

"Yeah! I bet Tonya would flip if she saw us. We'd better wash our faces right away incase she comes to the door. I am sorry, Ches, for not being here when you needed me. I'm sorry you were afraid."

"I'm sorry too. I shouldn't have lost my temper." A light gentlemanly tap on the shoulder acknowledged their forgiveness. "Guess we should clean up this place and figure out what to make for supper."

"Yeah. We ate the last of the leftovers last night."

After their favorite meal of peanut butter and jam sandwiches made from homemade bread and a tall glass of milk, they cautiously offered Tilda a few sips of cooled tea with a bit of sugar, which she "Mmmed" with approval. Then they changed her newspaper and repositioned her on her other side for the night. She barely opened her eyes and her breathing was still rapid and rattled, but no worse. They were so exhausted they fell asleep on the top of their bed with their clothes on.

In the morning, Tonya's persistent rapping on the back door startled them awake.

When they opened the door, she gasped and stepped back.

"What in the world happened to you two!" she said, cupping a gloved hand over her mouth. Their lack of response told her everything.

"Were you two at it again? That's it!" she said, turning to leave. "I'm not coming back until you learn to solve your differences without half-killing each other. You're like wild dogs, fighting over the same bone. I'm afraid that one of you is actually going to kill the other or that you'll kill me if I get caught in the middle."

"Don't go, Tonya," they begged, Tyler trailing her down the back steps, clasping her arm. "We know how stupid we are. We're sorry we scared you. Just don't leave, please."

Why she believed them, she didn't know. "Before I take another step into your house, you've got to promise me that you'll stop hurting each other like this. "PROMISE ME!" she screeched.

"Okay, okay, we promise," they mumbled, eyes down.

"LOOK AT ME AND PROMISE!"

"We promise, Tonya," Tyler whispered shamefully.

Unloading several of Tyler and Chester's textbooks and notebooks into Chester's chubby arms so she could hang up her coat and remove her boots, she said, "Here's the homework your teachers gave me. I would have brought it yesterday but I figured if my mother knew you were sick enough to be away from school for a few days, she would be over here taking a look at you herself. I had to hide them under my coat so she didn't see them this morning."

"What did you tell our teachers," inquired Tyler.

"They still think you have a bad flu – the vomiting and diarrhea kind. That was all the detail they needed. They just said to say, "Hi, and come back when you feel better.""

The drone of Tilda's rapid wet respirations echoed throughout the house.

"She's still doing that, eh?" noted Tonya.

"It stopped for a few minutes last night," Chester replied, making brief eye contact with Tyler that reminded him not to expand on that comment. "But she basically hasn't stopped since you were here yesterday."

With the confident air of a seasoned nurse, Tonya strode into Tilda's room, the boys close behind. "She seems to be getting worse. If we don't do something pretty soon she'll die."

"We know that, duh!" Chester reacted defensively.

"Chester, she's just trying to help." Instantly, Tyler had to fight the urge to tell him off. "Did you tell your folks yet, Tonya?"

"I did. But it wasn't easy. I couldn't look them in the eye. I pretended I was looking at the calendar on the wall while I was telling them. When they asked where I would be staying, I said here tonight and Kluskus tomorrow night."

"And do they think Atsoo's friend, Bill, is driving us?"

"Yes, they do. When my dad heard it, he kind of cleared his throat and raised his eyebrows. I don't know why. Then he said, "That should be interesting." "What about the appointment at the clinic today?"

"I'm going to it at one o'clock," replied Tyler.

"You'd better try to cover your mouth - your lips look like sausages."

Tyler turned to study his marred reflection in the bedroom mirror.

"I've always thought Tyler looked like a wiener," Chester smugly interjected, careful to shield his face and arms for a reaction that had caught him off guard so many times in the past.

"You'd better bundle up, it's ten below out there right now," said Tonya. "The radio said it could go down to fifteen below or lower tonight. I'll come back after supper." Then she left for school.

In less than twelve hours, she would be back, expecting them to be ready. There was much to be done; from finding the toboggan, packing their backpacks to insuring the house would stay warm while they were away. They dressed in their work clothes and started by heaping the wood box to over full. It had been their responsibility to keep the wood-stove burning day and night since they came to live with their atsoo. If they forgot and the fire dwindled to ashes, she would refill it, but the next time she saw them, she batted their ears with a rolled up newspaper until they were black with newsprint. The high-pitched scolding was enough to drive off a starving buzzard.

A couple winters ago, when they forgot to fill the stove before they went to town, the fire had gone out. When they returned, the taps were frozen. They didn't have running water for hours. Fortunately, the water lines hadn't burst or they would have opened the door to a skating rink in the middle of the kitchen floor.

Before they left for Kluskus, the firebox would be crammed with logs and the damper closed to a mere slit. That way the fire would burn much slower. Hopefully, there would be warm ashes in the firebox when they returned Friday night. To insure the pipes didn't freeze they would leave one tap barely trickling. Even with a woodstove burning, it was difficult sometimes to keep the house above freezing. Moving water doesn't freeze as easily as still water, was a principle known by everyone in the Cariboo. On those profoundly cold winter nights when temperatures plunged to minus twenty-five degrees Celsius, it was imperative to leave a tap running slightly. Every precaution would be taken.

# CHAPTER FOUR

# A SOCIAL VISIT

The clock on the wall read precisely one o'clock as Tyler stepped over the threshold of the dispensary into its warm welcoming waiting room. Tonya's mother greeted him and a few seconds later the doctor, a six-foot, partially grayed man cloaked in a white lab coat, opened the door to an eight-foot square office and ushered out a woman and her two squirming preschoolers. One of them had a cough that sounded like the bark of a dog. The other's eyes were swollen and red and both children had green mucous dried onto their noses and cheeks.

"Give them a teaspoon of this three times a day for seven days," said the doctor, handing the woman a little brown bottle. "If they're not any better in a couple days call my office for further instructions." Then the mother shuffled the two pint-sized mucous monsters ahead of her out the door as they wiped their leaky noses on their coat sleeves.

"Yuck," Tyler thought. "I hope I don't touch anything they've touched. Little kids can be so disgusting."

"My name is Dr. Duval," said the doctor, extending his right hand for a handshake. "What can I do for you young man?"

Tyler shrunk deeper into his parka so the woolen scarf he had draped around his mouth would stay put while he talked. "Well, nothing for me. It's for my grandmother, Tilda Chantyman. She usually comes to see you, but she can't today. She sent me to get her prescription refilled," he muffled sheepishly, trying not to make eye contact as he reached into his coat pocket for the white plastic medicine bottle.

The doctor removed the lid and stared inside. Tyler was sure he was counting the pills to see if he was telling the truth. Suddenly there was no saliva in his throat and he had to swallow repeatedly to keep from gagging.

Replacing the lid, the doctor returned the bottle to Tyler. "Why didn't your grandmother come herself?" he asked.

There it was - the question he most did not want to hear. The whole scam would be blown in an instant if he screwed up. He had to think of an excuse fast. An eternity past and nothing came to mind. "She's busy...at home," he finally blurted out. Then he started to cough and not just a little. He coughed so hard he blew the scarf away from his face exposing his sausage lips. With his gloved hands, he fumbled the scarf back into place, hoping the doctor had looked away at the crucial moment.

"What is she ..." the doctor started to ask when he noticed Tyler's face. Before he could react the doctor slid the scarf below his chin and stared at his lips.

"What happened to your mouth, son?"

"Hockey."

"Must have been some kind of game."

"Yeah!"

"What's your grandma doing today?"

"Packing," he said facing the floor. "We're going to visit her sister in Kluskus for a few days."

While he wrote something unrecognizable on a prescription pad, the doctor cautioned, "Tell her to take it easy. Her blood pressure is still pretty high. Remind her to call my office if she starts feeling dizzy again."

"You bet." The conviction was killing him. Sweat trickled down his temples and armpits. The war to tell the truth raged inside him. The doctor seemed caring enough, but could he be trusted? He didn't want to take the chance. At first, he was hot then cold. If he didn't get out of there soon he was going to faint.

"And by the way, young man?" the doctor added. Tyler held his breath and waited for the verdict, which he was sure would expose his secret.

"Tell Tilda to have a nice visit with her sister."

He turned to leave with a sigh that exploded like he'd been holding his breath for minutes. As he opened the door, a white woman, shorter than himself, with chin-length reddish brown hair stepped inside. "Do you know where I can find Tilda Chantyman's place?" she called. "My name is Ms. Phillips. I'm from the Department of Social Services. I'm just new to the area and I'm trying to get acquainted with my clients."

"This is Tilda's grandson, Tyler." Tonya's mother volunteered. "He can take you to her place."

Every ounce of blood in Tyler's body plummeted to his feet. He felt so dizzy he thought he would collapse. He stumbled backwards against the door then took a deep breath, shook his head and stood up straight again.

"Are you alright?" asked Tonya's mother. "You look a bit pale all of a sudden. And my goodness, Tyler what have you done to your face?"

"Hockey. I'm alright… turned too quickly. Happens all the time. I'll be alright."

"I left word at your school yesterday that I would be coming today," said Ms. Phillips. "But your teacher said you had been away from school with the flu. By the looks of it you're still a bit under the weather I'd say. Could you take me to see her?"

He had to think fast. If I don't take her, she'll be suspicious. If I take her... Then he remembered the social worker hadn't seen his grandmother before. She wouldn't know what she looked like, if she'd had a stroke in the past, if she spoke English or Carrier. Perhaps he could prop her up in bed and act as her interpreter. It was their only chance.

"Sure, come on over! It's on the other side of the dispensary. A two-story log house right against the bush," said Tyler. "I'll go ahead and let her know that you're coming. She's been in bed with the flu lately too and was trying to catch up on a few things around the house. She might be taking a nap. I'll just go see."

He ran out the door, trying to politely wave a calm goodbye. Inside his heart was beating so fast he felt dizzy. He dashed down the dispensary path then along the road in front of Tonya's place and up his driveway to the back door. His footprints were mere smudges in the snow.

"Chester! Chester!" he shrieked plowing the door open. She's coming! She's coming!"

Chester was stretched out on the couch watching Batman again. "Who's coming?" he muttered distractedly. "Shoot 'em. Get out of there, you idiot! Oh, for Pete's sake."

"The social worker, you moron." yelled Tyler. "The social worker is on her way here. She'll be here any minute. We've got to do something. Shut that stupid thing off and help me think of something."

For ten seconds all Tyler could do was pace back and forth in front of the television, four strides this way, and four strides that way. He was hyperventilating. Sweat trickled down the neck of his parka. His hands were clammy and his brain was numb with panic.

"She's never seen Atsoo, right?" said Tyler. "Maybe we could fix her up somehow. Or maybe we could dress.... He couldn't believe it. For once, it was he who devised the plan of salvation. "Chester! Chester, come here!" he squealed, dragging Chester off the couch towards Tilda's bedroom. Follow me! Put on one of Atsoo's skirts and kerchiefs."

They rifled through her closet until they found a red floral skirt, a navy cardigan and a red and white polka-dot kerchief for his head. Then Tyler helped him put it all on. From under the bed, he grabbed her favorite badly worn moccasins and shoved them onto his feet. From the top of her dresser he took one of her rather masculine-looking pairs of reading glasses, the ones with the broken arm of course, and balanced them on his swollen nose. Ah yes, with the glasses, the look was complete.

Tyler led Chester to the rocking chair and plunked a ball of wool and some knitting needles onto his lap.

"Now, pretend to knit and rock. Keep your eyes down and answer all her questions in something that resembles Carrier," ordered Tyler, tying the kerchief under his chin. Then he laughed.

"I wished you could see yourself, Ches. You look...If I told you, you'd kill me."

"How am I supposed to talk Carrier?" Chester protested. "I don't have a clue how to speak it."

"I think there's a lot of ITs and TENs at the end of the words. Just add a whole bunch of those sounds. Or make up your own words. Just so long as she doesn't know what your saying and I'll act as your interpreter."

"Oh, I don't know about this, Tyler," worried Chester.

Suddenly, there was a commanding rapping on the front door. "Just keep your head down and don't stop rocking," whispered Tyler.

Tyler took a deep breath to calm himself then opened the door. With his politest voice he said, "Oh hello again. Won't you come in? May I take your coat?" Tilda had taught the boys to always be on their best behavior when they had company. Take their coats and offer them the best seat in the living room she would say.

"Would you like to sit down?"

"Thank you. That would be very nice," she replied craning her head almost completely around. They raised their eyebrows at each other in amazement. They had never seen anyone turn their head so far and still have their shoes pointed forward. Tyler thought her gawking was positively rude and that she looked more like the periscope on a submarine than a human being. It was obvious that she was trying to determine if his grandmother had enough money to run the house and look after them but he had to ask,

"What are you looking for?"

"Oh nothing," she replied. "Ms. Chantyman my name is Ms. Margarite Phillips. I've just been assigned to your area and I'm trying to meet my new clients."

"Hmm," Chester grunted, criss-crossing the knitting needles feverishly and rocking the chair. "Him, click a lick, oten. Shim a duck a luck, oten."

"Oh, you don't speak English," said the woman. "I understood from your records that you spoke English quite well."

"Yes, she does," corrected Tyler respectfully. "But sometimes she gets so nervous around strangers she kind of forgets her English. She said she was happy to meet you."

"What happened to your grandmother's nose?"

There hadn't been enough time to disguise that little detail. Tyler didn't know how to answer her question. Suddenly, Chester faked three sneezes and buried his nose in a Kleenex he quickly retrieved from one of the cardigan sleeves. Tilda always kept tissue tucked in her cardigan sleeves. He blew his nose repeatedly until it honked.

"No wonder it looks so swollen and red. That's a terrible cold you have, Mrs. Chantyman." And she wiggled a little farther back in her chair, hoping, they guessed, to avoid catching what she had.

"Can you ask her if I can see your birth certificates?" said Ms. Phillips.

"Atsoo, Ms. Phillips would like to see our birth certificates."

For a few seconds Chester thought his heart had stopped. His eyes crossed and he couldn't breath. Then he leaned forward in the rocking chair and began to recite the most impressive piece of impromptu he'd ever contrived. There were few things he did better than Tyler, but acting was one of them. Each line of his oratory ended splendidly with OTEN or IT. It was pure poetry. When he was finished, he glanced over at Tyler for his approval. Their eyes locked in amazement. A gleeful smirk too large to hide spread over their faces. Victory was in the bag.

"Okay, Atsoo. Yes, I know where they are. I'll get them for you. You just save those sore old knees."

"I think it's wonderful that you can speak your native tongue. I've read most Indian children can't speak their parent's language."

Chester mumbled something back and rocked quick short jabs. Every time he spoke, it seemed the speed of the rocking chair doubled.

Tyler bound up the stairs to his bed where the zippered book was safely tucked under his pillow. He had intended to return it to Tilda's dresser and forgotten. He was so glad he had found it that day and knew where it was.

"What's the snoring noise coming from that room?" she asked, raising her voice and craning her neck like she was trying to peer into Tilda's bedroom. Her neck must be made of rubber, thought Chester. It's long and stretchy enough.

"Oh that's our dog, Butch. He's a pug. Sometimes he snores so loudly we can't sleep at night." Chester filled in with the dog's allergy to wheat and how overweight he was, the diet he started last week. On and on it went until Tyler returned to the lower floor, gracefully sweeping past the bedroom door and closing it incase she decided to investigate the nasal pooch for herself. Then he handed her the birth certificates.

She studied them painstakingly slow from top to bottom. When she was finished with Chester's she said, "Where's your younger brother, now? His teacher said he has been away from school sick too."

"Oh, he's in the bathroom," Tyler replied.

"He's been in there a long time."

"He loves to sit in there and read for hours."

Chester cleared his throat and nodded for Tyler to come closer.

"Oh yeah. Would you like a cup of tea, Ms. Phillips?"

"No thank you," she said hastily jotting down a few lines in a spiral-bound notebook she retrieved from her briefcase. "I think I should be going now. Everything seems to be in order here. I'll call again."

As she stood to go, an agonizing, hair-raising, "Yeowl..." coming from under the rocking chair pierced the mortuary stillness.

Chester blurted, "You stupid cat!" Then he caught himself and quickly jabbered, "You'ten scared'ten me'ten to death'ten!" Everyone laughed with relief. Surprisingly, even Ms. Periscope herself, had a sense of humor.

"We've been waiting for that to happen for a long time," giggled Tyler, cordially escorting their unwanted guest through the front door. "You have a good day too," he called out as he closed the door. "Next time, call before you come," he muttered under his breath.

When she was gone, Tyler and Chester collapsed on the couch laughing until they cried. "That was way too close!" Chester sighed.

A few minutes later, there was another urgent knocking at the front door. They stared at one another in horror. Was she back? Again, the blood in their heads dropped to their feet. When they opened the door, it was Tonya. Her arms were stacked so high with textbooks and notebooks she could barely see over the top. When she spotted Chester, she laughed so hard the whole pile tumbled onto the living room floor.

"What are you doing here?" said Tyler. "We weren't expecting you till tonight. You nearly scared us to death." We thought you were Ms. Margarite Phillips," mimicked Chester with a professional tone of voice.

"Well, as you can see, your teachers are really worried that you don't have enough homework. And I felt like stopping by."

As they picked up the books, the boys excitedly told her every hairy detail of the afternoon; the doctor's office, including a vivid description of the Mucous Kids and the social worker with a head that nearly twisted right off. But the highlight of the day, probably the month, with timing literally out of this world, was the cat's encounter with the rocking chair. They knew the performance would really be something and they weren't disappointed. They rolled on the floor in hysterics.

After a glass of milk and the oatmeal cookies Tonya brought from home, they sat around the table catching up on what was happening at school. Then they went to check on Tilda. When they opened her bedroom door there was a horrible stench.

"Ooh... That doesn't smell very good," declared Chester. "I hope that's not what I think it is."

Tonya slowly pulled back the blankets to expose what they feared most.

"That is so gross!" exclaimed Tyler, his eyes, like everyone's, riveted on the brown golf-ball sized monster. "Who's going to get rid of it?"

Nobody raised their eyes. After a long silence, Tonya finally volunteered. "I guess I'll do it. I've cleaned up after my cat lots of times. This can't be that much worse. Get me some toilet paper."

She unrolled the two-play and wrapped her hand until it was the size of a baseball glove, then she removed the fugitive with the delicacy of a surgeon.

"You guys owe me big time," squinted Tonya.

"Name it. You got it," said Tyler.

The newspaper wasn't very wet this time, but the skin around the base of her spine was reddened so she spread some mucky fish-smelling white ointment on it she found in the medicine cabinet. She changed her nightgown and the boys helped her reposition Tilda with the pillows. She was getting worse. Her limbs were more flaccid. Her respirations were more rapid and her skin was burning up.

"I think she's got pneumonia," said Tonya.

"Is she dying?" asked Chester hesitantly. Nobody answered.

"We've got to get her out of here tonight," insisted Tyler.

"I'm going home to pack and have supper. I'll be back as soon as I can."

After she left, Tyler and Chester started to collect the supplies. From the log shed in the backyard, they hauled the eight-foot aluminum toboggan and some rope into the carport and set them beside the snowshoes and the deer-hide tarp. Then they returned to the house.

The first thing they did was split the list in half, then they took off around the house in search of the items. Trip after trip, upstairs, down in the crawlspace, from the kitchen cupboards, they hauled armfuls to the kitchen and living room. On the couch, they unzipped and spread-open their backpacks. Beside them - a quilt, three wool blankets, their parkas, toques, deer hide mitts and, two pairs of socks (apiece) were stacked. Knee-high felt-lined winter boots, approximately twenty double sheets of newspaper, two flashlights, and four books of paper matches, (two each incase someone's matches got lost or destroyed) were heaped in the middle of the living room floor.

To the table; three quart-sized plastic canteens – two with water and one with apple juice for Tilda, two card-size boxes of raisins, four single-serving boxes of Sugar Pops and Fruit Loops, two one-cup portions of shelled peanuts twist-tied in plastic wrap, two hand-sized slabs of moose jerky and six mandarin oranges were delivered. And of course, no day would be complete without junk food – approximately fifty pieces of red licorice, the same number of red and green jujubes and Chester's favorite, an economy size bag of Cheezies.

When everything on the list was crossed off, a staggering pile lay there before them.

"It's going to take a miracle to cram this stuff into those two bags," sighed Tyler, shaking his head. "What won't fit into the backpacks, will have to go on the toboggan I guess. Speaking of toboggan – we need to bring it in the house so it can warm up. Otherwise Atsoo will freeze to death on that cold metal, even with the blankets and quilt wrapped around her."

Astonishingly, it did all go somewhere. The apple juice, newspaper and blankets would have to be tucked under and around Tilda. Chester's backpack wouldn't close completely because of the Cheezies, but nothing was left on the table, couch or floor.

"Do you really think this is going to work, Ty?" asked Chester.

"We have no other choice. This is our only hope."

# CHAPTER FIVE

# MOON MAGIC

A muffled tapping on the back door could barely be heard as Tyler and Chester scarfed down the last of their peanut and jam sandwich and a glass of milk. It was Tonya – six thirty, right on time. Belching and wiping milk moustaches across their sleeves, they sprung from their chairs, knocking them other over in an attempt to reach the back door first. While they jockeyed for front position, Tonya managed to remove a mitten, open the door and let herself in.

"I had a lot of explaining to do about all this stuff," she said, peeling off her bulging backpack and down-filled hooded parka. "I finally convinced them that I was just trying to be prepared. I sure hope they bought it. And, I sure hope we're doing the right thing."

"Right or wrong, we're doing it," stated Tyler. "No social worker is going to take us away from Tilda and make us live with strangers."

"Let me help you with your coat," Chester offered, hoping to impress her. His chivalrous gesture however, wasn't recognized with as much as a smile or a, "thank you." She was more enthralled with what Tyler was saying.

"Do you really think someone could be that heartless?"

"You have no idea," said Tyler. "Remember I told you about the woman I overheard in Jenz. I don't know who she was – I'd never seen her before. I think she was working for the Forestry because she got out of one of those green government pick-ups. They've been up in hills lately, looking at all the orange trees.

She said she'd seen it on the news the night before - more than seventy kids had been taken from their families and placed in foster homes. There were so many kids, they ran out of foster homes in Quesnel and the kids were sent to other cities, like Prince George and Williams Lake. When those cities ran out of foster homes, kids were being looked after in hotels. The news said social workers had been told to carefully screen low income and single-parent families for "kids at risk." I'm telling you, Tonya, we're at risk. We've got to get out of here!"

Tonya stared at the floor in disbelief. She finally understood why Chester and Tyler were so afraid. "Are you guys ready?"

"We're ready. After we put our dishes in the sink and load Atsoo, we'll leave."

"Well, what are we waiting for," insisted Chester. "Let's go....."

"Ches, you take care of the dishes while Tonya and I finish dressing her. Then bring the toboggan into the bedroom and help us load her. Oh yeah, and spread the rest of the newspaper on the toboggan before you bring it..."Tyler's voice trailed off.

"And another thing," Chester mumbled under his breath as he disappeared downstairs for the toboggan before he lost again it in front of Tonya, "Chester would you mind bringing me breakfast in bed? And would you mind blowing my nose?"

The pink polka dot flannel nightgown Tonya had put on Tilda in the afternoon was still dry as was the newspaper.

But they decided a couple of fluffy towels next to her skin might cut down on the chafing and cushion the bumps. A pair of wool stockings was pulled to her knees, and a toque on her head, and she was ready to transfer to the toboggan. In a few hours, she would be in a much softer bed.

"Okay, you guys – just like we did it on Monday - on the count of three. One, two, three…" And the move went as smoothly as it had the first time.

"You know, we are good," boasted Tyler.

They swaddled her with the blankets, quilt and finally the tarp.

Then the layers were secured with a lightweight nylon rope, leaving only her face exposed. A flap of tarp was left at the top to cover her face, in the event it snowed or became extremely cold. She had never been one to shy away from the elements – her weathered skin was a testament to that fact. No frigid wind or sultry heat, had ever kept her from the daily quarter mile walk to the mailbox. She loved to be outdoors, under the sky, with whatever it produced.

"That's an incredible job," said Tonya. "Ambulance drivers should take lessons from you two."

The supplies and Tilda were packed. All that remained was to put on their heaviest winter attire and double-check the list.

"Okay, let's make a last minute check," said Tyler.

"Food?"

"Check." replied Chester.

"Flashlights?

"Check."

"Snowshoes? Got your snowshoes, Tonya?"

"You bet," she replied. "How about the matches and newspaper?"

"Got them," answered Chester.

"Second thought; let me carry the matches, Ches. I'll take *really* good care of them," he said receiving them from

Chester and tucking them deeply into one of his inside pockets and patting them for extra emphasis.

"Do you have the map, Tyler?" asked Tonya.

He sifted through the other inside pocket and lifted it to the light. "It's right here." Then he gasped, kicked off his bulky boots and bolted upstairs, skipping every other step. "I almost forgot the little zippered book." From the loft, he bellowed down, "I just have this feeling we're going to need it."

"There," he said returning to the others. "I think we're finally ready to go."

"Did you take care of the stove and tap, Chester, like I asked you?" asked Tyler.

"Did you take care of the stove and tap, like I asked you to?" Chester teased.

Tonya held her breath. "Dear God, not another fight." When Chester saw her shutting her eyes and shaking her head, he burst out laughing.

"Just kidding," he said.

"You better be," she cringed.

"Yes master, I took care of them."

By eight thirty, the inside lights of the house had been shut off and the porch light turned on. The door didn't need to be locked because nobody broke into his neighbor's house. The dogs knew where everybody belonged and if they spotted something out of place, they'd bark their fool heads off until everyone in the village was gawking out their windows.

With cumbersome backpacks and snowshoes strapped to their backs, they started down a path behind the house in the bush - a different path from the one that led to the open field through the grove. This path would lead them well hidden, off the reserve to the Nazko Highway and eventually to the Kluskus Trail.

The pale blue full moon glowed dimly through a thin layer of cloud. It was easy to imagine a wolf lurking behind a snow-covered stump or a bear sleeping beneath a cluster of partially buried logs. Deep in the woods, several pairs of golden eyes blinked as the flashlights panned one side of the path then the other. Animal tracks, probably of wild rabbits, zigzagged across the trail.

The air was warmer than when Tyler had gone to the dispensary in the afternoon. Shuffling through the foot of undisturbed snow was like blazing a trail through mashed potatoes – mushy and sticky. To make matters worse, the path was overgrown and wide enough for only one person, so the effort of towing the toboggan could not be shared as planned.

Anxious to impress Tonya, Chester offered to pull it first. Tyler wasn't about to argue. He knew exactly how tough it was going to be. He had hauled firewood on the toboggan from the back of the property to the house in snow like this, lots of times. Before Chester went a hundred yards, he was so out of breath he had to stop.

Lagging behind, so he wouldn't hear, Tonya stressed to Tyler, "This is going to be impossible for one person."

"I know I know," whispered Tyler. "I wanted Chester to see that for himself so when we got to the highway and I suggested we take turns pulling, two of us at a time, he wouldn't throw a hissy fit and accuse me of trying to be The Big Boss Man. If we rotate every half hour, I think our arms will last longer." By the time they caught up to him, Chester had no problem with the half-hour shifts. He was happy to surrender the reigns to Tyler.

Fifteen minutes later, they reached the Nazko highway. The moon had risen high enough in the milky night sky to illuminate the road and they no longer needed their flashlights. Traffic throughout the day had packed the snow till the road was as smooth as glass and nearly as slippery. Tilda felt light, and pulling her, even for one person, was a breeze. But as they had agreed, two would tow while the other rested,

Tyler gladly handed the rope to Chester and Tonya, eager to massage the painful knots out of his arms.

"Hold up a minute – I want to check the map, again - make sure I've got this straight," Tyler said, pulling off his mitts and unzipping his coat. Carefully unfolding it, he held it out so the moonlight could spill over it. "Our first switch should be about nine thirty at the Michelle Creek Road. That's about two miles from here. Then, if everybody's in agreement, we'll stop for a snack at Fishpot Lake around midnight."

"Sounds good to me," Tonya and Chester echoed.

But that was still three hours away and Chester was starving. He knew the others would be furious if he snacked too soon. They would give him some line about using up food supplies or slowing them down, yadda yadda yadda. It was his food and he could eat whenever he wanted. When it was gone, it was gone.

He waited until just the right moment, when Tyler was walking on the other side of Tonya and they were deeply engaged in a discussion about a white boy and a first nation's girl from their class who were dating. When he was sure they weren't looking, with his left hand tightly gripping the rope, he slid his right hand into his pocket and removed the wrapper from one of three chocolate bars he'd hidden there just before leaving the house. Tyler was the last person he wanted to find out about his stash of chocolate bars. He was always bumming Chester's candy when his own ran out.

Piece by piece, he nibbled and savored the almond chocolate bar until it was all gone. It was the most delicious thing he had ever eaten. While he peered straight ahead, enjoying the bliss of his covert operation, occasionally interjecting an, "Uh huh," into the conversation, the wrapper crept out of his pocket and landed on the road behind him.

At nine thirty Tonya hollered, "It's time! Could someone please take spell me off. My arm is killing me! How far is

Fishpot?" Tyler picked up the pace and strode to her side so he could maintain the speed. "I think it's about five miles still, Tonya. Ches, your arm okay or do you what to trade sides to give your arm a break?"

"I'm good." The chocolate bar had given him a definite lift. Fatigue hadn't crossed his mind once.

A steady pace and four more shift changes and they would make it to Fishpot Lake easily by midnight. It was going well. Occasionally, Tilda opened her eyes. The sight of stars and the sensation of movement didn't seem to alarm her. She looked so peaceful – the cool night air tickling the loose strands of hair on her forehead. Her coughing had almost stopped. Perhaps the cool air soothed her lungs or the movement lulled her. It seemed clear now they had done the right thing.

As they rounded the final corner, the shroud over the moon lifted and Fishpot Lake came into view. They stopped and stared in awe. A blanket of glittering gold, orange and pink covered it. Clusters of sharply defined dark charcoal evergreens dotted its shore. The rolling hills surrounding it were iridescent lavender against the diamond-studded velvet black sky.

Time stood still as they drank in the sight. It was as though they had discovered a secret, carefully guarded by the adult world - one that children, sent to bed hours earlier, weren't permitted to find. Moon Magic...its beauty had a power they had never experienced before.

Tyler quickly laced on his snowshoes and started packing a path to the cross pole fence that circled the lake, roughly fifty yards away. Then he and Chester towed the toboggan to the fence and flattened an area so they could sit and eat.

"Whew, I'm tired," said Tonya. "But it's worth it. I can't believe how beautiful this is. Imagine - if this hadn't happened to your atsoo, we would have never seen this. What time is it anyway?"

"It's just before twelve o'clock," said Tyler. "We're right on time."

As they slid off their backpacks to dig out a snack, Tonya was sweating. She unzipped her parka to let the soft breeze fan her neck. Still not cool enough, she removed it, as well as her toque and mitts. Then with her fingers, she combed her ebony hair away from her flushed ivory cheeks and took off her fogged glasses.

Tyler and Chester couldn't take their eyes off her. Suddenly she was a beautiful stranger that gave them a very pleasurable feeling and they found themselves needing to sit close to her. Tyler was also overheated. He too removed his parka, mitts and toque. With a backwards toss of his head and a quick comb with his fingers, his shiny black hair handsomely draped his square jaw. Afraid she might notice him looking at her, he stared at the ground. Slowly, he peered sideways to see if she was looking. It was the most awkward feeling he had ever had. When their eyes finally met, all they could do was giggle.

Chester was disgusted. He wasn't going to sit back and watch him walk away with her without a fight. Then he thought of a way to impress her. "Hey Ty!" he shouted, "Bet you can't do this," as he clambered up onto the top log of the fence and started tiptoeing along it with his arms held out to the side.

"That's cool Ches!" said Tonya.

"Hmm, that worked pretty well," he thought. "If I walk around the whole lake maybe she'll be really impressed."

He kept his chin up and eyes forward, inching along the narrow log path until their voices disappeared behind him. He was uncomfortable with so much distance between them, but he was determined to succeed. The fence took him into a grove of stunted jack pine where the evergreen fragrance was mystical and his imagination could transport him away from his difficulties, as it often did. He and Tonya were riding bareback, on a spirited creamy white stallion along the snowy ridge of the highest mountain in the Cariboo. She was holding on tightly behind him and he was pointing to the miles of virgin forest he had just purchased for her.

In the meantime, Tyler and Tonya had forgotten about Chester and were enjoying cookies and apple juice. Afterwards, they sat up Tilda and offered her a cup of apple juice. To their amazement, she drank it all – the most she'd had in four days. Then they removed the damp newspaper disposing it in the garbage bag they'd brought for the chore and stored it beneath the tarp that lined the toboggan.

Then it was time for some fun - a snowball fight. As he dodged her poorly aimed shots, he imagined her in his arms and kissing her. They stumbled to the ground and he wrestled with her. They laughed and she playfully pushed him away. She seemed to have no idea of his intentions. She treated him more like a brother - at least that's the impression she gave.

Off in the distance they heard a faint peculiar cry, which quickly grew louder. It was Chester running up the road, hollering, "Help!" He was being chased. Somehow, he managed to flush a young moose with his mother tailing behind, out of the grove. The sight was too funny to take seriously at first. Then they realized Chester was actually in danger. Waving frantically, Tyler yelled, "Get on the other side of the fence Chester! Jump - over - the - fence!"

"Hurry Chester!" Tonya screamed. "Jump over the fence!"

When the sound finally reached Chester, the calf was barely off his heels. With an abrupt turn, he scampered down the bank into the ditch then dove over the fence.

The young moose stood on the road gawking at Chester. The mother, not far away, snorted a Keep Your Distance warning. Clouds of vapor puffed from her flared nostrils. Her protective duty done, she nipped the ears of her belligerent youngster to move on and they disappeared into the bush on the opposite side of the road.

Tyler and Tonya ran to help Chester to his feet. He was covered in snow. They brushed him off and everyone laughed with relief. Even he could see the lighter side of his near miss.

"Common on Chester - we don't have time for you to race the animals," Tyler teased. "We've got to get going or we'll never make it to the Trail by daylight."

# CHAPTER SIX

# DISASTER ON THE BAEZAEKO

It was one thirty when they started to move again. Tonya's turn to pull with Tyler, but there was something different about her. She seemed flustered and distracted. "Are you sure you're up to taking this shift, Tonya? You look a little bagged. Chester and I can do this one."

"I'm alright Tyler! Look, don't treat me differently because I'm a girl," she snapped at him, jerking the rope from his hand. "This trip was just as much my idea as it was yours."

"Geeze, what crawled into her cookies?" He didn't have a clue what he had done wrong. Perhaps he had said something to upset her or maybe she was just tired, like they all were. Girls were so weird. They could be as sweet as pie one minute, then ignore you the next. He never could figure them out - whatever. He wouldn't say another word.

The next major stop would be the Baezaeko River, where the road ended, approximately four miles ahead. On the other side was the Kluskus Trail. From stories they had heard about it, they were expecting twenty miles of steep winding road, frequently interrupted by the Coglistiko River and frozen muskeg. They weren't looking forward to it.

The direction of the wind began to change. Thick gray clouds were moving in from the north, smothering the moon. The chilled darkness fanned a fear they hadn't mentioned while the moon illuminated the road and ditches – the fear that something was lurking in the bush, studying them, and waiting for one of them to make the mistake of straggling behind.

"Tyler," said Chester. "What would you do if we were attacked by a pack of wolves?"

"Yes," echoed Tonya, "What would you do?"

He didn't answer at first, because he wasn't sure himself. His answer surprised even him. "I'm a Carrier. I would out-smart them."

He'd never really thought about his roots before or what it meant to be Carrier. But in school lately, they had been learning that Carriers were once a nation of mighty warriors and expert hunters who made an important contribution to Canadian history. He was surprised to hear Carriers had guided the intrepid twenty-nine year old Scotsman, Alexander Mackenzie, and a handful of men across the Cariboo to Bella Coola in July of 1793 in search of the Northwest Passage. In fact, it was a woman by the name of Kama from Kluskus, who took the men the final hundred plus miles to the coast.

On a path suited more to mountain goats, she led them along the Grease Trail. The Carriers had traveled the trail for hundreds of years when they went to the Pacific Ocean for oolican oil, the oil they used for lamps and other prac-tical purposes. He had heard about the Grease Trail from his relatives but his grandmother never mentioned the famous woman from Kluskus. Perhaps she didn't know herself.

Not having a father, he and Chester learned about local wildlife from their grandmother and her good friend Bill. He taught them how to fish in the Nazko River and hunt with a gun. Lining the fence in their backyard with tin cans, he showed them how to aim with the sight and fire his 22 rifle. He had bigger guns at home that he kept locked in a closet. But he wasn't in a hurry to show them how to use them it seemed. Whenever they asked about them, he always said the same thing - "Lots of time."

The only real bush experience they had had was on the trails of the Nazko Valley. Apart from the occasional sighting of a black bear, they'd never personally encountered anything bigger or meaner than a deer. What they knew about wolves, cougars or grizzlies came from stories.

"You worry too much, Tonya," taunted Chester. "Those wolves are probably just scrawny over-sized dogs."

"One of those scrawny over-sized dogs could probably haul your butt into the bush where the rest of the pack would chew you to pieces. When they're starving and scrawny, they're the most ferocious."

An hour later, it began to snow. Sparsely at first, then so heavily they couldn't see across the road. They pulled the tarp over Tilda's face for the first time, more so that she would stay warm, than be bothered by the flicking of snow-flakes. Tonya wondered if they should stop until the storm past. She urged them to start a fire so they could warm up for awhile but Tyler and Chester convinced her it was safer to keep going.

"This is grizzly territory," said Tyler. "Sometimes in the winter, they prowl these woods on the way to their favorite watering holes, the Baezaeko and Coglistiko Rivers. We're probably crossing one of their trails right now. The sooner we put some distance between us and those rivers the better I'll feel."

A few minutes later she stopped abruptly, frozen by fear. Oh my gosh!" she gasped, "I can't see anything – nothing! What are we going to do?"

"Maybe we should shine the flashlights on the road, like car headlights," suggested Chester. Her panic had unnerved him. Tyler worried they both were close to falling apart. That possibility bothered him more than the White Out they were trapped in.

Hoping to reassure them, he calmly agreed, "It couldn't hurt."

With one hand on the rope, Tyler and Tonya pointed their flashlights at the road just ahead of their feet. Chester walked alongside doing the same. But the flashlights were anything but helpful. Instead, the glare on the snow created a mesmerizing wall of blinding white.

"Oh, I really don't like this," whimpered Tonya. "It's way too freaky."

"Yeah," agreed Chester, nervously peering into the void. His powerful imagination saw something on the road heading towards them. It was enormous and it was ugly. He stopped and blinked repeatedly so he could focus better. "Do you see what I see?"

Straining to see through the snow, the others also stopped and stared in disbelief. It was massive and right in the middle of the road blocking their way. Perhaps it was a grizzly standing on all fours. Perhaps it was two. Cautiously, they proceeded to get a better look, holding their breath and glancing over their shoulders at one another for moral support. Whatever it was, they hoped it recognized they were frightened puny human beings and that a little mercy, like stepping aside and letting them by, would be surely appreciated.

A few yards farther, the beast came into focus. Ten, maybe twelve feet tall, it was the burnt hollowed out carcass of a colossal ancient cottonwood tree. The road appeared to divide in front of it. Tyler couldn't remember a Y on the map, and he feared that in the White Out, they had veered down the wrong road.

He unzipped his parka and took out the map. "Man, am I ever glad I brought this thing. I don't have a clue where we are. This is the first time I've been past Fishpot Lake."

"Me too," said Tonya. "We've ridden the horses throughout most of the valley, but never this far. They huddled together at the foot of the toboggan, to create a windbreak for the tattered old forestry map, and then carefully unfolded it.

"Give me some light Ches," said Tyler.

Pinpointing their exact location with a flickering, slowly dying flashlight made the task nearly impossible, as did the sloppy half-inch snowflakes blurring the ink. But there it was – a divide in the road.

"Why didn't we notice that before?"

"The road seems to branch around something. Obviously around that tree, but maybe it's somebody's property," said Tonya. "Maybe there's a cabin in there that hasn't been drawn on the map." A quick survey with their flashlights however, ruled that out. All that was behind the freakish stump were other blackened stumps and a thriving young forest of 3 to 6 foot spruce trees, whose tender boughs were heavily burdened with snow.

By now, Tonya was becoming acutely aware of a situation she had been trying to ignore for the past hour, and this stump was exactly what she needed. While she contemplated what to tell the boys, the faint barking of several dogs could be heard from the direction of her bushy outhouse. "Oh great! How am I supposed to go in there now?"

To skirt the issue she casually mentioned, "Somebody with dogs must live near here."

"Those aren't dogs," said Tyler. "Those are wolves. They won't bother us as long as we keep moving."

"Look, you guys," she blurted out. "I've got to go, bad! And I don't want to go into the bush by myself."

Having no experience with sisters Chester suggested, "Why don't you go stand behind that big stump over there. What's the big deal?"

"Chester, girls don't operate that way!" she snapped.

Then the light went on. "Oh...." he grimaced. "That would be cold."

She danced on one foot then the other, putting it off for as long as she could. Then she quickly unstrapped her snowshoes and backpack, dumping them on the road, and hobbled into the bush warning, "You guys turn around and talk loudly. And I don't want to see the whites of your eyes until I come back here." They snickered the whole time she was gone, but they did as she asked, like true gentlemen.

When she returned she was much happier, until she heard the howling of the wolves. They were getting close.

"Come on Tonya!" shouted Tyler. "Help me pull this thing. We've got to get out of here. We've got to outrun them to the river."

Suddenly the fatigue they'd been battling disappeared. It was as though a reservoir of energy had been tapped. In spite of the snowshoes and bulky backpacks, they ran so fast the toboggan swayed wildly behind them. It was a ridiculous sight. Chester started to laugh. Then they all laughed until they were so weak they were forced to slow down.

Straggling in the rear, Chester glanced over his shoulder. Four black wolves were loping up the road about a hundred yards behind him. "Run you guys!" They're catching up to us."

Even though his unlaced boots felt like they had been lined with lead, Chester managed to run faster than he had ever run in his life. The trees on the sides of the road flew past in a blur. Then he tripped and fell face down on the icy road. He tasted blood and his lip stung sharply. Raising his head to see where they were, tears blinded his eyes. "That's it," he thought. "I'm done."

"Tyler!" he hollered. "They're going to eat me!"

Tyler and Tonya turned just in time to see the wolves skidding to a halt around Chester's motionless body in the middle of the road.

"Help him!" screeched Tonya.

Tyler dashed into the ditch and brought out a long sturdy pole from a pile of slash, and then he tore down the road towards them, hollering and swinging wildly. He managed a couple jabs into the backside of one of them. The yiping appeared to startle and disorganize them, dispersing them into the bush.

Tyler helped Chester to his feet then he and Tonya took turns hugging him. Chester was shaking uncontrollably. "Oh man," he said. "I thought I was a goner." While he brushed the snow off his parka, he spotted a shiny piece of paper at his feet. It was the wrapper from the chocolate bar he had eaten earlier.

"This is amazing!" he said, picking it up and examining it for teeth marks. "It must have fallen out of my pocket and they carried it here; that was near the Michelle Creek turn- off."

"Wow, that's got to be ten miles," said Tonya.

"Ten miles is nothing for a wolf," snapped Tyler. "You're lucky they weren't hungry for more than chocolate. If they'd been hunting you, I never would've been able to scare them away. That was really stupid Chester."

"You think I don't know that? I didn't do it on purpose." Chester felt bad for causing so much trouble and he knew Tyler was right, but did he have to say it in front of Tonya? Couldn't he, just once, not embarrass him? It was all he could do to not smart mouth him back.

"Come on. Let's get out of here," said Tyler. "I have a feeling we haven't seen the last of those guys."

When they rounded the next bend, they could hear water rushing. It was the Baezaeko. Once they were on the other side they would be safe. As they approached the bank, they started looking for the bridge. They walked a hundred yards in either direction, but there was no sign of a bridge.

"Are you sure this is the right river?" asked Tonya.

"Good question Tonya." he replied, slightly irritated by her lack of trust. "Come on Chester, let's see if we can find a way across this thing."

Chester was still nursing his own grudge. "Yeah, yeah, I'm coming. Don't get your girdle in a knot," he grumbled under his breath. He hated Tyler telling him what to do. All he wanted was a little respect - was that too much to ask?

Steadying themselves with protruding roots on the bank, they navigated the slippery rocks and slash to the river. Then they scanned the riverbed and both banks with their flashlights. "I see it!" yelled Chester.

A dozen or more moss and snow-covered sawn timbers, approximately fifteen feet long, and attached by a rusted steel cable, were leaning against the opposite bank.

"That's got to be the bridge. It's right here in front of us."

"Well at least we know we've got the right river," Tyler said disappointedly. "This isn't going to be easy."

In the dark it was impossible to tell exactly how wide the river was. With the snow outlining the edges, they guessed maybe fifty feet across at the narrowest point. The banks on both sides were roughly eight feet high and steep. Most rivers this time of year were silenced by a six to twelve inch crust of ice. But the Baezaeko's bubbly chatter was crystal clear. Down river, out of sight, was the ominous vibration of a thunderous current. And that wasn't the only unnerving sound - the wolves they had supposedly frightened away a few minutes ago, were wailing not far behind them.

"Do you think we can do it, Ty?" asked Chester.

After a lengthy pause he replied, "I hope so."

When they returned to Tonya and the toboggan, Tilda was whimpering. Tonya was shining her flashlight on the old woman's face. Her forehead was wrinkled and there were tears in her eyes. Whenever they had checked her before, she'd been sleeping or staring at the sky. This wasn't like her.

"Are you in pain, Mrs. Chantyman?"

Again she whimpered. But this time louder.

"I think she's trying to tell us something," said Tonya. "Maybe she was hurt when we were running down the road back there."

"Well we can't stop now. We can check her when we get to the other side. Right now we've got to get ahead of those wolves. Make sure the tarp is tied securely so the water can't get inside, ordered Tyler."

"Tyler! Come on man, this won't take a minute. Let's give her a drink or unwrap her and see what's wrong. It's been hours since we've checked her," insisted Chester.

"No! We'll check her on the other side."

"You sure like being the big man, don't you Ty!" taunted Chester.

"Why don't you grow up, Chester!"

"Why don't you make me!"

"Look you guys! You can argue after we get her to her sister's," urged Tonya. "Let's just get there."

With his back to them, Tyler bent over to check the tarp knots. "Yeah, you're right. I think me and old Ches are gonna have us a little chat when we get there."

It was all Chester could do to keep from kicking him in the rear so he would fall flat on his face and look like a fool. But he restrained himself for Tilda's and Tonya's sake.

"You could help me Chester," Tyler sneered with a backwards glance.

"I could help you alright," he thought, "right into the river."

83

"Chester, go ahead of us and steady the foot of the toboggan. Tonya and I will lower the head from up here."

Chester wanted to suggest that he and Tonya catch it from the bottom, but seeing he had made such a fool of himself in the last hour, he felt he couldn't risk it. He scampered halfway down the bank and dug his feet into a mound of dirt and waited for the others to get into position.

"Let us know when you're ready," Tyler shouted over the roar of the river.

Chester rechecked his grip and called back, "I'm ready!" And they started to let it down.

The weight of it surprised him. He staggered backwards and lost his footing, falling onto an obtuse ice-flanked boulder. A sharp pain shot up his left arm into his jaw, momentarily stealing his breath. In the effort to save himself, he inadvertently jerked the toboggan rope out of Tyler and Tonya's hands. The toboggan dropped the last three feet to the ground and shot onto the ice out of control.

Had it been carrying any other cargo, going down any other slope on any other day they might have cheered, but it was an eight-foot metal toboggan doing what it did best, sliding down a sheet of ice. In no time it was out of sight, heading for who knew where - rapids, the Pacific Ocean?

Tyler charged down the bank and onto a shelf of ice after it, slipping and tripping all the way. Chester and Tonya were not far behind hollering, "Atsoo come back! Come back!"

Finally, he spotted it and with a giant lunge, he dove onto it to try to stop it. His weight sent them crashing through the ice into the frigid water. They tumbled over and over beneath the water. When he surfaced he gasped, "Grab the rope!" The current and his soaked clothing kept sucking him under until his energy and air were nearly gone.

Chester and Tonya ran between the slippery shore and the ice yelling, "We're trying! We're tryin!" Every step on the ice was warned with a terrifying, "Crack!" They could feel the icy water rising inside their boots and its spray drenching their gloves and faces. "Oh God, please help us!" cried Tonya. "HELP US!"

Then, as suddenly as the toboggan had taken off, it stopped, getting jammed between two boulders - its foot lurching into the air then landing with a splash. To Tyler's amazement, the water was only knee-deep. He lay in the middle of the river, his head spinning, trying to catch his breath. When Tonya and Chester reached him, he was on his knees, jerking the rope and trying to boot the toboggan free. He was fuming. "Help me get this thing out of here!" he screeched. Frantically he shook the rope, but his rage made it worse. Tonya noticed the rope was looped around one of the rocks and managed to free it, then the three of them hauled the toboggan out of the water and up the bank on the other side.

"Chester!" he ranted, "Help me unwrap her!"

"Why would you want to expose her to the cold?" questioned Chester. "Wouldn't it be better to...?"

Then something snapped. "Alright, that's it!" he yelled. "Chester you're dead!"

"Come on dirt bag," Chester hollered back, "Let's see what you've got! You're so tough! Let's see how tough you really are!" He didn't feel cold or pain, just fury and it felt great. He was going beat Tyler until he got some respect.

They fell to the ground rolling repeatedly, punching and kicking. Their lungs burned with exhaustion. Every time he swallowed he tasted blood. Tyler was sick to death of being second-guessed all the time. There wasn't a thing he asked Chester to do since their grandmother got sick that hadn't been met with resistance. He wasn't backing down until he got the respect an older sibling was due.

They pounded each other, both of them wincing and puffing, "You give? You give? Had enough yet?" Tonya begged them to stop but they ignored her.

In the distance, the mournful howling of the wolves could be heard. Above them, Tonya's helpless sobbing. In the fracas, they managed to block out every plea but one. From under the tarp came a muffled familiar, "Quit dat! Quit dat!"

Dazed, they stopped and listened intently. They couldn't believe what they were hearing. On their knees, they scrambled to the toboggan to find Tilda trying bat off the tarp and wiggle free. When they uncovered her, she was frowning and shaking her head. Her blue lips were chattering a string of Carrier words they didn't recognize and probably not allowed to repeat.

"Atsoo," they shrieked, "you can talk!"

# CHAPTER SEVEN

# TREE HOUSE

They knelt around the toboggan, marveling at Tilda's miraculous improvement and contemplating what to do next. According to Tonya's watch, it was four a.m. It had stopped snowing but the wind was building and it had become fiercely cold. Their clothing was frozen stiff and they convulsed with shivering. Their faces were so numb their lips could barely form words, but it wasn't enough to keep Tonya from telling them exactly how she felt. "I can't stand either of you. I believed in you. I thought you were mature enough to handle this, but I was wrong. Let's build a fire, dry off and take her back."

They were quiet for what seemed forever, but it was likely only five minutes. Their eyes never left the ground until Tyler, lost for words, sheepishly broke the silence, "I'm sorry Tonya. You're right. We should go home. I'll build a fire if you guys can help me find some firewood."

"I'm sorry too Tonya," said Chester remorsefully. The idea of going back now, after all their preparation and the near miss with the social worker was incredibly sad but what their fighting was doing to Tonya made him feel worse. She was a good friend. She deserved better than this. Why they couldn't keep from fighting, even in front of her, he didn't know. It was like they had no control over their temper and their actions at times. He wondered if it had something to do with the Fetal Alcohol Syndrome they were supposed to have. Whatever it was, it scared him. If it didn't stop, who knows what they might do in the future.

The gnawing ache in Chester's left forearm, which disappeared during the fight, returned. His wrist and hand were swollen and couldn't be bent. Everything from the shoulder down throbbed mercilessly unless it was held up by the other hand. He had never broken a bone before but he was sure this was how it would feel. "My arm is killing me."

With a somewhat guarded tone of remorse Tyler asked, "Did I do that?"

"Not exactly. I fell on a big rock down by the river when the toboggan slipped," Chester winced, raising it for Tyler to see. "I can't move my wrist. I think it might be broken. I need a sling."

Tyler was relieved to hear this hadn't been his doing. However, pounding a broken bone couldn't have helped it. As he examined the swollen discolored hand without touching it, he felt like a bully. "That must hurt."

"Yeah."

Tyler slid out of his backpack and lowered it to the ground so he could look in the first–aid kit for a sling, where he thought he saw one. To his dismay, the backpack's zipper was torn apart and everything inside had fallen out. The first-aid kit, his food supply, the newspaper and matches were all gone. Fortunately his hunting knife was in the holster on his belt or it would have been swept away too.

"This is bad, real bad," he whispered to himself, trying to stay calm and not show his alarm. "I can't believe this! What next?"

He remembered putting an extra book of matches with the map into the inside pocket of his parka. He patted the pocket for the map and felt nothing. He didn't know which would be the greater loss, the map or the matches. Frantically, he fumbled down the zipper and fingered through the pocket, but there was nothing. Then, digging a little deeper into the corner – there they were, half-dissolved but there. He heaved a sigh of relief.

Not knowing how long he could keep the news from the others he decided to be upfront about it. "Tonya! Chester! We need to talk. Something has happened." They gathered around him, noting the furled lines of concern across his brow. "When I was in the river, the zipper of my backpack must have ripped apart. Everything fell out - the first-aid kit, the food, water, newspaper, and matches. Furthermore, the map is gone too. All that's left are these," he said holding up what was left of the matches.

"Look in your backpacks and check your supplies."

The shocking news of the loss sent a bigger chill up their spines than the icy clothing. They shrugged off their backpacks and unzipped them. "The fruit's okay," said Tonya, "but everything in the boxes, like the crackers and dried cereal is wrecked."

"Same here," said Chester.

"You don't have anything else, Chester?" asked Tyler. "No chocolate bars or candies?"

Chester didn't answer right away. He didn't want to divulge what he really had unless it could buy him some favor with Tonya. Then he thought about Tilda. On many occasions, she had given him the last piece of gum in her purse. At least, that's what she had said.

Grudgingly, he tossed the items onto the toboggan. "Here's my water, oranges, jujubes, licorice and Cheezies, they're a bit crunched but they're still good."

"Here's my apple, orange and my water too," added Tonya.

"Check your pockets too Chester," ordered Tyler.

Deftly, he fingered one of the two drenched chocolate bars behind the torn liner in his pocket then pretended to thoroughly probe both, pulling them inside out. If Tyler didn't believe him, he would check the pockets himself, as he had often done in the past. Acting belligerently, he flipped the other chocolate bar onto the ground near the toboggan, not on it, hoping to convince him that he was being robbed.

"It's not much," Tyler grumbled, "but it'll have to do. Tonya you're going to carry the food in your backpack."

Chester wasn't comfortable with the insinuation but at least the insult wasn't spoken. He would give him credit for that.

"Chester, how are your matches and do either of you have any newspaper?"

They dumped the remainder of their backpack contents onto the ground and feverishly picked through them while Tyler held his flashlight overhead. But there were no matches or paper.

"I can't believe you guys. Where did your matches go Chester?"

"How are we supposed to start a fire?"

"You said you were going to take care of the matches Tyler, remember?" Tonya reminded him, patting her pocket.

"I know! I'm sorry alright?"

Stirring beneath the tarp, Tilda began to cough, clear her throat and try to speak. After several unsuccessful attempts, Chester knelt on the ground beside her.

"What are you trying to say, Atsoo?"

Repeatedly, she mumbled the same thing but he couldn't figure it out. "It sounds like she's saying, "Matches in your hair."

"That's what it is," exclaimed Tonya. "She's trying to tell us to put the matches in our hair, so they'll dry. Carriers used to do it years ago when their matches got wet. My father told me about it."

"My hair is drenched," said Tyler, handing the matches to Chester. "Your hair always dries faster than mine."

At least his frizzy mop was good for something. He tucked the damp book of matches as close to his scalp as he could then secured it with his toque, which for some reason had managed to stay reasonably dry. Then he pulled the hood of his parka over his head for added warmth.

"Now, paper?" said Tyler. "What have we got for paper?"

Pausing for a second, suddenly it came to Chester, like divine inspiration. "I know where we can get some, under atsoo."

Tyler hummed and hawed, "I don't know…" It was a good idea. It just wasn't his.

"It might be our only option," Tonya giggled. "Help me check her."

"Alright, why don't you help her, Chester? I'll go look for a place to set up camp." Trust Tyler to leave when the dirty work had to be done.

When they untied the tarp, they discovered the newspaper, in fact everything but Tilda's braid was dry. The underside of the tarp was certainly cool, but her clothing as warm as though she was lying in her own bed. The only newspaper that was remotely damp was the layer right next to her. After they removed that piece, they took all but a couple layers and bundled her again.

The road, which had been a two-lane logging road on the other side of the Baezaeko River, was little better than a glorified cattle trail on this side of it. Tyler hadn't wandered far in the knee-deep snow when he spotted something with his flashlight. Ahead on the right side of the trail, was an entrance. A few yards in, the passage opened into a circular den with a powdery dirt floor. The lush boughs of an immense cedar tree formed a roof ten feet above. The dense stand of half-grown conifers surrounding the den created a windbreak not even a howling windstorm couldn't penetrate. By the look of the charred remains in the shallow fire pit, the small stack of firewood nearby and several wooden blocks, others had also enjoyed this sanctuary.

Ecstatic with the find, Tyler yelled to Chester and Tonya, waving them in with his flashlight. Chester and Tonya ran with the toboggan to the clearing and parked it beneath the tree.

"Wow, this is unbelievable Tyler! It's like it's been prepared just for us! Look over there," said Tonya pointing to the firewood. "Dry wood - it must be a courtesy thing; you replace what you use."

"Well it's a start, but we're going to need a lot more than that." Then he meekly suggested, "Chester, why don't you stay with atsoo and rest your arm while Tonya and I find some more fire wood."

"You think you could you help me sit her up so she can look around before you go?"

"Right after we get the fire built Ches," he said leading Tonya deeper into the bush on the trail that had brought them there.

He could only imagine what Tyler had in mind. But he was in too much pain to protest. His arm throbbed like a toothache and the fingers were so swollen the tips were numb. He sat cross-legged next to the toboggan, rocking and sniffling, holding his arm to his chest. It seemed to hurt less when it wasn't hanging down. If only he had a sling and something for the pain.

First-aid classes in school had taught him how to protect a fracture by immobilizing the joint above and below it with a splint. Reducing swelling and pain could be accomplished by applying cold and elevating the part. Something cold was obvious – it was all around him, but a sling. He knew he had seen something somewhere that could be reconfigured into a sling, but where...Then it came to him. Tilda had been wearing a red and white kerchief around her neck when they loaded her onto the toboggan.

"Can I borrow your kerchief Atsoo?" he said leaning over her. "I need to make a sling for my arm."

With the nod of approval, he gently untied it and slid it from around her neck. He played with it for a while but couldn't remember how to fold it.

"You make a triangle." Tilda croaked softly. "The long side runs down the middle of your chest with the arrow pointing to your sore arm. Put your arm on the kerchief and tie the pointed ends in a knot at the back of your neck."

After a few frustrating attempts, Chester finally had the sling tied securely. His arm still throbbed but it felt better.

"Now put some cold moss on it," she said, "Dat will take the fatness out of the fingers. The moss will be on a dead tree, like dat one over dare."

As Chester headed for the stump she was pointing to, he noticed Tonya, too far away to see clearly, sitting on a log staring up into a tree. Tyler was hanging upside down from a branch about six feet above her. Suddenly, a clump of snow dropped from a branch above him, dousing him and her, nearly knocking him to the ground. Tonya fell backwards on the snow in hysterics.

Tonya had always been Tyler's friend, truthfully his best friend, but after she started coming to the house to help with Tilda he noticed that she was a girl. Then at Fishpot Lake when she took off her coat and glasses, and he saw how beautiful she was, his feelings changed. He was consumed with the desire to kiss her. He had trouble thinking about anything else.

He swung to the ground and sat next to her, their parkas just touching. This was it - his opportunity to kiss her and there wouldn't likely be another for weeks, perhaps months, depending on how things went with is grandmother. He had blown it at Fishpot and she pushed him away. He couldn't bring himself to look at her incase their eyes met and she wasn't ready for his message and she rejected him again. He wanted to say so much. After a few moments of awkward silence and staring at the bush, all he could think to say was, "Sure is a nice night."

"Yeah," she replied.

"What a stupid thing to say," he berated himself, sweat running down his temples, heart somersaulting and a lump in his throat so big he could barely swallow. He was lucky he could say anything at all. If he couldn't think or speak, how was he supposed to get up the nerve to kiss her? He decided a surprise approach might work best. He would turn towards her, position his lips, close his eyes and wait.

Cautiously, he turned his head towards her. Suddenly, she turned hers too and their eyes met. It surprised him. He wasn't ready. His heart raced out of control. Panicked, he leaned forward and pushed his lips towards her, closed his eyes and waited, waited for their lips to touch. But nothing happened.

Bewildered, he opened his eyes and she was gone. In fact, she was twenty feet away already picking up twigs, humming like she hadn't even noticed.

"Come on Tyler. Let's get the firewood," was all she said.

He was too embarrassed and mad at himself to respond. He felt like a five year old sneaking a kiss in the coatroom on the first day of kindergarten.

With his hunting knife, he angrily hacked several two-inch thick, six to eight feet poles from a heap of brush near the "love nest". Then he dragged them back to the camp-site where he stomped them into two-foot lengths and added them to the pile. Oddly, the sweat of physical labor was a relief from the heat of his passion.

While Tyler built a tiny stick teepee in the fire pit, Tonya brought him handfuls of crumbled newspaper. When he was satisfied it would ignite with a half-decent match he summoned Chester. The matches had had an hour to dry next to his scalp. It was time to see if the Carrier trick worked.

Working from the outside of the book towards the middle, Tyler plucked off a damp match and struck it against a boulder in the fire pit. Each time as he feared, the head ripped off. Several more failures and the prospects were fading - until he reached a match in the middle. One swipe and it lit.

Carefully, he cupped the precious flame in his hands and carried it towards the newspaper. Everyone stared as the transfer was made, hoping for a miracle. Slowly, from the paper, a delicate smoke lady began to gracefully dance into the night sky.

"Way to go Ty!" everyone cheered, including Tilda. Then as he had agreed, Tyler helped sit Tilda up against the trunk of the cedar tree so she could see the fire.

By the time the fire was hot enough to dry their clothes, the first sign of dawn was gleaming along the eastern mountain range. They were supposed to be starting the Kluskus Trail now, not camping. But all they could think about was sleep and staying warm. After they snacked on a few Cheezies, shared some of Tonya and Chester's water, they curled up on the ground around the fire and fell asleep.

# CHAPTER EIGHT

# OLD BILL

"Are you nearly ready for breakfast honey?" hollered Tonya's mother, as she frantically scurried between flipping the eggs and bacon, lifting them to plain white dinner plates and buttering the toast. "Hurry up and come to the table. These eggs aren't going to wait forever."

"Mmm, that sure smells good Nat," called Rick from the bathroom. "I could eat a horse. Go ahead and pour my coffee. I've just got to run upstairs and grab the pager." When he strode into the kitchen, the pager was clipped to the leather belt of his neatly pressed black uniform trousers.

Natalie eyed her handsome husband from head to toe, smiling. Whether it was the uniform or the adventurous man she fell in love with, he still made her heart flip. "I thought you said you weren't going to do anymore trades with Jim for awhile Rick. You said you were tired of one-day weekends."

Straddling his chair at the table and taking a quick slurp of his coffee, he replied. "I know I know. He said his mother needed him to help her look at this apartment in town or something and…Well, when he came at me with those sad puppy dog eyes, I couldn't resist."

"I've heard the story a million times Rick," the tone of her voice now sounding more like a nagging wife than the flirtatious schoolgirl she usually was when he was near. "I was hoping you would help me shovel the barn today."

"I'm really sorry honey. You know how much I've been looking forward to helping you shovel a month's worth of …."

Just then the pager chirped twice.

"That'll be dispatch," Natalie whined. "Well, there goes the day."

Leaning sideways till the legs of the chair were airborne, Rick plucked the receiver from the radiophone mounted on the wall.

"What's up Linda?" After a minute of nodding his head and rolling his eyes, he answered, "Okay, I'll check it out."

"What's going on?" asked Natalie.

"The band leader at Kluskus just called and said some guy was chasing his wife and kids around the house with a gun; that he locked them out the house and was hollering at them from the inside. Apparently, the woman and the kids were wearing only pajamas and nothing on their feet. Linda said she sounded pretty upset and asked if someone would come out right away. It's probably nothing. Teddy's likely just horsing around again. Little too much…" he said, miming an upended glass to his mouth.

"Isn't that where Tonya and the Chantymans are going?" asked Natalie. "Tonya said Tilda had to go out there to visit a sick sister or something."

"Who was driving them, Old Bill?"

"Probably. He's usually the one who takes her places. Maybe you should try to catch up to them. They might be heading into something dangerous."

"I'm sure it's nothing Nat. Please don't worry. But I'd better get going. I've got to fuel up the Blazer and put a bit of air into the spare," he said gulping down the last of his breakfast and coffee.

"Is that the vehicle with the winch and flares?"

"No dear. It's the one with the bald summer tires."

"Well that road makes me nervous, especially in the winter. They say there are so many wolves and moose this time of year. And the weather can change so fast. One minute it's clear, the next - it's snowing so hard you can't see your hand in front of your face. Let me pack you a lunch, Rick. It'll only take me a minute."

"Got no time. I'll pick something up at Jenz on the way out of town," he said drawing her to his chest and pecking her forehead.

"Isn't there supposed to be a second officer when you confront someone with a weapon?"

"Don't worry. I'll call you as soon as I get there," he reassured, pulling her off him. As he flew out the door with his navy blue uniform jacket under his arm, she managed to thrust a brown paper bag with a couple of egg sandwiches, some chocolate cookies and an apple into his hand.

He drove to the one-room police station, a kilometer away in the Nazko village, where he opened the door of the one bay heated garage and started the Chevy Blazer. While it warmed, he slipped into the office for a weather update, a forestry map, and his duty bag. When he returned, he started the pre-trip check.

On the dash, all the lights that were supposed to be off were. The fuel tank was full and the radio check produced a perfect static-free, "Keep in touch," from dispatch. In a large compartment on the floor in front of the stick shift were extra bullets, pepper spray, handcuffs and the first-aid kit. From the holster on the floor next to the passenger door, he pulled out the short handled shotgun, checked the bullet chamber to make sure it was loaded and reset the safety, praying it would stay that way until he came home.

Then he got out and went around the back and opened the rear doors so he could inspect the survival gear. Behind the back seat was a 4'X3'X1' chrome box, with a hundred foot nylon rope, four flares, box of wooden matches, sharpened hatchet, compass, approximately twenty pages of newsprint, small bundle of dried kindling, two-man nylon tent, box of two dozen packaged dried fruit and granola bars and a dozen bottled waters.

When he was confident he had everything, he headed to Jenz's gas station next door. Allan Jenz was a retired US army mechanic. His intrigue with northern Canada and Alaska was something his New Mexico roots couldn't explain. As near as he could figure, it started after he watched the movie, Never Cry Wolf, while he was in the army. He vowed once he got out of the service he was going to move to Alaska with his wife and young son and build a gas station with a convenience store. And twelve years ago, that's what he started out to do.

On the way through Quesnel, he took a wrong turn and ended up on the Nazko highway. Black bears scampered in and out of the ditch nearly every bend in the road. Finally, a pack of wolves darted in front of their overloaded pickup. One of them, he nearly hit. He said just days before, he had dreamt he saw three wolves running across the highway and he believed it was a sign telling him where they were supposed to live. Moving to Nazko was the best thing he'd ever done, he often told his customers.

Al usually ran the pumps, but if he was tied up servicing a vehicle in the one-bay garage, his eighteen-year old son Danny filled in. Otherwise, Danny was behind the cash register and his mother in the cafe.

"Going someplace today Constable Clement?" asked Danny politely.

Squinting to see the young man's face in the blinding sunlight he replied, "Yes, I've got to make a run out to Kluskus and settle a little dispute."

Leaning over the windshield to clean the window Danny said, "Guess you heard about the big storm moving in eh? Heard about it on the radio ten minutes ago. They're expecting a heavy dump of snow and fifty kilometer winds this afternoon. Supposed to drop to fifteen or twenty below tonight."

"So I heard." He looked over the backseat to make doubly sure he had remembered to throw in his goatskin mitts, fur lined boots and Old Faithful; a ten-year old down-filled hooded parka that had taken him through several blizzards since he'd started with the force.

There wasn't a cloud in the sky and the sun was so intense that Rick had to remove his jacket and put on his sunglasses. It was hard to imagine the weather was going to change that drastically. Ominous forecasts like this usually turned out to be false alarms but to be safe he thought he should warn Natalie that he might have to stay the night in Kluskus. He would do it right after he backed up to the air-hose on the side of Jenz' garage, filled the spare and checked all the tire pressures.

As he was pulling onto the highway and calling Natalie on his two-way, sixty-two year old Bill Wilcox turned into the gas station in his 1968 Ford pick-up. It was a smoky noisy cornflake of a wreck. Bill didn't believe in mufflers. He said they would only get knocked off. Though it's faded red and white body was half riddled with rust, Al Jenz said the beefed-up suspension and over-sized tires could chew through more snow and mud than most all-terrain vehicles ever dreamt of.

Bill was the oldest man on the reserve. Just under six feet, slim, with shoulder length silver hair tied back in a ponytail and a handsome face that bore the scars of several bar fights and logging mishaps, he went nowhere without his reddish brown buck-skinned fringed coat and his foot-long hunting knife. He never married and he never returned from a hunting trip skunked. After he turned fourteen, he said there hadn't been a sober day in his life. That is until five years ago when he met Tilda and got saved. Since then he was known for the miniature black Bible he carried in his pocket instead of the whiskey bottle.

He met her at one of the monthly meetings in the sixty-year old reserve church. Catholic priests and protestant ministers took turns conducting the half-hour Sunday after-noon service in the otherwise abandoned rather run-down twenty-seat sanctuary. Usually there were only a handful of elderly folk. Sometimes it was just Bill, Tilda and the service leader. If the preacher didn't make it, they'd go to Tilda's for a time of Bible reading and prayer. They'd sit around the table, giggle over a cup of tea and eat something she had baked for him earlier in the day.

Marriage had come into the conversation a couple of times. Bill thought the boys needed a father but Tilda admitted she could never love another man the way she had loved her deceased husband, so they just remained good friends.

Rick rolled down his window and waved him to his side. The bewildered expression on his face gave Bill the hint to not roll by and find out what he wanted. He stomped on the brakes and stalled the sputtering blue-smoke spewing engine.

"I thought you were taking Tilda and her boys to Kluskus today to visit her sick sister."

"I don't know about that," replied Bill. "But I was supposed to stop by and take her garbage to the dump."

"Tonya's with them. Maybe we should stop by her place and see what's going on.

"Maybe she's left a note on the table. She usually does that if she's expecting me and has to go out."

Rick rolled up the long unploughed driveway with Bill close behind. Then they stomped the snow from their knee-high boots, entered the house and tiptoed over to the table. The only note on the table was the piece of paper with the list of scratched off supplies for the kids' trip.

"What do you make of this?" asked Rick, holding it up for Bill to study too.

"Toboggan, deer hide, snowshoes," said Bill, "This doesn't sound like Tilda. She was having trouble walking to the mailbox let alone walking to Kluskus. Boy, her sister sure must be sick."

"That's crazy! Let's go out back and see if we can see anything."

"That's a good idea. I'll get the garbage while we're there."

Behind the house footprints had been trampled in the snow to the shed and into the bush trail. "I hate to say it," said Rick, "but it looks like they went somewhere on foot."

"I just want to check something in the shed," said Bill.

They unlatched the unlocked shed door and shuffled inside. Pushing past the half-dozen bulging black plastic garbage bags, broken furniture, watering cans, hoses, push mower, shovels and rakes they managed to reach an empty space on the floor.

"This is where the toboggan usually leans against the wall," said Bill.

They stared at each other, shaking their heads in disbelief. "Why would they do this and not tell anyone?" muttered Rick. "We'd better keep this to ourselves. I don't want Natalie worrying," he gestured for Bill to keep the secret.

"I won't tell a living soul. Do you want me to come along Rick?"

"No, you'd better stay here in case they return. If they do come back, will you please get a message to Linda, my dispatcher, so she can let me know where they are? I have enough to contend without wondering about them."

After they loaded Tilda's garbage into the back of Bill's pick-up, they drove off in different directions. Rick radioed the time, nine forty-five, and his location to Linda then headed for Kluskus.

# CHAPTER NINE

# TILDA TALKS

Shafts of welcoming sunlight beamed through the snow-laden boughs of the giant cedar. Tyler squinted at the brilliant blue sky and dazzling white snow on the branches above. For a moment he found himself believing he was in bed beside Chester. The occasional crackle of the campfire and waft of wood smoke took him home where his grand-mother was humming and shuffling about in the kitchen, stoking the stove and stirring a pot of bubbling oatmeal. White homemade bread was toasting in the toaster. He could almost taste it.

He looked at his watch and couldn't believe his eyes – it was nine thirty. The others were still sleeping. He stood slowly then stretched and groaned. Every joint in his body was stiff and achy. He stirred the ashes in the fire pit with the charred pole Chester had used before he fell asleep. From the stack of branches Tonya piled near the tree, he picked out the driest twigs and bunched them on top of the still-warm coals then gently blew. At first there were only a few sleepy embers but with a little coaxing and some thicker pieces, they erupted into hungry hot flames.

With the heat, he began to feel the tips of his fingers and his toes again but with an intense itching and burning that nearly drove him insane. He found the only way to cope with it was to walk around and try to think about something else. Then it came to him, to search for the Kluskus Trail sign. He shuffled through the snow back to the road. Everything had been shrouded by the heavy deposit of snow. For an instant, he thought he spotted it about twenty feet away, on the edge of the road. He waded to a hump and excitedly gloved away the snow. It was a wooden post alright - half-rotten with rusted nails but not a hint of the sign that had been ripped off. He dug around it until his gloves were packed with snow and his wrists ached from the cold. Finally, he gave up. This has to be the road.

Baffled and slightly discouraged, he returned to the others. Chester was sitting cross-legged by the fire massaging his sore arm and poking the fire with his stick. The tarp over Tilda's head was moving slightly and Tonya was rubbing her eyes in the sunlight.

"I'm starved," she said.

"Me too," added Chester. "What's for breakfast?"

"We need to dig out the food and divide it up," said Tyler. "We should be there by suppertime so that means three meals."

Tonya unzipped her backpack and dumped the contents onto the toboggan over Tilda's legs and Chester did the same, then she and Tyler began to count the pieces. There was a bag of jujubes, and one of red licorice, about twenty pieces in each, six oranges and the remainder of Chester's Cheezies - approximately three cups worth.

"That should be half an orange, two pieces of licorice, two jujubes and about five Cheezies each per meal," said Tyler.

"I think you counted wrong Ty," she said rearranging the piles. "And I thought you were the math genius. Actually, there will be only one and a half pieces of licorice and the same for the jujubes per meal and two left over."

"Divide those in half and we each get a piece – doesn't that work out to two pieces each?"

"Yeah." She was baffled. There were twenty pieces, four people and three meals. 12 times 2 equaled 24. How did he make 20 pieces work? That's weird.

"How will we ever hold it all," mocked Chester.

Just when the day's rations had been neatly sorted into four piles, Tilda moved her legs and the piles rolled together into a jumbled heap. Before they rolled onto the ground, Tyler quickly caught the edge of the tarp and the others shoveled the candy onto a sheet of newspaper. Then he pulled back the tarp to see what was bothering his grandmother. She was frowning and muttering what had to be a lecture of some sort.

"What's wrong Atsoo?"

"Help me get up!"

"Tilda," said Tonya. "You can't get up - you've had a stroke."

"You guys better help me, but quick!"

"Tonya, help me sit her up."

"I have a feeling she wants to do more than just sit up," warned Tonya.

"You boys help me stand up, Now!"

"I don't know about this," worried Chester.

The three of them pulled away the blankets and tarp exposing her to the frigid air. As Tyler and Tonya gripped her arms and supported her to a sitting position, she shivered.

"Man, dat cold; must be twenty below. Help me over dare," she said pointing to the bush with her nose."

"You mean walk you over there Mrs. Chantyman?"

She was at least twice Tonya's weight before the stroke but she hadn't eaten in four days, with the exception of a few swallows of apple juice. It was likely she had lost some weight, but if she couldn't stand on the good leg, they doubted they would be able to raise her to her feet. One thing was clear; she wasn't taking, "No," for an answer.

"Tonya, you get under one arm and I'll get under the other," said Tyler. "Chester, stand behind her in case she starts to fall backwards. Then on the count of three we'll stand her, alright?"

"Ready? One...Two...Three...Stand!"

At first she was a dead lift. Her legs buckled and everyone staggered.

"Come on Tilda, you can do it," Tonya coached. "Put some weight on your good leg."

"Come on Atsoo," echoed the boys.

Puffing and grunting, she managed to stretch her left leg to the ground and with assistance, straightened it. In her ankle-length flannel nightgown and stocking feet, she stood, bent over and teetering, but supporting her weight. Then she dabbed the ground with her right foot. It buckled repeatedly until she balanced precariously on the side of it. Her right shoulder could rotate but most of the arm was a useless as wet spaghetti. With her arms wrapped around Tyler and Tonya's necks and her right leg trailing behind, she nodded for them to head into the bush.

Beyond the view of camp, beneath another tall sheltering tree, she spotted a log. When they reached it, she frantically flapped and cawed for them to leave, insisting that they not come back until she said so.

"Here, at least wear my coat Atsoo," urged Tyler, slinging it over her shoulders. He didn't dare tell her how foolish it was for her to be left alone – that would have been disrespectful and probably incurred an embarrassing yank of his ear when he least expected it.

Fifteen minutes later, she was staggering back, on her own, crouched over a stick she had dug out of the snow. "Tilda," they shouted, running to her, "What are you doing?

Let us help you." But she waved them away, scolding them in Carrier, for trying to help her when she could do it herself.

Two steps later, she was on the ground and her nightgown was tangled around her cold bluish white legs. They stood her, shook the snow off and limped her back to the toboggan where they wrapped her again in blankets and propped her against the tree. She beamed like a boy riding his first bicycle. Once they removed her wet stockings, she went to asleep.

The stockings were hung by the fire to dry and the candy, Cheezies and oranges were again counted and sorted into piles on the foot of the toboggan. Then each person received their breakfast ration and shoved the rest into their backpacks; Tyler put Tilda's with his own.

"This calls for a celebration," said Chester. "Let's eat."

"That would be your idea of a reward," jeered Tyler.

While they warmed by the fire, contentedly munching on the snacks and waiting for the socks to dry, the woeful lament of the wolves could be heard in the distance. They had heard them after they crossed the Baezaeko, but assumed they were on the other side. This sounded much closer, and strangely, like they were ahead of them now.

Tyler and Chester shot glances at one another. The color in Tonya's face disappeared. "I don't like the sound of that," she said.

Tilda chuckled, "Don't worry Tonya." Dey not going to hurt you. Don't worry bout dem four-legged ones - worry bout the two-legged kind. Dey much worse."

"How come you're not afraid of wolves, Mrs. Chantyman?"

"Been round dem all my life. Sometimes I go out with my father to the trap lines, and dey close by. Dey don't hurt us. Dey don't like it when you catch dare food. Sometimes dey try to take it back. Dat scare me, not my father. He shoot 'em."

"Did your father and mother teach you not to be afraid of wolves?"

"Dey teach us bout all the animals and fish too. I grew up on a big lake with bush all around. Dare were wolf, bear, deer, moose, muskrat, skunk, rabbit, beaver, fox, coyote - all kinds. No roads to town, no pick-ups. We went to town by boat twice a year for sugar, tea, and other stuff. The kids have to sit very still. The boat was very tipsy."

"Where did you go to school Tilda?" asked Tonya.

"The government make us go to residential school far away from home when we were seven or eight years old. We did not see our parents for many months. We live at school with the priest and nuns. Dey look after us and teach us. Some of dem were mean. Dey slap us for speaking our language and for crying at night. Dey tell us if we speak our language, we can't be a Christian. I know dey wrong. No body can take Jesus away from your heart.

Everyday we get porridge for breakfast - no milk, no sugar, sometimes lunch too. Suppertime we have moose or chicken, vegetables from the garden when we pick 'em. Sometimes we have rabbit when the boys catch 'em. But we were always hungry."

"Why didn't you run away?" asked Chester.

"Our parents say we have to go because the government, the police, and the priest tell 'em we have to learn to read and write."

"That must have been horrible," said Tonya.

"It wasn't all bad. We learn about God and Jesus. We sing songs dat make us happy. We learn to pray and go to church. I know God loves me. He always heps me. He will hep you too."

Tyler was furious. He had never heard Tilda's story of residential school abuse. She never brought it up and he never thought to ask. He'd heard from his relatives how the First Nations people had been deceived and mistreated by some government and religious leaders, but never experienced it. Now, though not from racial bias, he was being forced to outrun Social Services in the dead of winter, towing his fragile grandmother over one the most rugged regions in the province to keep his family together. He was more determined than ever to make it to Kluskus.

It was eleven o'clock by the time the socks were dry and they had finished their meager breakfast. The sun was high and the sound of howling wolves was farther away. They smothered the fire with snow and restocked the stash of firewood by the tree then headed for the road. The trail inclined sharply and before they walked a quarter mile, they encountered the best and the worst road conditions they had ever seen.

Beneath a canopy of cottonwood trees, whose snow-laden branches arched over the road from both sides, there were numerous foot-deep ruts, some ten feet long, glassed over with smooth black transparent ice. It was impossible to avoid them. They ran the entire length of the dense hundred yard deciduous tunnel. The brow in the middle was too rounded and slippery to navigate, as were the shoulders on the road. Nowhere was it easy to find enough traction to tow the toboggan. When they emerged, the sun shone with unbearable glare.

The one-lane road wound upwards for miles, it seemed, over steep red lava rock. Numerous sets of fresh moose and deer tracks zigzagged up and down the banks and across the deeply rutted road. Footprints of big-footed rabbits dotted the shallow ditches. This was the extent of any sign of life or traffic. No one had been up or down the road to pack it in days. They were blazing their way through two feet of untouched snow. Tonya and Chester weren't able to pull more than five minutes at a time. The only way any progress could be made was if two pulled and the other pushed.

By two o'clock, they finally reached the top of a long tree-lined hill which Tyler figured was, "Kookenay Hill." The locals had labeled it this because they said, if you didn't make it up the hill after several tries, you probably weren't going to. Either your gas or your engine would burn up in the attempt. It was wiser to bring out the beer and camp because you weren't going anywhere until somebody towed you up.

It was a long ways to the bottom, at least fifteen minutes by snowshoe they reasoned. But somebody had a much better idea.

"We should go down there on the toboggan," suggested Chester. "You took the words right out of my mouth," agreed Tyler. "I heard there was a river at the bottom," said Tonya. "You're not going to let a little river bother you are you?"

"What are we going to do with the snow shoes?"

"Let's leave them here Ty. We'll pick them up on our way back."

"I don't want to take a chance on loosing them, Ches. They belong in the old trading post. What if somebody comes while we're at Kluskus and thinks they're garbage?"

"Nobody in his right mind is going to be out here today. It must be twenty below."

"No Ches, I think we should sit on them. We'll cover them with blankets and sit on them. Help me roll Atsoo," ordered Tyler. "I'll steer, you be our brakes in the back and the girls will sit in the middle. You have to protect your arm."

"My arm's alright. How about you sitting in the back and I'll do the steering," insisted Chester.

"How're you going to steer without two hands on the rope?" said Tonya.

"I don't use my arms, I use my weight and lean."

"Okay, man. Have it your way. I'll sit in the back." Tyler was counting on his response. He had hoped all along to squeeze in behind Tonya and wrap his arms around her. He was confident too, that they could steer it by shifting their weight. They had steered this way for years. Unfortunately, it registered for Chester too late that he had missed his opportunity to sit behind Tonya.

When everyone was neatly tucked aboard, and the toboggan strategically perched on the crest, Tyler backed up and sprinted to the toboggan then leapt on. Initially the fresh snow resisted, but it was no match for five hundred plus pounds of aluminum thrust on a twelve percent grade. Halfway down, the slope leveled briefly and the thing was airborne.

When Chester yelled, "Lean!" they all leaned. The hoods of their parkas and hair flew straight back and the biting wind whistled past their ears. The snow was so brilliant their eyes were closed half the time. The boys hollered, "Yahoo!" and Tonya hollered for help. Tilda's wide toothless grin spelled it out. It was just a great day to be alive.

It was the most fun Chester had had in days, perhaps the whole winter, until he noticed something glistening at the bottom. The closer they came, the faster they went. He stared at it, blinking tears out of his eyes. Over the final rise, with less than a hundred feet till impact, what he feared became crystal clear; a pick-up was stuck sideways across the road.

About the time Chester spotted it, Tyler also realized their dilemma." Launch it, Chester, launch it!" he yelled. The words weren't even out of his mouth, when Chester yanked the front of the toboggan backwards with both hands and shouted, "Lean to the right...!"

He squeezed his eyes shut, and braced for impact. Instead, they were airborne, vaulting over a ten-foot bank then careening down the ditch towards a frozen pond with a beaver hut, dead centre. Before they had a chance to react, they collided with it. Brittle branches snapped like an explosion. Its thick mud walls were like concrete. The impact projected them into the person in front and Chester's sore arm took the brunt of it.

He cried out in agony, rocking and bracing his arm. "Oh my arm, my arm!" he whaled. It was nothing like the pain when he first hurt it – that was a bruise by comparison. An intense boring pain penetrated his left chest, arm and neck and he passed out.

Tyler and Tonya quickly pulled Tilda out of the way, wrapping her in a couple blankets and the tarp and dragged her to the shore. Then they carefully uncrossed Chester's legs and pulled him straight on the toboggan. His face was frighteningly pale and his respirations were so shallow he looked dead. Tonya panicked and began to cry. Tyler bent over him and watched for his chest to rise. He learned that from the CPR video he saw in gym class.

He felt awful for not insisting that Chester sit in the rear. Chester had complained so little about his arm the past few hours, he thought that it had somehow healed itself or hadn't really been a big deal from the start. Obviously he was wrong. His mind went blank. All he could think of was the ABCs of his CPR training:

A is for Airway.
B is for Breathing
C is for Circulation

Is he breathing? It was difficult to tell, but when he looked hard he could see his clothing rise and fall. Did he have a pulse? He grappled with one of his gloves till he could palpate his wrist about an inch above the thumb. It was there but faint and it seemed slow. He checked his own. It was about a hundred and forty. Chester's was about eighty. It worried him. He couldn't see anything wrong but he didn't know what else to do but yell at him. "Chester, Chester, wake up!" Tonya and Tilda stared silently in disbelief.

# CHAPTER TEN

# THE DINNER GUEST

B y two p.m. Richard Clement had his own problems. Arriving at the Baezaeko River he discovered, as the children had the night before, that the bridge was gone. His only way over the river was to winch the truck over.

He put on his parka, toque and gloves and got out of the still-running vehicle. Jerking the half-inch steel cable and hook from the winch, he headed towards the riverbed like a fireman lugging a fire hose. He had hoped to loop the cable around a trustworthy tree on the other side but to his dismay, it was at least twenty feet too short.

He cursed the cable and the biting north wind numbing his lips, nose and ears, then he shuffled back to the truck, flicked the winch switch and watched the cable recoil.

"Well at least the darn thing works," he grumbled. "But how am I supposed to get up the other side?"

He paced up and down the river in search of its narrowest point, like the kids had done. To his amazement, he found three sets of tracks and what appeared to be a toboggan impression. The boots were the size and brand the kids wore. He was relieved to see they had made it this far but couldn't understand their need for the toboggan or where Tilda was in all of this. Bewildered, he radioed dispatch.

"Linda, this is Rick...are you there? Over..."

There was a long pause then a faint static-riddled response which was barely audible.

"T..HI........S......DIS...PA.........OME..IN"

"Linda what in the world is going on? You sound like you're on the other side of the world."

"THERE'S....BA......STOR......ICK...OVER.." she hollered.

Then slowly and distinctly he shouted into the receiver, thinking she would have a better chance of hearing his message, "I'M..AT...THE BAEZAEKO...RIVER. THE... BRIDGE...IS...OUT! THE...KIDS...HAVE...BEEN... HERE.

I...SEE...THEIR...TRACKS. BUT...IT...IS... BITTERLY...COLD. DO...YOU...COPY? OVER."

"CO..Y, RICK. IT EX..MLY..OLD AND WIND ...ERE.. TOO, OVER."

"I'LL...CALL...YOU...LATER. STAY...BY...YOUR... PHONE,

OVER."

As Linda was returning to her desk, she remembered the call she received from the Kluskus bandleader twenty minutes earlier, telling her to advise Rick that his help was no longer needed. All was quiet. The perpetrator apparently, had left the reserve in his pick-up. But by the time Linda got to the radio, Rick was outside the truck again. After several attempts, she gave up and decided to try later.

He secured the rewound cable to the winch then climbed back into the truck and decided to four-wheel it over the river. He put it in the lowest gear and began motoring towards the river. Descending was no problem – the steep icy bank and gravity took care of that. Missing the boulders was another story. The first couple nearly drove him through the roof, even with the seatbelt on.

All of a sudden, he came to an abrupt stop, his head whipped backwards and forwards. From the spinning tires, he knew exactly what was wrong - he was high-centered on something, probably a boulder. He jumped to the ground which was a lot further and wetter than he anticipated - a good two feet wetter. The river was all but spilling over the tops of his knee-high boots. Underneath the pick-up, he could see a four- foot pole jammed between a couple boulders suspending the front axle just above the water.

He grabbed the axe from the back of the truck and knelt in the rushing frigid water, hoping to beat the log free or bust it apart.

"Jim, I swear this is the last time I ever take one of your shifts. The next time you ask me to...Ah, you stupid piece of junk!"

Everything but his chest, back and head were soaked and excruciatingly cold. His arms were so numb he could barely feel the axe let alone swing it with any force. He swung blindly managing to club something, though he had no idea what until he heard the hissing of his left front tire.

"This is unbelievable, absolutely unbelievable. Did I walk under a ladder last night in my sleep?" he snorted. "I guess I'd better get some help."

Water spilling over his boots, he climbed back into the truck to radio Bill. He wasn't the only one in Nazko with a four-wheel drive pick-up and a winch, but he was the only one with a radio and who had the skill he needed to help him out of the river. But there was no answer at his place. After several tries, he decided to change his boots and jeans, a pair which Jim had forgotten in the Blazer the last time he worked – his only redeeming quality at this point. Then he started the truck, turned the heater up to high and ate the lunch Natalie had forced him to take. He was so glad she had won out over his stubbornness.

In the meantime, old Bill was inching his way home down the Nazko highway in white out conditions. The snow was falling so heavily he couldn't see beyond the windshield without hanging his head out the window. The tracks of vehicles ahead of him were filling in nearly as fast as they were being made. He seemed to be driving forever and getting nowhere.

Through the dense fog of falling snow, he spotted a pair of faint red taillights.

The closer he came; he could see they were the taillights of a small foreign car that had veered off the road into the right ditch. The engine was still running, its rear tires were in the air and spinning, vapor was puffing out of the exhaust pipe and the dome light was on inside.

Pulling in behind it, he saw a woman sitting behind the steering wheel, talking into a cell phone and looking at a map. He got out of his truck, leaving it running, and knocked on her window. She was desperately trying to convince someone, a towing company he presumed, to tow her out of the ditch.

"You look like you could use some help," he said as the power window lowered. "Is a tow truck coming to help you?"

"You've got to be kidding," she chuckled flipping her cell phone closed. "I've just been told the only tow truck in Nazko is going to be tied up for the next four hours. They suggested I try someone in Quesnel. Who knows how long that will take?"

"Would you like me to pull you out?" asked Bill.

"Could you do that?"

"No problem. Me and my girl have pulled out lots of people in our day, haven't we Jess?" he said patting the rusty snow-covered hood. "Come on, hop in and I'll pull you out."

Reluctantly, she crawled into the cab of his truck. In all of her forty-nine single years, Margarite Phillips had rarely spoken to a complete stranger outside of work, let alone accept a ride from one.

"I don't normally take rides from strangers," she said. "But you seem sincere. I hope you don't take advantage of my trust."

"Oh, you don't have to worry about me ma'am," he said, producing a worn out black New Testament from his buckskin coat pocket.

"Once upon a time, when I carried a mickie of whiskey in my pocket, you would have had to worry - not any more. I'll tell you about it sometime."

He went back to the truck and lugged the rusted winch cable and hook to the rear axel of the car. With the car's bumper three feet off the ground, the axel was easy to locate. Then he ran back to his truck, jumped behind the wheel and gently applied the gas.

At first, his tires spun on the slippery road, but gradually, they began to chatter and dig in. He hoped no one was coming because he was across both lanes of the highway. As the car slowly crept up the bank, the rear tires slumped to the ground.

"Thank you Lord, and thank you Jessie," he whooped. "We've done it again!"

Margarite glanced at him briefly, then turned her eyes forward, trying not to stare at the man, who could if he wanted to, overpower her and haul her off to who knows where. Hastily reaching for the handle of the door to let herself out, she arrogantly said, "Thank you very much. How much do I owe you?"

"Nothing. Nothing at all. Except to allow me to make supper for you."

"Oh no. No, I could never do that. I should be heading back to town."

"How far do you think you're going to get out there tonight? I'll tell you...just as far as you got the first time. Why don't you have supper at my place first? Maybe the storm will pass and you can head back to town with a belly full of food."

She couldn't resist the logic, but to go to the home of a perfect stranger for a meal - that was unthinkable, way out of her comfort-zone. But there was something different about Bill.

"This is really crazy, but, yes, I accept your invitation for supper."

"Real good. Just stay in my tracks and follow me into my driveway."

As they opened the front door of Bill's twenty-year-old 12' x 52' trailer, Rick's staticky voice came over his police scanner. Bill often had it on in the evening for entertainment or on nights like this when the weather was bad. They both stood silently listening to Rick's predicament at the Baezaeko. When he got to the part about finding Tyler, Chester and Tonya's tracks and where they were heading with Tilda her ears perked up.

"Bill, I could sure use your help right about now. Is there any way...?"

"You don't need to ask."

"How soon can you get here?" "Should be there in about an hour; two at most."

"Good. Could you please bring a geri-can of gas, some extra blankets, water and food? I've got a feeling it could be a long night."

"No problem, Rick. See you in a bit, over."

At the end of the conversation she casually mentioned, "Is that Tilda Chantyman from Nazko?"

It sure is," he beamed. "One of the finest women on the face of the earth."

"She must be. I met her two talented grandsons yesterday when I visited their home. One of them is quite the little actor. He was dressed up in his grandmother's clothes and pretending to be her. They didn't fool me, though. I knew she wasn't around but I figured if they loved her enough to protect her like that they must be in a pretty good home."

"You seemed to know a lot about Tilda and her boys."

"I should. I'm the new social worker for this area. I know all about the clients out here."

Suddenly, the light went on. He understood exactly who she was and why she had come to Nazko. She was one of nearly two dozen social workers hired by the government to screen families on social assistance for children "at risk." Rumor had it that over seventy children had already been apprehended. Some kids had been placed in homes in other towns and their parents didn't have a clue where they were. No wonder the kids were headed for Kluskus - they were trying to hide.

Now, here he was, standing face to face with the enemy. Didn't the New Testament say, "Love your enemies? Do good to those who persecute you. Overcome evil with good." But all he could think about was driving her and her car back into the ditch and telling her, "Have a nice life!"

Like a thick cement wall had been erected between them, he tried to make conversation. "Coffee?"

"Yes, thanks. That would be nice," she replied with cool reservation.

Sensing her awkwardness, he felt a bit sorry for her and his attitude warmed slightly. "So, you're new to these parts then?"

"Yes and no. Yes, I'm new to the Cariboo but no, I'm not new to cold winters and snowstorms. That's why I thought I could drive back to town. I've driven in lots of bad weather like this before. Originally I'm from northern Ontario."

Before she could finish her pathetic arrogant history, he angrily interrupted, "Why did you come here? Why have you all come?"

"Someone stumbled upon the truth," she snapped defensively. "The truth that there are a lot of teenagers out there looking after their babies in poorly furnished apartments, barely surviving on junk food. Elderly disabled women are being shackled to a mitt-full of preschoolers while the daughters disappear for a week or a month. Believe it or not, we do care."

"I don't have time to hear your lame excuses. I've got to help Rick."

"Let me come with you. Maybe I can help."

"I think you'd better stay here. You're the last person they need to see right now."

"If I'd been in the picture before now, this might not have happened."

"It's because of you and your kind that there *is* a picture!" he retorted.

"Look, whether you like it or not, I've got a job to do and there's nothing you nor I can do about it!"

Bill made some sliced cheese sandwiches and threw them in a bag. Then filled his thermos full of coffee and headed for the door. Margarite grabbed a couple of blankets off the couch and followed close behind him.

"You'd better fasten your seatbelt," he snarled. But inside he was thinking, "You'd better hang on lady because you're in for the ride of your life!"

## CHAPTER ELEVEN

# RICK'S RESCUE

For the next half hour, nothing more than the occasional engine hiccup and Bill's dry cough could be heard in the cab of the truck. Not even a platitude about the weather, which was severe, was exchanged - though it should have. The visibility was so poor he misjudged the edge of the road twice. Had it not been for four-wheel drive, they would be driving to the Baezaeko River in the ditch.

Most people sitting next to Bill were uncomfortable with the speed he drove, even on dry roads. He expected Margarite to nag him about his speed, but she didn't and that impressed him.

"The roads are getting a bit slippery," he mentioned casually, a bit unnerved.

"I noticed."

"You like driving in the snow?"

"I'd rather not but if I have to I do."

Her cool self-confidence intrigued him. She was so petite and feminine yet fiercely independent. Why was such an attractive intelligent woman not at home snuggling her husband on the couch or reading her children a bedtime story on a night like this?

"You married?"

"No."

"Ever married?"

"Came close once - How about you?"

"Came close once too. When I was nineteen, there was this girl. She was barely seventeen; kind of cute and petite, like you. Well let's just say we spent a lot of time together. She got pregnant. We talked about getting married but her parents talked her out of marrying me and into letting them help her raise the baby. They said I was too young and stupid to be a good father. They were probably right. I liked to drink and party a lot in those days. You ever a party girl?"

"If you mean did I ever get drunk with my friends? The answer is no. It wasn't that I didn't drink – I drank when I was under age, but I didn't get drunk. I saw enough of that at home. My dad was an alcoholic. He floated in and out of our lives for as long as I can remember."

"I grew up in a good family in Northern Ontario. My parents believed in doing unto others as you would to yourself. They loved to get together with relatives and neighbors for picnics and sing-a-longs. There was always practical jokes and boisterous laughter. But they also loved their wine. Dad worked away from home as a faller but on the weekend, he came home. There was never an abundance of money but if an appliance broke down or one of us needed new shoes, somehow there was always enough."

"Things were going well for us until one day, when I was nine; he came home in the middle of the week. He slammed the back door and threw his work boots at the kitchen wall. He had liquor on his breath. When my mother asked him what was wrong, he yelled at her to leave him alone and he broke down and cried at the table."

"Later that night my mother told my two brothers and me that our father's partner had been killed in the bush that morning and my father felt he was to blame. He said he was away from the landing refueling his chainsaw when a gust of wind blew the tree the man was falling on top of him. Said if he'd been there, he could have warned him. His partner had been a faller for fifteen years. It wasn't like he didn't know the risks of falling in windy weather. But somehow, my dad couldn't get past the notion that he'd abandoned his partner. It took him weeks to work up the courage to face his co-workers again."

"In the meantime he hit the bottle hard. Each day he would drink until he passed out. By the time we came home from school he was asleep on the couch. He would get up around seven in the evening, stagger into the bathroom then collapse on top of his bed. When he got up the next morning, he was really grouchy and hung-over. He would slam the refrigerator and cupboard doors and yell at my mom to make his breakfast. They would argue and she would run off into the bedroom crying until he went in there and sheepishly begged her forgiveness and they would make up and be happy again. Our house became a roller coaster of laughter when he was drunk and crying when he was sober, calm when he was away at work and stormy when he was home. Amazingly, he always managed to go to work on Monday morning. I'm sure nobody at work knew what his home life was like."

"It wasn't like that for me. I had a terrible time in school. I had trouble concentrating and reading. Finally, in grade nine, my teacher referred me to the school counselor. She and I had quite a few sessions together. At first we talked about school; did I like it, and then we talked about home. I was afraid to tell her about the weekends and dad's drinking in case she brought in social services and had us kids removed from our home. She must have known I was holding back but she never pushed it."

"Eventually I trusted her enough to confide in her and I spilled the beans. She said she would help in anyway she could, but unless there was actual physical abuse her hands were tied. More importantly, she told me if I ever needed someone to talk to, she would be there. Had it not been for her I probably wouldn't have made it through high school. It was her that inspired me to help other kids who are going through what I was and become a social worker."

Bill was speechless. He stared at the mesmerizing snow pelting the windshield, trying to understand why their lives had intersected in this way, tonight, of all nights. She wasn't a monster, she was a survivor.

"What about you Bill? What was growing up like for you?' I'll bet you have a few of your own stories."

"I grew up in the Chilcoltin, the highlands about eighty miles west of Williams Lake. Parents were Carrier, very poor but happy. We lived in a tiny village, which basically consisted of my father's relatives, on a river. There was no road to bring in outsiders or help, so we had to rely on one another. Couple times a year we would go to town in canoes to trade pelts and buy stuff like sugar and tea, oil for the lamps, tools and treats such as a bag of apples and some hard candy for the kids."

"It was a wonderful adventurous life for a young boy. I loved messing around in the bush with my younger brother, watching the black bears and grizzlies dive into the river for salmon in the fall, the moose and deer nibbling the leaves off the trees near our house in the summer. I loved listening to the woodpeckers tapping on the trees first thing in the morning, the coyote pups whimpering at sundown and the wolves howling at night. And in the winter, when the moon was full, I loved staring out my bedroom window at the long black shadows of the cottonwood trees on the white glittering snow."

"In the spring all the mothers planted gardens and the fathers trapped and fished. We used everything we caught or hunted. Either we ate it or we wore it. Vegetables from the garden and wild berries like blueberries and raspberries were canned or dried then stored in a root cellar for the winter. We had a cow for milk. How they got her in there, I don't know, and a horse that couldn't be ridden by anyone but my mother. We had more fun trying to catch and ride that poor old nag."

"In the evenings, especially during the winter months we visited our relatives a lot. We drank tea and chewed pemmican, told stories and laughed. I remember we laughed a lot."

"Then one September day, everything changed. An Indian agent came to our village and told the elders that all children, seven years and older, had to go to school to learn to read and write. He said we would be boarded in a residential school, taught and looked after by the nuns and a priest. My parents told him they weren't sending my brother and I, that they wanted no part of it so he left."

But three weeks later, he came back with an RCMP officer and a priest and they said they weren't leaving without us. A bunch of us were hauled away kicking and screaming, crammed into a canoe between the cop and the priest, and taken to the residential school in Williams Lake. We didn't see our parents for eight months, until they came to bring us home for the summer. The school didn't even have the decency to bring us back at the end of the school year. And that's how it was from the time I was ten till I turned fifteen when I got too big for them to force into the canoe."

"Then one summer, in the late forties or early fifties, the government punched a road through the bush to our village. At first it was great; we could drive to town for supplies. My dad and I built a wooden wagon and bought a couple more horses. A few others did the same. And we rode to town. It was a three-day trip. We would camp beside a river or a lake and catch fish for supper. Afterwards we'd sit around a fire, talk and laugh. Those trips were the happiest days of my life."

"But then the grown ups started bringing home whiskey and there were all night drinking parties, arguments and fights. People visited less and went to town more but not with other families. On one of those trips, while my brother and I were away at school, my baby sister contracted the measles and died. Before the deadly epidemic had run its course, half of the village had been wiped out including my parents. My grandparents, who were away from the village at the time, visiting relatives at the coast, showed up at school in May to bring us home. Measles had shut down the school for a month but nobody died. We hadn't heard a thing about our village or the many others that had been devastated by the measles. It was a terrible shock."

"The summer I was fourteen, when we were home from school, my uncles decided to make moonshine - man that stuff stunk. You could've stripped paint with it. They drank some and went a little crazy. They laughed and hollered. It looked like they were having a lot of fun so my brother and I decided to try a little. We snuck the bottle out behind the house, poured ourselves a glass and drank it in a hurry so we wouldn't get caught. But we did anyway. When my grandmother smelled our breath and saw us staggering around and giggling - did she let us have it? "You two are going to be so sick." And, boy was she right. Later that night and half the next day, we barfed until our guts fell out."

It wasn't long before I forgot the hangover and remembered only the laughing. The moonshine experience, however, did teach me not to drink until I passed out and I soon figured out that if I did chores for the right people, the next time they went to town they would buy me a bottle of whiskey. I got pretty handy with an axe and a shovel."

I would sneak the bottle out of the house under my shirt and tell my grandmother I was going for a walk. At first, those walks were only on the day we came back from town. Pretty soon, I was going for a walk every night after supper.

I didn't fool my grandmother, though. She warned me to stop before I hurt myself but I didn't listen. I thought, "What does an old lady know about drinking?"

"When I was about eighteen, some friends and I started to go to town on our own to buy liquor and look for girls, that's when I met that girl I told you about. We would camp by a lake and party; have some fun. Then, one night, things got out of hand. A rancher who lived in the area was going by and got a bit nervous. He had a gun and was a little outspoken, like us. There was some pushing and shoving. I don't remember much after that. They said I blacked out - I was awake but my mind and my memory were shut down- I had done that a few times. When I woke up, I was in a cell. The police told me I had shot and killed the guy."

"I went to jail for nearly ten years for that stupid mistake. By the time I got out, my grandmother was gone. I didn't even get a chance to tell her I was sorry and how much I appreciated everything she had done for me. I was more depressed and bitter than when my parents died. The only way I could numb the pain was by working hard and drinking. For the next twenty years, I worked on the biggest ranches or in the steepest forests in the Cariboo. I worked until my hands bled in the day and drank until I passed out at night. Nothing could stop me from lifting the bottle until I met Tilda."

Then he choked up and grew quiet. Tears spilled down his cheeks. Margarite was speechless.

The trip had flown by. The ghostly headlights of the Rick's blazer suddenly appeared in the dense swirling snow. A steady plume of exhaust rose from the rear of the vehicle hinting that it had not yet run out of gas. Bill rolled to the river's edge, left his truck running, headlights and parking brake on, then climbed down the bank. He stepped from boulder to boulder in the river until he reached the blazer then tapped on the driver's door window. It looked like Rick had fallen asleep against it; the tapping startled him to an upright position.

"Bill, you made it."

"Sure did. How can we help?"

"Is someone with you?"

"Well, I don't know how to tell you this. It's one of those social workers the government sent to Quesnel."

"What's she doing here?"

"I'm not sure myself. She was at my place when you called. When she heard you say you were going after Tilda and the boys she suddenly insisted on coming along – said she might be of some help."

"I can imagine how much help she's going to be, especially when Tyler and Chester find out who she is."

"I know, but we've had quite a long chat on the way here and I think we should give her a chance."

"If it was coming from anyone else but you Bill, I'd insist she go right back to town."

In the meantime, Margarite had managed to navigate the bank in her $200 high-heel leather winter boots and was standing at the edge of the river hollering, "Is he alright?"

"Yes ma'am - fine as you and me."

"Thank goodness. What an awful night to be stuck way out here," she yelled for Rick's benefit. Can I help in some way?"

"No thank you," Rick bellowed back, climbing out of the blazer, pulling on his work gloves and wading to rear of the vehicle. "I think Bill and I can handle it."

As the men bent down to survey the problem, icy water splashed their faces and soaked their jeans. "Mercy that's cold!" yelped Bill.

"You think you can winch me out partner?"

"Depends on which way you want to go. I thought you were heading to Kluskus."

"I am, but not for police business anymore. I radioed Kluskus half an hour ago to see how things were and if the kids had arrived yet. Theresa, the bandleader said not to come because Teddy was gone. He sped off the reserve in his truck about noon, madder than blazes, saying he was going fishing and not coming back. She also said there hadn't been any sign of Tilda and the kids. My gut is telling me we need to find them fast."

"Well if you want to go to Kluskus I'll have to winch you out from the other side of the river, which means I have to get there first."

"How are you supposed to do that?"

"If I can't drive over, I'll fly over."

Bill grunted and huffed his way back up the bank to his truck with Margarite following closely behind him. After he reassured himself with a visual check of the four-wheel drive lockers on his front tires, he climbed behind the wheel. When Margarite opened her door he suggested, "It might be safer for you to stay on the ground. This could be dangerous."

"I'll not be treated differently just because I'm a woman," she retorted indignantly. "If you can do this, so can I."

"Okay, have it your way. Get in and fasten your seat belt."

Bill revved the engine and they rumbled over the crest of the bank until the nose of the truck was pointing nearly straight down. Margarite braced the palms of her gloved hands on the truck's roof and her boots on the dash, so she wouldn't slide off the seat.

"Hold on!" Bill yelled.

The engine screamed, rocks battered the floor and water sprayed behind the pick-up like a rooster's tail. They must have hit every boulder and log in the river, each time their heads barely clearing the roof and the steering wheel ripped from Bill's grip. Then they started up the bank on the other side. Half way, the tires began to whine and the motor suddenly died. Bill tromped on the brake, shoved it in gear and tried to restart it. Gravity had its own way of handling things and the truck soon lilted backwards to the river. When it came to rest in the mud, their backs were pressed against the back of the seat and their feet were in mid air.

"Well, this is interesting," smirked Margarite.

"Wouldn't that frost you," Bill muttered, pounding the steering wheel and trying to release his seatbelt.

"Now what?"

"I'm not sure. This has never happen to me before," he wanted to tell her, but his pride wouldn't let him. Instead he growled, "Nothing to worry about. Just stay put."

He worked his hips forward and reached for the handle then kicked the door open. When he jumped down, his boots quickly sank in the mud. He braced himself on the sides of the truck and pulled his boots out one by one planting them on the first level rock he found. Stepping from one rock to the next, he made his way to the front of the truck and the winch.

He lugged the heavy steel cable over his shoulder up the bank, slipping and struggling to stay upright. He pulled until it reached the trunk of the closest sturdy tree then he looped it around and secured it with the giant metal hook on the end. When he was satisfied it would hold, he ran back to the truck and turned on the winch. Slowly, as the cable recoiled, the truck inched its way up the bank and over the crest, with Margarite still stubbornly sitting and smiling inside.

Safely on the Kluskus side of the Baezaeko, Bill turned his pick-up around and faced it towards Rick's. Then he ran the winch cable down to the Blazer's front axel. When he switched on the winch, the steel cable barely moved. Both vehicles creaked and yawed from the strain warning them not to push any harder.

"I don't think it's going to budge Bill, unless we get rid of that pole. We're going to have to wedge another one under the axel, hoist the Blazer and knock the pole out of the way."

"Maybe we can wrap the cable around the jammed one and pull it free," suggested Bill.

"Let's give it a try."

Bill climbed back up the bank and into his truck and floored it. All that did was change the Blazer's direction; now it was facing down river with water flowing into the exhaust pipe. Bill didn't like the look of it. Numb from cold and the bewildering turn of events in the presence of *her* was enough to make a man cuss.

Margarite had stayed out of it at Bill's request. But the men's precarious circumstances unnerved her and she was powerless to keep her mouth shut. She leaned out the window and hollered, "Why don't you wedge a pole under the axel, wrap the cable around the jammed one and winch it out. You guys can push and I'll drive the Blazer."

The men stared at each other. They had thought of pounding the jammed pole free but they hadn't thought of her driving the Blazer while they pushed from behind. It was actually an excellent idea. However, the last thing they wanted to do was concede defeat to a woman, in high-heels no less. But they were gentlemen - brought up to respect the gentler sex. They were big enough to accept a suggestion. Not to mention they didn't have a better one. "Okay." snarled Bill. "We'll give it a try."

Margarite got out of the truck and descended the bank, snagging her heels on roots protruding through the snow. When she reached the river the men each took a hand and guided her to the step of the Blazer.

"Is it in four-wheel drive?" she asked.

Bill looked at Rick and Rick returned the stare. He had completely forgotten to put the truck in four-wheel drive. Afraid she would see his reddened face; he turned away from the headlights as he made his way to the front tires so he could turn the lockers in.

"Margarite," Rick chuckled shaking his head, "I had you pegged all wrong. You are definitely not just another pretty face. I owe you one."

"Make it two," Bill echoed.

They lassoed the stubborn piece of wood with the cable and when Rick was positioned behind the Blazer, ready to push, Bill switched on the winch and gave Margarite the order to, "Hit it!"

She dropped it into the lowest gear and the cable began to recoil, swinging the Blazer around. While Rick pushed, Bill tugged on the pole with the little strength he had left. "God," Bill cried in his thoughts, "we need your help."

No sooner were the words spoken when he felt it release, but not before both men were drenched by a giant rooster-tail of water. When Margarite glanced in the side mirror and saw them standing there dripping wet, she burst into hysterics. She could hardly hold onto the steering wheel she laughed so hard. Whether it was a stress release or the fact that it was her naïve suggestion that made the rescue successful, she couldn't tell. She was just grateful the truck was moving and that she had won some respect.

She wasn't so sure about driving up the bank. Fortunately, she didn't have to because Rick was behind the wheel, shoving her to the passenger seat and steering them over the top before she quit laughing.

When they came to a stop, she looked at him and cracked up all over again.

"What is so funny?

"You."

And that was all she said. By the time Bill joined them they were doubled over in their seats. He couldn't figure out what was so funny. Whatever it was, it was bigger than all of them. He burst out laughing too. Nobody ever did figure it out.

# CHAPTER TWELVE

# UNWELCOME COMPANY

"Y ou tryin to raise the dead, kid?" slurred the man's voice from the top of the bank.

Tonya gasped at the sight of him. All of six feet, his lanky shadow cast an ominous presence over them. His raven shoulder length hair and face looked like they hadn't been touched in days. Even from a distance, she could smell alcohol on his breath. His gray and white wool knit sweater flapped in the icy breeze displaying a navy T-shirt with numerous large tears and a distended abdomen. Around the crotch of his half zipped blue jeans was a dark stain. Holes in the toes of his black rubber boots revealed bare feet inside.

"You want some hep wiff the kid?"

"I think we'll manage okay," Tyler replied, trying to politely and wisely not rock the stranger's obviously unstable boat.

"Let me hep you, kid. We'll take you to town in my pick-up."

"We don't want him to go to town," Tonya insisted.

When he spotted Tonya, he lost his balance and tumbled down the bank, landing not far from her feet. "Silly bitch!" he chortled.

"Teddy, you watch your mouth!" Tilda barked. "What wrong wit you? Why you drinkin' so much?"

He staggered to his knees, attempting to stand but collapsed again. "You kinda cute," he said to Tonya. "How old are you? You got a boyfriend? Want one?" Then he laughed maniacally until steam and the pungent odor of urine rose from the front of his jeans.

"You're disgusting," she muttered under her breath.

Chester moaned on the toboggan, his eyes flickering against the porcelain white clouds that were filling the sky. As the color returned to his face so did the intensity of his pain and once again he was writhing and sobbing.

"Whas wrong wiff him?' slurred Teddy.

"He broke his arm last night, then hurt it again a few minutes ago when we slid into the ditch," explained Tyler.

"He needz a doctor… Come on, I'll take um to town in my pick-up."

"No, thanks!" Tyler stated emphatically. "We'll take him to Kluskus."

"I can't take um to Kluskus. I'm in a lotta trouble wiff my ol' lady and the band. They told me to get out so I'm going to town. I'll take um wiff me."

As gently as possible, Tonya firmly asserted, "We are not going with you. You are too drunk to drive."

Her words infuriated him. He swayed to his feet and lunged towards her, grabbing her by the hair and pulling her to the ground.

"Leave her alone, you big jerk!" yelled Tyler, kicking his hands away from her hair. "Or I'll kill you!"

A vacant stare came over Teddy's face. "Huh! We'll see about that, kid."

Knees wobbling, he crawled over the crest of the bank and disappeared.

"We've got to get out of here before he comes back," shivered Tonya.

"But where're we going to go? We can't take the road, he'll find us!"

They scanned the bush around the pond hoping to spot a path that would lead them out of sight. All they could see was a steep deer trail ascending the Kluskus side of Kokanee Hill.

"I don't think we can make it up there," said Tyler glancing down at Chester.

"I can make it," said Chester.

"No Ches. We'll find some other way."

Studying the shoreline at the opposite end of the pond, Tonya spotted an arch made by bowed cottonwood and willow trees. "Maybe there's a campsite or something down there," she pointed, "where we can hide until he goes away?"

"What if he doesn't go away, Tonya? What if he comes after us? I think we should put Chester and Tilda on the toboggan, strap on our snowshoes and see if it's a trail and where it goes."

"No," Chester protested weakly. "I can walk. Just help me with my snowshoes."

They bundled Tilda on the toboggan and laced Chester's snowshoes before putting on their own then waded through the powder sea to the boreal archway. To conceal their tracks, Tonya lightly swept behind them with an evergreen bow.

The swish of the toboggan seemed to linger forever. The deeper into the gray forest they went, the more gloomy it became. Biting gusts lashed at the barren brittle branches, snapping them and showering the last surviving leaves across the path. Shadows took on eerie shapes. Whistling, hollering or singing to stave off hungry predators and calm fears was not allowed on this expedition.

Each one retreated to his own world of contemplation. Tyler envisioned an all out confrontation with Teddy. His wrestling experience from school would help but Teddy had at least fifty pounds on him. What if he had a gun and in his drunken stupor, imagined they were wild game – meals for his table, trophies for his living room wall? He didn't want to go there.

. Instead, he forced himself to meditate on more pleasant daydreams. When Tilda was well and they were home again, he was going to ask Tonya to be his girlfriend. He would show up at her door one night after supper with a pair of skates in his hands, instead of textbooks, and invite her to skate with him on the pond. On the way there, he would cautiously take her gloved hand in his. After a few laps on the ice, they would sit on a log and gaze at the stars. A few minutes later, she would slide towards him, giving him the queue to kiss her. The timing would be right.

Chester's daydreams also included Tonya. By silently enduring the throbbing pain in his arm, one heartbeat at a time, he hoped his bravery would not escape her attention. If only she knew how much he cared for her. He would cut his arm off for her if she told him to.

Tonya wondered if her parents had figured out that she lied to them. She didn't know how they could – she had been gone less than twenty-four hours, well within the three days she said. She hated lying to them. They didn't deserve it. They had always been up front with her. If they promised something, they delivered - good or bad. The guilt was eating her up. But Tyler and Chester were important to her too. They needed her help. She only hoped her parents would understand and forgive her and that it wouldn't take the rest of her life to win back their trust.

Tilda reminisced about her father. She loved to revisit a treasured memory of him; the day he took her to the trap lines with him, the winter before she started school. Her mother had strongly protested saying she was too young and would wander into the woods, get lost and freeze to death while he was distracted with the traps. But he won over her fears by sweeping his daughter into his arms, kissing her on the cheek and reassuring, "I won't let her out of my sight."

He pulled her in the toboggan for what felt like hours. Big-foot floppy-eared white rabbits hopped across the trail in front them and whiny wolf pups yipped in the distance. After they had checked several traps and tucked the pelts of two beavers and as many mink into a burlap sack on the toboggan beside her, they stopped for lunch at a campsite they often used in the summer.

From the woodpile left behind by other campers, he arranged a stack of sticks in the fire pit. A handful of dried twigs and leaves stuffed beneath it, he ignited it with a match he took from a tiny metal box he kept in the pocket of his parka. More twigs, thicker sticks and the flames were soon too high and too hot to sit close to.

When the flames died down, he pulled a small aluminum pot with a long black handle, two tin cups and the lunch her mother had packed for them out of the deerskin knapsack. He filled the pot half-full with water he poured from his goatskin bag then set the pot on a flat rock near the centre of the fire pit. After the water boiled, he stirred in loose black tea. When it was steeped to a deep orange color, he stirred in just the right amount of sugar. Sitting next to him, sipping tea, like a grown-up, watching the fire dance in his eyes, with his undivided attention, was one of the most wonderful times of her life.

When she, like all the other school-age kids, was taken to the residential school, she never felt far from his love. At first, the white man's school terrified her, but there she learned about the love of another father, The Heavenly Father. Thoughts of his protection had comforted her many times since then, as it was now.

When they felt far enough ahead of their predator, they stopped for a snack. They undid their backpacks and pulled out another allotment of Cheezies and candy. It wasn't enough but the thought of a hot meal at Kluskus in a few hours satisfied their gnawing hunger pangs, everyone but Chester. For him, no pain was worse than the pain of hunger. He still had one more ace up his sleeve; the chocolate bar he'd been saving for precisely this kind of emergency. He fumbled around in his pocket and gently unfolded the foil, faking a cough to disguise the crinkling. In the dead quiet, not even one's breathing was a private affair. He just needed two bites to silence the screaming in his belly.

Suddenly, two gunshots rang out and Teddy bellowed from behind them. "You can't sneak away from me, you old whore! Those kids are mine too! If I can't have um, you can't have um either! I'll kill all of you!"

"Is he talking about us?" questioned Tonya.

"I think he talking about, Rosy, his wife and kids," answered Tilda. "My sister Mary, say he diabetic - take insulin. She say, sometime, when he don't eat right or drink too much, he go crazy."

"Well, she got the crazy part right," mumbled Tonya.

"So he thinks we're his wife and kids? I'd hate to be them!" said Chester.

It was snowing heavily now and with the gusts, their tracks were obscured in the fading light. Soon they would need to resort to what was left of Chester's flashlight. And while it would temporarily help them, unfortunately, it would help Teddy too.

"Maybe the dark is our best defense," suggested Tyler. "If we can out pace him and hide up ahead until he goes by, maybe we can double back to the road and lock ourselves in his truck. By the time he gets there, it'll be dark. Hopefully he wouldn't see us and eventually pass out in the snow. After that....I don't know."

Rick, Bill and Margarite sat in the Blazer, with the heat on high, until their clothes started to feel dry and Rick couldn't wait any longer. It was nearly dark and his gut was telling him that they shouldn't waste any more time. He felt the kids were still on the road somewhere. With the wind building, he was certain extreme cold and heavy snowfall weren't far away. Fifteen minutes later, while he and Bill were replacing the punctured tire with the spare, his suspicion was confirmed. It was snowing so heavily he could hardly make out the other side of the road.

As they headed towards Kluskus Rick thought he could smell raw gas. He noticed it a couple times while the truck was climbing out of the river but past it off to the rocking and an overfull gas tank. "Do you smell gas?"

"Yeah," they replied.

"I thought I could smell something back at the river," said Bill checking the gas gauge. "Was your gas that low before, Rick?"

Glancing at the dash, he was alarmed to see the needle just above the "E". "No it wasn't, Bill."

"I'd say you have a hole in your gas tank, Officer Clement."

Rick pulled over to the side of the road and the two men hopped out. Snow pelted their faces. Frigid gusts quickly penetrated their still damp clothing. A brief inspection under the truck revealed a steady reddish trickle onto the snow. "That pole must have punctured the tank. Fortunately I have a spare gallon in the back." Then he remembered. He had put it on the ground when Margarite got in the Blazer and forgot to put it back. His heart skipped a beat. His blank stare said it all.

"You left the tank at the gas station?"

"Just about as bad – I left it at the river. I put it on the ground to make room for You- Know-Who," he spoke discreetly. "She got us laughing so hard I forgot about it."

"I knew bringing her along was a bad idea."

"You can say that again."

"I guess we'll have to go back to the river and get your truck Bill."

"How are we supposed to get seven of us into the cab of my truck?"

"I don't know but that's all we've got. Hopefully we have enough gas to make it there."

They jumped back into the Blazer and pretended nothing was wrong.

"Hole in the gas tank, eh? You can't fool, You-Know Who," she whispered forcefully. "I was going to mention the gas container was on the ground before we drove away.. Sorry, I forgot."

Half way back to the river, the engine began to sputter then died.

"Well, guess that's the end of the ride boys and girls. Looks like we're walking from here."

"If you don't mind, I think I'll wait here. It's ugly out there."

"You'll freeze to death."

"I'd rather freeze to death in here. You never know what's prowling around out there."

"Guess you got a point there, lady."

They were just as happy leaving her behind anyway. If it hadn't been for her they wouldn't be in this position. Yet, to her credit, if it hadn't been for her, they would still be trying to climb out of the river. Why was that anyway; sometimes the people you need most in life are the most infuriating?

As the sound of their voices and footsteps faded, she felt more alone than she had in a long time. The cold gradually crept through the layers of her parka, gloves and long johns and she began to shiver. Despite the darkness, she could see the snow beginning to build on the hood. If she didn't stay warm, she knew she could freeze to death.

She remembered learning how to conserve body heat and prevent hypothermia in fourth grade swimming lessons. By curling into a ball, the instructors taught, you could protect the major heat-loss zones of the body - the neck, chest, armpits and groin. If others were in the water with you, you were supposed to huddle together and tread water.

The huddle drill was her favorite part of the lesson. If she planned it right, she got to huddle next to the cutest boy in the class. When he touched her arm, it took her breath away. Sometimes, to make her stomach look flatter, she would hold her breath for the entire two-minute exercise and nearly pass out. Kyle was his name. She wondered whatever became of him.

As she reminisced about the old days, she found herself drifting off. She couldn't remember if she was supposed to keep moving or allow herself to fall asleep. Gradually the painful cold in her hands and feet disappeared and the shivering stopped. The world seemed far away. She was powerless to fight the pleasurable urge to sleep. It was seducing her. One second she was in the Blazer, the next she was in her nice warm apartment, curled up on the couch with her black and white cat, reading a novel and sipping hot chocolate. An apple cinnamon candle was burning on her coffee table.

She roused briefly to the sound of faint knocking. Somebody must be at the door, she thought. Maybe he'll go away if I don't answer. No, I better get it. A child might need my help. "I'll be right there," she mumbled.

Something startled her, her voice perhaps. She had no idea how long she'd been asleep. Something was bumping the door beneath her shoulder. Then she heard sniffing and snow crunching outside. She wasn't worried. Bill and Rick were probably just messing with her and she drifted off again. Suddenly, wolves were howling disturbingly close by.

She had often examined their fresh tracks and watched them high-tail it off a back road into the bush near their rural northern Ontario home. But never had she seen one up close.

When she glanced up at the window - a massive furry face was staring down at her. His mismatched blue and green eyes, snarling top lip and long white fangs nearly stopped her heart. Six-inch wide paws were sprawled across the top of the window. She tried to scream but nothing came out.

Repeatedly, she tried to shoo him away by flicking her hand and pounding the glass, but he wouldn't leave. Then she spotted three others, slightly smaller, pacing around the Blazer like security guards. For some unknown reason, the leader was fascinated with her. If they all decided to jump on the hood or the roof, she was afraid the windshield would cave in and they'd attack her. Peering outside, she saw what resembled someone's bloodied gloved hand in the mouth of one of them.

"That's it!" she shrieked. "This has gone far enough. Next, it'll be my hand or worse if I don't do something."

She bolted over the front seat and laid on the horn. The big one jumped down and skipped away with the others close behind, tails between their bony legs. A safe distance away, they turned and faced the vehicle, patiently sat on their haunches and howled a symphony of protest. Every time they stood or tried to creep forward, she would hit the horn. They were annoying, but she didn't have trouble staying awake anymore either.

## CHAPTER THIRTEEN

# TEDDY

B lowing drifting snow had erased all signs of snowshoe and toboggan tracks. Instinct and the broken branches under the cottonwood trees, however, told him they were ahead of him.

It had taken more effort to climb the steep bank and return to the truck for his rifle than Teddy anticipated. He was dizzy now and his boots felt like they were filled with cement. He couldn't stop fumbling and dropping his gun. Nauseated all day from a hang over and eating only a handful of potato chips with the morning's insulin was a mistake. So was leaving his toque and gloves at home.

The darker it became, the more alone he felt. Depressing thoughts soon haunted him. "My life is a mess. I'm sick all the time. I have no job and no money. My wife and kids hate me. Everybody hates me and I hate them."

Usually the bad talk came when he first awoke in the morning, when his mind processed yesterday's failures. Shouts of guilt and condemnation came over his thoughts like a loud speaker. Often they made him cry. When he'd been drinking, it was worse. Without the alcohol, he couldn't shut them out and there was rarely a reprieve from the sadness.

He crumbled to the ground and sobbed, "What's the point? I have nothing to live for. No one will miss me. I'm going to die anyway if I don't get food. If I blow out my brains, at least it will be over with fast."

Vision blurred by tears, he unlocked the safety and steered the end of the gun into his mouth, pointing it to the top of his head. Reluctantly, he began to squeeze the trigger when the pick-up horn echoed through the trees. A minute later, there was another and another. Then wolves answered. He wasn't alone.

Perhaps someone was coming from town or heading to town, and would give him a ride. His truck was stuck across the road. To maneuver around it wouldn't be easy. It might buy him the time he needed to get back to it – if he had the strength. Staggering to his feet, he stumbled in the dark towards where he believed the road was.

Crouching behind bushes not far away, Tyler and the others had been listening to Teddy crying and talking to himself. While they waited for him to abandon the pursuit or kill himself, they nearly froze to death. Their faces and extremities were numb from the cold and it was getting harder for them to move their limbs. When they heard the honking, they too, had been struggling to stay awake. It revived them. If they reached the road before he did, perhaps they could flag somebody down and get help.

They weren't sure how far into the bush they had gone; only that it hadn't taken long to get to there. Chester scanned the bush with his failing flashlight until it went out - long enough to see that the freshly fallen snow had disguised the trail back to the pond and made the dense brush look frighteningly unfamiliar and impassible in every direction. The only light left was the whiteness of the snow.

Getting lost, particularly in the night, was a possibility Tyler hadn't even considered. He was barely managing his own urge to panic when Tonya whimpered, "Are we lost?"

Seconds later she shrieked, "We're lost! Oh my gaud, we're lost. We're going to die!" Hysterical, she began to hyperventilate and she couldn't catch her breath. "Oh no, you guys, I think I'm going to pass out."

"No you're not!" shouted Tyler. "You're panicking and if you don't stop it, you will die!"

Her reaction triggered his. Panic clutched his own throat, robbing him of any common sense and reason. For a minute he couldn't construct one complete thought. Then he remembered the acrostic for *lost* that one of the teachers had taught them last fall when the entire school went on a hike; STOP.

"Remember what Mr. James taught us about being lost the day we hiked up the mountain behind the school, Tonya?"

"He said,

"S is for Stop. Stay put. Don't move until you figure out what to do.

T is for Think. Calm down and think clearly.

O is for Observe. Look around. Remember. Try to identify smells, sounds and sights, like where the sun was when you came.

P is for Plan. Plan the best possible route and if that fails, plan to build a shelter for the night and conserve heat until help arrives."

"We've got to sit here for a minute, calm down, and just think."

"And pray," added Tilda.

They sat without speaking for several minutes while Tonya cupped her gloved hands over her quivering lips. Soon she relaxed and the dizziness passed. She could think clearly again. "Let's see if we can find Teddy's tracks," she said. "Maybe he's found the trail back to the road."

"Do you honestly think he's with it enough to find his way back to the road in his condition?" jeered Chester.

"Do you have any better ideas?" barked Tyler.

That was the first time in hours Tyler had been rude to him. Chester thought the old Tyler had grown up or gotten lost in the bush. He was actually more comfortable with the old Tyler. At least he knew how far to push.

Tripping over the underbrush and swatting back sharp branches as they scraped their faces, they headed towards where Teddy's voice had come from. When they figured they were close, Tyler and Tonya knelt down and groped the snow for tracks and an indentation in the snow where he had been sitting.

"I found them, the tracks!" she screeched. "They'll take us back to the pond. From there we can follow the shore back to the road. Yahoo!"

"Yahoo!" repeated the others.

It was impossible to tell how far from the pond they were, but it felt like three times longer than when they hiked in. They couldn't understand why they hadn't arrived at it yet. Teddy's tracks were still ahead of them, though they looked more like something being dragged. Finally, Chester in the lead, stopped. "I have this ugly feeling…"

"That he's lost? I didn't want to say it," agreed Tyler, "but I've been thinking it for the last five minutes."

Knowing better than to panic this time, Tonya took a deep breath. "So what should we do?"

"We have to keep going and hope he found the way out," replied Tyler.

A few yards farther they spotted him collapsed on the ground, gun still in his hand. From a distance, he appeared to be unconscious and barely breathing but they wanted to observe for a while before they went any closer. After five minutes with no movement, Tyler decided it was safe to move in and take the gun.

Cautiously, he approached him, softly speaking reassuring words while the others waited behind. When he was barely within reach, Tyler crouched down and gently patted his shoulder so as not to startle him. Then he shoved him repeatedly and shouted at him - still no response. One finger at a time, he pried the tightly clenched fist from the barrel of the rifle. When it was done, he stood to his feet, haggard, as though he'd just disarmed a bomb. "Whew! Well, he's down for the count. For how long I don't know."

"Now, what are we going to do with him?" asked Chester.

"We can't leave him here, he'll die. He needs a doctor," said Tonya.

"He needs to be off the ground," said Tyler.

"He needs sugar," Tilda added.

"Where do we get that and how do we feed it to him?" said Chester. "He's unconscious."

"We need to get him to Kluskus and get him some help," Tyler stated.

"Give him some sugar!" ordered Tilda. "Get a candy and hurry up!"

"But he's unconscious, Mrs. Chantyman. Our first-aid book says not to feed the victim if he's unconscious," Tonya insisted respectfully. "We're supposed to turn him on his side and keep him warm until help comes."

"He gonna die anyway. Do what I say."

They fumbled through their backpacks and Tonya pulled out what was left of her rations - a few Cheezies, a couple jujubes.

"Chew the candy until it mushy," she said. "Put it inside his mouth, in his cheek, and den rub his throat. But first, get him off the snow."

They undid the rope that secured the tarp and spread the tarp on the ground next to him. Then they rolled him onto it, keeping him on his side.

Tonya chewed a jujube until it was slimy then she tucked it inside his cheek and stroked his neck under his chin. Like a reflex, he began to move his gums and swallow. She waited a few minutes and checked his mouth. To her amazement, it was gone. Then each of them took turns doing the same until all the jujubes were gone. And again, they waited for a response - eyes opening, fingers moving, speech. But nothing happened.

"Maybe he has hypothermia," suggested Tonya.

"We gotta save Teddy!" hollered Tilda excitedly. "He my nephew and we gotta hep him. Hep me up!"

They stared at her as though she had gone mad.

"Don't just stand dare - Hep me up, stupid kids!"

Muttering under their breath in quiet protest, Tyler and Tonya uncovered her and helped her to her stocking feet. "Now, put him on the toboggan and hurry up!"

"What about your feet, Atsoo? You have no shoes."

"Give me his shoes and a blanket, den wrap him up."

The blankets were still warm. They wrapped one of them around her shoulders and shoved his bulky rubber boots onto her tiny feet. Next, they rolled him onto the toboggan, tucking his arms and his gun, out of reach, by his side, and covered him with the remaining two blankets and the tarp. Finally, they bound him with the rope.

"This was a good idea Atsoo," said Chester. "He's not going to bother anybody for awhile."

"Tonya, you and Chester walk with Tilda and I'll pull Teddy. I think we've missed our ride to Kluskus, but at least he won't bother us. Maybe when we get back to the road we can warm up in his pick-up."

Pressing the backlight button of her watch, Margarite squinted to see the time. It was quarter to nine, nearly four hours had passed since Bill and Rick left. "This is ridiculous," she fumed. How long can it take to walk a few miles and drive back here? They probably went to Rick's place for a roast beef dinner and are watching a movie, hoping I'll freeze to death."

She managed to work herself into a full-blown pity party, with sniffles, when the lights of Bill's pick-up lit up the tops of the trees and blinded her in the rear view mirror. As they did, the wolves loped away into the woods in different directions like mythical creatures. When she unlocked the doors, and the men climbed inside, they were met with more frigid air than an Arctic Front.

"Where have you two been? Go to town for Dinner and a Movie?"

"Actually, we haven't eaten yet. We had trouble at the river. That's why it took us so long," explained Bill.

"Has there been any sign of the kids?" asked Rick. "It's strange we haven't seen any thing yet. I'm going to radio Kluskus again to see if they're there."

Rick radioed the Kluskus Band office - letting it ring ten times before he hung up. "They must have gone to bed. Looks like there's no choice – we'll have to drive all the way there. Probably won't get there before midnight. Before we leave the Blazer, we should get something to eat from the back. Margarite, would you be so kind as to crawl over your seat and dig out some snacks and water from the survival chest?"

"There was food and water? It would've been nice to know that, before you left." Trying to be brave about her brush with death, she indignantly mentioned, "Four wolves have been hanging around here all night - is that why?"

"Nah," said Bill. Then he muttered under his breath, "They probably heard about your love for animals and all your other endearing qualities."

She loaded her arms and distributed the plunder between them as Rick locked the Blazer and they headed for Bill's truck.

"Men are such pathetic creatures," she fumed.

The step into the old Ford was farther than she remembered. With her arms full, she wasn't able get in without putting something down or allowing them to help her. She wasn't about to ask for assistance and surrender her feminine independence that easily.

While she stood there, pondering the dilemma, Bill shoved her from behind. She and her baggage ended up sprawling somewhere between the floor and the seat in a most unladylike position. "Sure are an ornery little cuss," he chuckled.

Fortunately, it wasn't far from Kokanee Hill or she would've slugged him or burst out crying. As they drove over the top, the men laughed about the hole in Bill's gas tank and the duct tape repair that would have made Red Green proud. It had stopped snowing and strong gusts were driving glittering eddies across the road. Silvery cotton ball clouds drifted away and the brilliant full moon appeared. It had become a spectacular night. As badly as she felt, even Margarite was forced to say so. Suddenly, the men stopped talking.

"I hope that's not what I think it is," said Rick.

Leaning over the steering wheel to study it better, Bill shifted into neutral and tapped the brakes to slow their descent. Half way down, the problem became clear. A pickup was straddling the road - bumpers hanging over both ditches. They looked at one another and Bill stated, "Only one thing to do; take the ditch."

"Do we have to do that? Couldn't we shove it out of the way with your truck?" Margarite asked.

"No way!" snarled Bill. "That would wreck my truck."

"Rolling your truck in the ditch would be better?" she came back.

There it was again, that dad blasted infernal logic of hers that drove him crazy. Of course she was right but he wasn't letting her know that.

"I'm going to gently slide past the pick-up into the ditch. After we get around it, we'll winch the pick-up to the side of the road so no one else will run into it, if that's okay with everybody?" he said glaring at Margarite.

"Sounds reasonable to me," agreed Rick, winking at Bill. "Let's give it a shot."

He actually agreed with Margarite, but he wasn't going to abandon his buddy in his darkest hour and concede the battle of the sexes, especially to this overconfident little snippet from the city.

Bill's true plan was to get the speed down and take the ditch on the left side, the shallower of the two ditches. Just before they struck the deep snow on the shoulder, he would gun it, steer over the edge and drive along the steep bank. To do it in the two hundred feet that remained, he would have to go against the number one rule for controlling a vehicle on icy roads and hammer the brakes. Some paint was going to be sacrificed, that was a given. He had pulled it off before. No reason to think it couldn't work again, unless there was something hidden under the snow.

They braced for impact and Margarite squeezed her eyes shut. As the tires chewed into the snow, the engine faltered and the old truck shuttered violently, nearly rolling over. Margarite screamed. The men gasped.

When they landed, she was very impressed. But she was so infuriated that he had scared her half to death that she decided not to puff up his already over-inflated male ego and keep it to herself. Later, if she still felt the same and he was a little nicer, she might say something like, "Well done or good job."

They got out to search the early nineties extended cab 4X4. Its aqua and white paint was still in surprisingly good condition. From the description Theresa gave him, Rick was positive this was Teddy's truck. The doors were unlocked and the keys were gone. Two dozen empty beer cans and a bag of potato chips were scattered throughout the cab. More disturbing was the half-used box of rifle bullets on the front seat.

"I don't like the look of this," said Bill holding up the box.

"Can I take a look at those Bill?" Rick took the box and pulled out one of the lead-tipped brass-colored bullets then reinserted it back into its slot. "These are big enough to drop a bull moose a quarter mile away." His heart flopped in his chest.

Bill could see the alarm on his face. "Do you think this is Teddy's truck?"

"Yeah." he sighed.

"Should we take the time to move it off the road Rick?"

"I don't really want to but it's gotta be done sometime. I have to tell you Bill," he said as they walked back to Bill's pick-up for the winch cable, "I'll feel a whole better when I see those kids."

While the men inched the pick-up to the side of the road, Margarite stood out of the way on the bank that overlooked the pond. Nervously, she studied the bush on both sides of the road for the four wolves. She was sure she hadn't seen the last of them and it would be just her luck to get eaten alive while two able-bodied men stood by distracted with man toys like trucks and wires.

As she peered over the bank, enjoying the pale blue glow of the snow, something caught her eye not far from her boots - a myriad of half-concealed footprints leading down to the pond.

"Look at this!" she shouted shuffling down the bank towards the imprints. "You've got to see this."

At first, they ignored her babbling but when she disappeared over the bank, they thought they should see where she went and what all the fuss was about.

"Look down here. Tracks – lots of them," she hollered. "I think it's them!"

With arms out-stretched, the men rode the powdery wave to the bottom like world-class snowboarders. All of a sudden, their boots stuck fast and the rest of them went sprawling, face down, embarrassingly close to her.

"Where is a camera when you need one?" she said, hand on her hip, vengeful smirk on her face.

After they dug themselves out and brushed off enough snow to build a snowman, they saw why she was so excited - Tracks; boot tracks, several sizes and a toboggan impression. It had to be theirs.

# CHAPTER FOURTEEN

# GUARDIANS OF NAZKO

It was eleven o'clock and the moon had crept high into the twinkling black sky. The pond glittered like a field of polished gems. Shadows were short and well defined. Even white rabbits were easy prey tonight. Several wolves barked and howled excitedly, likely with the message, "Humans are coming!" When they were quiet, they were circling, sniffing from a distance. One minute they were fearlessly sneaking up behind, out of sight on the trail, the next, they were clumsily tumbling over each other ahead of them. Margarite recognized the chorus. With Bill walking in front and Rick close behind, she wasn't afraid.

Like a spotlight on a canvas, the moonlight illuminated each half-buried footprint in the snow. It was clear where the kids had gone. Why, was another story. When she heard his voice Tonya yelled, "Dad, is that you?"

"We're coming Tonni!" he hollered back.

A few minutes later Tyler pushed the snow-lined branches aside and Rick and his two companions came into view. Bill, he recognized instantly by his tall, lanky frame and ambling gait, but the other person, much shorter, was following too closely to see.

Then he saw her. It was Margarite. He froze on the spot. From the euphoria of being rescued, he plummeted to bewilderment and rage. How had she managed to beguile them? What could she possibly have said or done to convince them to let her come? She could turn her head almost all the way around without losing her balance. Did she also possess some demonic power of persuasion?

"Tyler, what on earth are you doing?" said Tonya, stumbling over the foot of the toboggan. "Why did you stop?"

"Look who's here," he whispered hoarsely.

"Is that who I think it is?"

"Oh no," moaned Chester. "It's the social worker. We're in big trouble man."

When they got a little closer, Margarite could see them keeping their distance and whispering to one another. "What's wrong?" she said, "You guys look like you've seen a ghost."

"Worse," said Tyler.

Tonya hugged her dad and Bill patted the boys on the shoulder then he picked up Tilda, hugged her and pecked her cheek.

"Tilda," he said, examining the drooping side of her mouth and her floppy right arm and leg. "You've had a stroke. So that's why you guys are running away."

"Looks like you've had quite the night," Rick said stooping to the toboggan and pulling the tarp away from the unconscious man's face. "That would be...."

"Teddy, my nephew, Mary's boy," said Tilda.

"I would have guessed that by the smell. Did he pass out from the alcohol?"

"Mrs. Chantyman says he's a diabetic and that he takes insulin," offered Tonya. "We tried to feed him some candy because we thought he had low blood sugar. When he didn't respond, we wondered if he had hypothermia so we wrapped him in blankets. He won't wake up, Dad. We think he needs to go to the hospital."

"Can I see the flashlight Rick?" asked Margarite. "I worked as an ambulance attendant a little while when I was going to university in Toronto. I'd like to take a look at him."

Rick helped her roll down the tarp and she checked his pulse. She couldn't feel one at his wrist, only in his neck. Then she opened his eyes and waved the light across the vacant stare. The pupils were sluggish but equal.

"This guy's in bad shape. He's in shock. If he doesn't get to a hospital soon, he'll die."

"Well duh, I could've told you that," sneered Tyler.

"Tyler Ernest Chantyman, you don't talk like dat to your elders," exclaimed Tilda.

"She's not my elder, she's a social worker."

"She's come here to take us away from you Atsoo," added Chester.

"What you talking about?"

"It's true Dad, she wants to take them away from Mrs. Chantyman."

"I know that's what you think, but you need to know more about what we're doing in Quesnel," said Margarite. A crossfire of accusations soon followed which escalated to an all out shouting match.

"Look you guys," calmed Rick, "Let's just get out of here. You can tear each other apart when we get home. Tilda, get on my back. I'll carry you."

"No Rick, I'll take her," Bill insisted. "We've been taking care of one another for a long time." Then he crouched in front of her and presented his back. "Climb aboard Tilda. Grab my neck and hang on tight."

With Tyler's assistance, Rick hoisted her onto Bill's back so she could wrap her good arm and flop the other one around his neck. Then he removed the bulky rubber boots and helped her coil her exposed legs around Bill's waist. Her right side, too weak to hold on, kept sliding down, so Bill had to support her with his crossed hands.

"Aren't these a little too big for you?" joked Rick.

"Doze are Teddy's."

"I figured as much."

Taking the rope from Tyler, Rick said, "Let me pull for a while. You look like you could use a break. Why don't you lead us out of here."

"Fine - just keep me away from her."

She usually didn't take a slam like that personally. It went with the job. But his words struck too deep to merely blow off. She found herself unsuccessfully choking back the tears. Perhaps it was fatigue, or the kids' devotion to Tilda that reminded her of her own family when they were struggling to stay together.

"I'll stay out of your way," she said softly, trying to disguise the sniffling. Then she fell between Bill and Rick in the line-up. She could see Tyler leaning over to Tonya and whispering something then giggling. She assumed it was about her. It hurt.

It surprised her that Chester wasn't more involved in the clucking session. He hadn't said a thing, with the exception of some muffled moaning. Then she noticed him clutching his left arm and walking stiffly. He was obviously in a great deal of pain. It was odd that neither he nor any of them mentioned it. Was it a cultural thing? Was this how Carriers handled pain? Was it a dignity issue? Or simply that if you don't talk about it, it doesn't hurt? Then the light went on - they were trying to hide it from her because they didn't trust her.

She waited until she was back at the truck then she casually strolled alongside him, "Bet that hurts, hey?"

As she went to touch it, he flinched, generating a sharp pain that forced a loud involuntary, "Ow! Don't touch it!" His abrupt reaction startled her and she gasped and stepped back. In the moonlight, he could see she was crying. Her mascara had run down both cheeks. He thought it very strange. She had come to hurt them and she was crying? All he could figure was that she was a girl - they cried all the time.

"I'm just trying to help," she sniffled.

"No you're not!" retorted Tyler. "If you were trying to help, you wouldn't be here! Leave us alone. We can look after ourselves."

"Tyler Chantyman. What got into you? Why you talk so bad?"

"I think I can explain Tilda," said Bill. "Last week, a bunch of social workers came to Quesnel. Rumor has it they're taking dozens of kids away from their parents. Some have even been taken in the middle of the night. Tyler and Chester were afraid if they found out you'd had a stroke, they'd be taken away too. That's why they were taking you to Kluskus. Is that about right you guys?"

"Yes," they agreed.

"So if you were heading to Kluskus, why were you in the bush?" asked Rick.

"Him!" they pointed to the toboggan.

"He was drunk and he came after us with his rifle. We had to hide," said Tonya.

"Look, I have a job to do," Margarite stated emphatically. She may as well have declared war, because what followed closely resembled it.

"I want a piece of her right now!" Tyler shouted a foot from her face.

"Me too!" added the other two, standing right behind him.

"Quiet!" yelled Rick, getting between Margarite and the kids. "Listen to me! If we're going to save this man's life, I need your co-operation. We'll work on the other problem later."

"Tyler, have you seen the keys to his truck?"

"No. We were hoping to find them too. We were going to sit in the truck, turn on the heater and try to stay warm until help came." The truth was, Tyler fully intended to drive the truck to Kluskus. He had had some experience behind the wheel; Bill let him back up and down the driveway whenever he came to visit. He was confident he could manage the drive to Kluskus.

"Okay everybody, fan out and look for the keys," ordered Rick.

They hadn't searched long when Chester spotted the keys on the bank where Teddy first stood. A glint of metal in the moonlight wasn't difficult to see. He alerted the others, hobbled back to the pick-up and handed the keys to Rick.

The engine was cold and hesitant after sitting in sub-zero temperatures for several hours. The fuel gauge was low but Rick figured there was enough gas to get them to Kluskus. "Help me load Teddy into his pick-up, Bill. And would you mind taking Chester, Tilda and Margarite in your truck? I'll take Tonya and Tyler with me. That way maybe we'll have peace for awhile."

"There'll be peace - when she leaves Nazko," Tyler growled at Margarite.

It was two a.m. when they sped away with Rick in front. The mood was somber for the first few miles but the beauty of the night gradually eased away the previous hours of tension. The narrow road wound through wooded hills with hypnotic repetition and the whine of the winter tires soothed them like a lullaby. Chester was soon fast asleep.

"I haven't seen anything this beautiful since I left home," commented Margarite. "I had forgotten how beautiful a northern winter night could be." She stared out her window hoping to sight the glowing eyes of an animal in the bush but what she beheld was the luminescent dancing of the Northern Lights.

"Oh my gosh, the Northern Lights! It's been years since I've seen them. They look like waterfalls of lavender and aqua and mint green. It's glorious."

"You can almost imagine angels dancing up there, can't you?" said Bill. He paused for a minute then added, "Imagine, God made this for our enjoyment - so we would see him in his handiwork."

"I believe in something," said Margarite. "If you call him God, I couldn't disagree with you."

"You see this little lady sitting right here? She's the one who told me about God, the Creator. He reached into his coat pocket and pulled out a limp faded black New Testament about the size of a deck of cards then handed it to her. "This changed my life. Turn to the marker and read what's underlined."

She turned to the page and began to read:

We are made right in God's sight when we trust in Jesus Christ to take away our sins. And we all can be saved in this same way, no matter who we are or what we have done. Romans 3:22"

"You see that?" he said excitedly. "God wipes our slate clean. He forgives all our sin when we have faith in his son, Jesus. We can start over no matter what we've done. Isn't that the most wonderful news you've ever heard?"

She closed the book and handed it back to him then sat quietly thinking about what she had read and what Bill said.

"Years ago, Bill, when I was studying anthropology in university, the Carrier people fascinated me; how they were called Carriers because they grieved a loved one by carrying a small piece of bone in a tiny pouch for a year. Recently, I learned the Carriers of Kluskus led Alexander Mackenzie to Bella Coola in July 1793. Since then, it's been my dream to meet these unsung heroes and hike their famous trail. When I was given the opportunity to come to Quesnel, I jumped at it. I didn't come here to shatter families and lives, I came in search of a great people and I have found them and much more."

They stared through the front window for several minutes, spellbound by the radiant narrow twisting road. Then Tilda spoke.

"Our people have suffered many years in the good land God gave us. We have suffered at the hands of the government, misguided church leaders and our white brothers. We have been treated like dogs, especially the women. Only now do our children read dat it was a woman from Kluskus, Kama, who showed the explorers the way to Bella Coola. First Nations people have led the way, in the river, in the trail, and in the ways of peace, patience and forgiveness. I believe God has heard the prayers of the grandmothers."

"The night of my stroke, while I lay on the floor, I had a strange dream. Chester was standing on a stage, looking over a large crowd of people – mostly First Nations. It was dark. Dare were bright lights shining on him, and the others with him. His hair was long and tied back and he wore a beautiful coat like Bill's. His hands were raised to the sky and he was leading the people with songs and prayer. The fringe on his sleeves was rippling in the breeze."

"Den I saw Tyler. He was riding a beautiful white and brown horse beside a four-lane highway. Cars and big trucks were speeding by. The sun was shining and the air was warm. He had no shirt on and his long shiny hair was streaming behind him. He was riding towards a city with tall buildings, waving a piece of white paper and singing a Carrier hymn. He was going to an important meeting where the leaders of our people from all across the country were going to make a decision dat would change history forever."

She paused then looked up and softly pleaded, "Margarite, please take care of my boys. Don't hurt 'em."

# CHAPTER FIFTEEN

# IN THE DISTANCE

In the other pick-up, Tonya and Tyler had also fallen asleep though not before they had interrogated Rick about his reasons for following them to Kluskus and hotly questioned his judgment in bringing Margarite with him. It had been a long day, with more headaches than he had bargained for, in a shift that should never have happened. But the outcome had been good and it was nearly over now. Teddy had been a nuisance but done nothing worth the added paperwork of a formal complaint. He groaned softly, occasionally breathing erratically. Rick wasn't sure what that meant. The sooner the guy was on a chopper heading for Quesnel or Prince George, the better.

The kids were at least safe now, and Tilda was obviously recovering from her stroke. After they reached Kluskus, he would radio for a helicopter to pick up Teddy; they would have breakfast, a bit of a rest then head back to town. When the Blazer was fuelled, they would somehow cross that infernal Baezaeko River – even if it meant jumping it. He had to chuckle when he thought of Bill suggesting it, and Margarite screaming, paler than death when they nearly rolled his pick-up earlier. He wouldn't have missed it for the world.

The relief, the soothing purr of the engine, and the gentle twisting around countless bends were powerful sedatives. As were the warm cab and two snoring companions. His thoughts drifted to Natalie waiting at home for him, hopefully asleep in their bed. She looked so beautiful when she slept. He loved how she curled one arm under her head and the way her thick wavy hair spilled over the pillow. Suddenly, it was gone - the sound of the engine and the road. At first it startled him and a rush of adrenaline revived him.

Bill mindlessly gazed at Teddy's pick-up wandering repeatedly to the right shoulder, a rooster-tail of powdered snow showering the road. Rick was probably showing the kids a good time. Then it registered; Rick was falling asleep.

He sat on the horn hoping to rouse him, but it was too late. The right tires caught the deep snow, instantly flipping the pick-up onto its side in the four-foot ditch.

Margarite had also been drifting in and out of sleep, when the horn startled her. She opened her eyes and witnessed the pick-up leaving the road and she screamed. Her scream awoke Chester and he sprung to attention. Rubbing his eyes, the image of spinning tires, a vertical bumper and glowing red brake lights, all out of place in a cloud of settling snow confused him.

Bill slid in behind the downed pick-up and parked with his headlights on it. Then he and Margarite jumped out and ran to the up-turned driver's door. From the edge of the road, the window was at eye level. Rick was hanging over his seat-belt and trying, unsuccessfully, to reach around and release it with his left hand. His right arm appeared to be pinned underneath him.

Tonya and Tyler lie in a twisted heap against the door and the toboggan stood on end with Teddy's legs and feet at the top. His head, likely under the seat entangled in the blanket, was out of sight. Tonya pushed herself off Tyler, looked around and began to cry for her dad, softly at first then hysterically when she saw Tyler. There was still no sound from Tyler or Teddy, but Bill could see blood on the dash and the passenger window.

He sent Margarite back to the pick-up for his flashlight and reassured Tonya. "It's okay honey, we're going to get you out as quick as we can."

When Margarite returned with the flashlight he took a closer look at Tyler. His face was pale but he was starting to open his eyes and move his head. His arms and chest were wedged tightly between the seat and the door and his legs were curled under the dash. Rick was getting panicky.

"Rick, hang on. I'm going to tip the pick-up so we can get you out. Just stay put for a minute. Leave the seatbelt."

"Okay Bill. Hurry, it's cutting into my gut!"

Bill drove ahead thirty feet and turned to face the overturned vehicle. Then he unwound the winch cable and hooked it to the front axel. As he climbed back into his pick-up, a horrifying thought haunted him, "What if Teddy's rifle had fired when they rolled?" He couldn't remember seeing Rick check the safety or hearing him ask Tyler about it before they loaded the toboggan into the pick-up. When Rick and Margarite were examining Teddy earlier the tarp had been pulled back. Perhaps he had taken a moment to perform the routine police maneuver.

As the cable began to wind, the pick-up wouldn't rotate, only slide along the ditch. The pull wasn't coming from the right angle. Bill was afraid of this. Plan B was more complicated; the cable would need to be attached to the frame near the driver's door and pulled at a ninety-degree angle. This meant positioning his pick-up so it faced the opposite bank. There was scarcely enough room on the one-lane road to drive forward let alone park sideways. That left, at the most, four feet between Rick's door and the winch. It wasn't enough room. He looked up the bank to see if there was a tree he could wrap the cable around. And there was - at a perfect right angle to Rick's door.

He set the emergency brake on his pick-up then he and Margarite lugged the cable up the steep bank to the tree, wound it around and brought it back to Teddy's truck. With a flick of the switch, the cable slowly claimed its prize. The vehicle flopped back to the road, shaking a cloud of compressed snow free from the wheel wells.

As the cable rewound, Bill and Margarite ran to Tyler's door. Carefully they opened it and he slumped lifelessly into their arms. His right shoulder was drenched in blood. By now Rick was alert enough to unbuckle himself and he led Tonya, crying and shaken to Bill's running pick-up. Fortunately, the bloody mess had been hidden by the angle of the pick-ups. Tilda and Chester looked on, scared and stunned by Tonya's hysterical sobbing. They knew something terrible had happened to Tyler.

When Rick returned, he and Bill unzipped Tyler's parka, exposing what they feared – a bullet hole high in his right upper back. They laid him gently on his side, stretching him across the front seat, while Margarite applied pressure to the wound. A small firm rectangular object in his coat pocket, beneath her palm, made applying pressure easier. "It must have nicked an artery," she said. You'd better pray there's a helicopter in the area looking for something to do. How far are we from Kluskus?"

"Maybe ten minutes."

"Go there and radio for help. And bring back whatever first aid supplies you can find. I'll apply pressure until you come back."

"I think we should drive him there," disagreed Rick. "At least we'll have light and heat and a clean bed to look after him in."

"I suppose you're right. Are you able to drive Rick?"

"I've got no choice.

"What about Teddy?"

"Give me a minute and I'll check him. Take my place Rick, and maintain pressure on the wound."

Ominously, the toboggan had flipped face down. Margarite and Bill looked at one another with deflating hope for the unconscious man. She tried, with Bill's help, to turn it over, but she didn't have the strength. With a nod, she and Rick traded positions and the men managed to right it. When they pulled back the tarp, the man appeared to be dead. They couldn't feel a pulse or see any respirations so they covered his face again.

The vehicles pulled away from the accident scene spinning from one side of the road to the other. As the pickup ahead disappeared around the winding turns, Tonya's heart went with it. Time had ceased. The night was endless. Would the lights of Kluskus ever appear? She wanted to say so much to Tyler. "Thanks for being her best friend, which she never told him. Thanks for helping her with her math and walking her home in the dark. But especially, thanks for making her feel beautiful."

No one had ever done that for her before. To the other boys at school, she was just one of the guys. She hadn't been blind to his attempts to kiss her earlier in the night. The pleasure of being pursued was unlike anything she'd ever experienced and she just wanted it to last. To think of him out of her life was unbearable, like the pain in her heart.

There was no pain in Chester's arm. It had succumbed to the distraction of thoughts of loosing his best friend and brother. Why had he been so mean and disrespectful to Tyler? Why hadn't he ever told him how much he loved him or that he always felt safe when he was around? It was impossible to imagine him gone from his life. The thought of it made him wretch.

Bill gripped the steering wheel as though his whole driving career had been preparing him for this one sprint. He feathered the brakes into each corner and accelerated out. His turns were smooth and precise. Never had he been so anxious behind the wheel. Every second counted and was possibly too late. Tears blurred his vision.

While Chester and Tonya leaned on each other against the passenger door, Tilda leaned against Bill. He was her support. He had always been there for her. If she needed to go to town for groceries or one of the kids had a doctor's appointment he never said no. She couldn't understand why such a handsome educated man would want her. She made it clear from the start of their five and half year relationship that she wasn't interested in marriage. Yet here they were again, walking through another crisis together.

He reached down and squeezed her hand. The sensation hadn't yet fully returned from the stroke, but their souls were entwined. She felt that in her heart.

Her mind replayed the images of the past four days and nights, though not without gaps or with perfect clarity. What she recalled most clearly was Tyler's lionhearted determination to care for her and Chester. Truly, in the fire, he had proven he was no longer a boy. She wouldn't allow herself to think about loosing him. Instead, she prayed for his safety and healing. She was confident the vision for his life would be fulfilled. Perhaps this was how.

A dim porch light, which they presumed was coming from the band office, flickered through the trees as they drove the final yards of the rutted trail to the village. Margarite's hands, front of her coat and slacks were red with blood. The stench of it was nearly suffocating. Rick flicked on the dome light to briefly study the scene in the back seat through the rear view mirror. It was one of the bloodiest he had ever witnessed.

"How's he doing?"

"He's still here. That in itself is a miracle."

They roared to a stop in front of the band office and sat on the horn. Thirty seconds later, when there was still no sign of life, Rick leapt out of the truck. His fist still pounding the horn, he hollered, "HEY! WE NEED HELP OUT HERE! WAKE UP!" When Chester and Tonya arrived, they jumped out of their vehicle and screamed the same desperate pleas for help.

A few minutes later, a short middle-aged woman ran out of the house next door. Fumbling to cinch the belt of the faded pink housecoat around her stout middle, she combed the strands of long grey hair away from her face. As she unlocked the band office door and turned on the lights, she introduced herself as Theresa then led them inside. Behind the closed door, Rick could still be heard excitedly describing the rollover, the accidental shooting, Tyler and Teddy's conditions and the need for a radiophone so he could call for urgent helicopter airlift.

The muffled sounds of harried voices seemed far away to Margarite. In the black stillness of the night, Tyler's labored breathing and her own rapid heart beat were all that were real. Her brain was numb with fatigue and stress. Then she felt something in her back. At first she thought it was her imagination. The next time it happened however, it was accompanied by an unmistakable muffled, "Hey."

"Teddy is alive? How is that possible?" She had seen bodies, dead for hours, look better than he did. Boy, had her assessment of him been out to lunch. She had done what she often warned junior colleagues not to do, "Never Assume."

It was ironic. Here she sat with a social work degree and paramedic experience; knowledge that was supposed to help people in times of crisis and she was pinned, powerless to help, between Tyler and Teddy.

The door of the band office swung open and Rick and Bill ran out with a canvas stretcher and Theresa trailing closely behind. The men carefully lifted Tyler from her lap, lowered him to the stretcher on the ground and covered him with blankets.

"Margarite," said Bill introducing Theresa, "This is the band leader. Her name is Theresa. She said we could stay at her house until the helicopter from Terrace arrives. They figure it will be here about daybreak. And get this - the pilot is bringing a doctor with him – his brother-in-law, who just happens to be visiting from Prince George."

Teresa led Rick and Bill into her bedroom where they laid Tyler on a tidy quilted double-sized bed. In the midst of shuttling people between her place and the band office, two younger men and an old man with a cane arrived at her door. When she greeted them in a mixture of Carrier and English, they listened with noticeable respect. Then Rick asked the young men to follow him outside.

He led them to Teddy's pick-up, where Margarite was still sitting, trying to collect her thoughts and wiping the blood from her hands on a T-shirt she had found on the floor. After Rick confirmed the ownership of Teddy's pick-up with them, he solemnly proceeded to inform them that Teddy had passed away, and asked them where his body could be stored until the coroner arrived and funeral arrangements made.

Margarite was horrified. "Shouldn't we, at least, have the doctor look at him before we bury him?" she blurted out. "I felt him nudge me in the back and mumble something a few minutes ago while you were inside."

"You're kidding right? He's dead. Trust me, I know *dead*."

"Well, check for yourself."

Rick pulled back the tarp and shone the flashlight directly at the man's eyes, hoping to generate a reaction. His eyelids flickered then his lips parted and the odor of stale alcohol filled the cab.

"Well, I'll be a....! You're right. He is alive. Let's get him into the house. The doctor can look at him too."

The endless night was almost over. Sunlight gleamed along the eastern horizon. As the minutes went by, the gloomy charcoal blue hills gradually turned softer shades of mauve and pink. The moon faded behind the snow-covered trees in the west. Far in the distance, sleepy coyotes yipped. Hungry crows cawed from the lids of metal garbage cans behind the house.

Inside Teresa's kitchen, Rick, Bill, and the men crowded around the table slurping mugs full of freshly boiled coffee. Politely, they passed a plate stacked with cinnamon and sugar sprinkled toast, which she had made when she wasn't rotating between the bedrooms, where Teddy and his mother were, and Margarite and Tilda sat with Tyler.

Chester and Tonya were huddled together on the couch in the living room. A pole lamp dimly illuminated the room from the corner. As the rising sun began to filter through the dark floral curtains, the light from the lamp grew faint. But not faint enough to hide the dust on Teresa's bookcase filled with her college textbooks, First Nations periodicals, lay persons medical books, household and auto maintenance manuals, romance novels, recipe books and many others.

On the cushioned seat of a scuffed wooden rocking chair, near the airtight wood stove, a matted black and white terrier was snoring. Suddenly, he lifted his head, straightened his ears and let go with a piercing high-pitched howl. He jumped from the chair, bolted to the door and paced in front of it, barking incessantly to be let out. A few seconds later, the ground began to shudder and the drone of the approaching helicopter could be heard. Teresa jogged to the door, opening it for a better look, with Rick on her heals, and the dog ran out, thankfully.

Helicopter landings were not new to Kluskus. Once a month, Dr. Duval visited the village with its one hundred fifteen residents, fourteen houses, tiny school and health centre. The helicopter pad was well maintained. But it had never seen a machine like this. As the mammoth yellow Griffin approached, its four-bladed rotor violently shook the trees far below. Crystalline clouds swirled a hundred feet in every direction as it descended to the snow-packed pad with a commanding crunch.

The walloping blades decelerated and lowered. The pilot and doctor crouched and ran to where Rick and Teresa were waiting beyond their reach. While they were led to Tyler, Rick introduced himself and Teresa then gave the two well-groomed men in black starched coveralls a brief history of Tyler's accident and Teddy's condition. Stretching out his hand to shake Rick's, the pilot said, "I'm Chris Adamson and this Dr. Mike Calvington."

When they saw Tyler's ashen face their alarm couldn't be hidden. They glanced at one another and Mike cleared his throat passing the blood pressure cuff to Chris. As he pulled a stethoscope from his black carry-on bag Margarite asked, "Is there anything I can do? I used to work for the Toronto Metropolitan Ambulance Service."

"Yes, you can write his history," he said handing her a generic pre-printed history form. "Starting with his name, address, next of kin, allergies, write whatever you know about him and what's happened tonight." She filled in the lines, asking Tilda for his age and address while the pilot initiated the automated blood pressure machine. The pressure read 65/48, his pulse 122. His nail beds and lips were cyanotic and his skin was cool and damp.

"He's in shock," the pilot announced.

"Hopefully, his kidneys haven't shut down. I'll start a infusion then we can load him into the chopper while you examine the other guy."

A needle was threaded into the vein at the bend of Tyler's right arm. The tubing hanging from the liter bag of saline and dextrose was unclamped so the infusion would run wide open then it was taped in place. Margarite changed the last of several dressings she'd applied since he'd been carried to Theresa's bedroom two hours earlier. Then Rick and the pilot transferred him to a stretcher on the floor of the warm running helicopter.

After the doctor examined Teddy, he said, "May as well load him up too," and Rick and the pilot carried him to another stretcher in the cavernous passenger area.

Hurrying from room to room, the doctor noticed Chester holding his arm. "Let's see your arm son." A brief assessment with a wince of pain when the arm was slightly moved and the doctor ordered Margarite, "Put a sling on him and load him on too."

"This little gal had a stroke a few days ago. Maybe you should look at her too," piped up Bill.

"Tell you what; I think we'll take the four of them to Terrace for a little check-up."

Bill helped Tilda limp to the helicopter then he kissed her cheek. As the pilot carried her aboard and belted her into the seat next to Chester's, Bill called to her, "I'll see you in a day or two, good lookin'."

With seatbelts over each passenger and the doctor, the pilot began his pre-trip walk about. While the hydraulic steps were folding up into their hold, Tonya came running from the house. "Wait!" she shouted.

She leaned over to her father, briefly whispering into his ear then hollered, "Chester, come and stay with us until your atsoo comes home." Chester was ecstatic. The most beautiful girl in the world was asking him to come and stay at her house.

The pilot was sliding the door across when she yelled again, "Wait, I need to do one more thing." Trying unsuccessfully to lift her leg the four feet so she could climb into the helicopter, she asked her dad to help her up. When she was in, she knelt beside Tyler and whispered, "Tyler, I love you. I will be waiting for you." Then she softly kissed his lips.

In a moment, amidst the swirling snow, the helicopter ascended into the cloudless morn with everyone waving until it was out of sight. Staring up into the clear blue sky Bill declared, "They're in good hands."

The doctor glanced over his shoulder and turned around in his seat. "Would you look at that."

"Look at what?" replied the pilot.

"Those four goofy-looking wolves down there - they look like they're running after us."

"They probably are," said Chester. "They've been following us from the beginning."

# CHAPTER SIXTEEN

# KLUSKUS FLIGHT

As the Griffin rose into the crisp morning air, waves of glittering ice pellets showered the windshield. Turbulent arctic gusts from the northwest soon began to strum the rotors and pat its aluminum belly. The clear plastic I.V. bag hanging above Tyler jiggled and twirled from its pole. The sounds of flexing metal echoed throughout the spacious chamber where the two passenger seats and two stretchers were bolted to the floor.

In the cockpit, Chris gingerly poured a cup of steaming coffee from the thermos Theresa had packed for them, trying not to spill any on his slacks or hands. Chester listened as the pilot and his brother-in-law reminisced and laughed about some of their wilder missions together on the blustery west coast. He also observed how they reacted to the down drafts and the rattling of the aircraft - they didn't seem to notice. The closer they came to the coastal mountains however, the rougher the ride – deeper down drafts, louder banging, and harder landings in the seat. When the helicopter penetrated the clouds, they were tossed about like ping pong balls in a bingo cage. The chatter upfront didn't miss a beat until there was a complete loss of vision. Then, there was unnerving silence.

As if he suddenly remembered his own first experience with turbulence, Chris removed his headset, turned around and looked at Chester. "Are you alright? Your eyes are as big as saucers."

"This is my first time in the air."

What he really wanted to say was, "Take me down - right now!"

Tilda, who had been dozing by the time they reached cruising altitude, was now sitting straight up. Teddy, also awakened by the violent jolts, began to wrestle beneath his blankets. When Chris noticed him in the observation mirror, he was sitting up, swaying like a palm tree. Somehow, he had managed to undo the lap belt and was working on the one across his ankles.

"Hold on there buddy," Chris cautioned with a startle. "Mike, you'd better go back there and check on him. See what he wants."

"I know what he wants. He wants to take a whiz. Do you have a urinal?"

"Of course."

He fumbled around under his seat for the lidded plastic bottle he usually carried but couldn't feel it. "It must have slid…" he said stretching a little farther, neck straining against the shoulder restraint. Then it dawned on him. "I took it out at Kluskus to empty it and forgot it in the house. He should be able to hold for half an hour, shouldn't he?"

"I hope so."

Staggering in the turbulence, Mike grasped the security straps dangling from the roof for balance, as he made his way to the farthest stretcher. He was almost afraid to approach Teddy. His acne-scarred beard-stubbled skin looked more like a mask than a human face. His soiled navy T-shirt and blue jeans stunk of body odor and urine and his breath stilled reeked of old beer. His bulging biceps had no doubt been toned by countless confrontations with others who also had

had one too many. Denying him this basic need under these circumstances wasn't wise.

In his calmest voice, Mike asked him what he wanted.

"What do you think I want, man? I need to take a leak. Get me outta here! I gotta go!"

"Do you know where you are?" questioned Mike, trying to buy some time.

"Of course I know," he slurred, "I'm at the Cariboo, havin' a few beer."

"We're actually in a helicopter - flying to Terrace. We should be there in about twenty-five minutes. Can you hold it a little longer?"

"We better get there in ten minutes or I'm gonna 'splode. Just get me to the friggin' gas station or I'm hurting somebody, alright?" Then he collapsed back onto the stretcher, whimpering something unintelligible.

When he reached his seat, Chris informed him, "We've just had a weather advisory that your friend's not going to like; Terrace and Smithers are both socked in. We have to go to Prince George or Vancouver."

"It doesn't matter to me. Which ever one is the closest."

"Prince George it is then."

Like a timer had gone off, ten minutes later, Teddy was crawling off the stretcher. Mike hadn't restrained his wrists when they brought him on board thinking it would be better for his confusion. He wasn't sure now that was the right thing to do.

"I gotta go. Take me to the can! Who are you guys, the police?"

"There's nothing we can do. We don't have a bottle. You just have to hold it," stated Chris firmly.

A violent disoriented patient, who wouldn't take no for an answer, was definitely not what they anticipated this trip. Under better circumstances they might have looked for a spot to land so they poor guy could relieve himself but they were flying between mountains in poor visibility.

They looked at one another. "You don't happen to have anything in that little black bag of yours, do you, Mike?"

"You mean like drugs? I was expecting to treat a critically ill patient not someone who needs chemical restraint because he's detoxing. The only sedative I've got is a Reader's Digest."

By now, Teddy was groping his way around the floor trying to stand between down drafts. The turbulence was suddenly their ally - but not for long. He managed to stand holding onto the backs of Chester and Tilda's seats then found the security straps and started to work his way towards the front.

"You've got to keep him out of here Mike! I don't care how you do it."

"Is there no way we can set this thing down and let the guy out?"

"If I veer twenty feet, in any direction, they won't find us until June."

Mike didn't appreciate the dilemma he'd been given. Lives were placed in his hands daily. But this was different. This was about a critically injured boy and his family, their own lives, a multi-million dollar helicopter, years of investigations and mountains of paperwork if they crashed.

He stood almost toe to toe with the man not knowing what else to do. Perhaps allowing himself to be a physical barrier was all he could do. Then Tilda spoke up, "He's a diabetic. When he needs sugar, he goes crazy." Like a Broadway marquee flashing the title of a new show, her words illuminated the solution.

When he was preparing for the trip and heard they were taking a diabetic, he had thrown a couple vials of rapid acting insulin and some syringes into his bag. If he could keep the deranged man out of the cockpit long enough to draw up some insulin and somehow, inject it, he might be able to put him into a controlled insulin coma. It was all he had and he would only get one crack at it.

Mike backed into the cockpit fumbling through his bag for the insulin and a syringe, calmly conversing with Teddy about the hockey game between the Edmonton Oilers and Vancouver Canucks the night before. Then with his back turned to him, he loaded the syringe. By now, Teddy was standing on the thresh hold, clutching the doorframe and swaying with the turbulence.

"Ever been up in one of these things before?" asked Chris, trying not to show alarm.

"I went to Prince George in one, one time," he slurred. "I got in a car accident in town. Or was it an ambulance. I'm not sure. I was pretty tanked. I don't remember. I puked out my guts in the back anyway."

For a short time he seemed content to stare out the front window and talk. Then the urgency to urinate overpowered him again and he became extremely agitated and irritable. He swung his left fist towards Chris's head and lost his balance landing on the floor between the seats. With his backside up, Mike pulled down his trousers, exposing a buttock, and fired in the insulin. Enraged, Teddy reached back and grabbed Mike by the throat, choking him so that he couldn't breathe. With one lucky blow, Chris managed to backhand the man across the side of the head, stunning and driving him to the floor.

Mike shrugged his shoulders a couple times then sat up in his chair. He was trembling as he rubbed the back of his neck and throat. Teddy lay there staring up at the ceiling. His eyes lids soon flickered and closed as the insulin dropped his blood sugar. In a few minutes, he was snoring between them.

Mike turned him on his side, in the recovery position, and observed his airway. "I think it might be easiest to keep him here for the duration of the trip. I'll top him up with a couple units as soon as he starts to move."

Mike had maintained a vigil of Tyler's vitals every fifteen minutes, when Teddy's behavior allowed. The liberal flow of oxygen and I.V. fluid had kept Tyler in a moderate degree of shock. He would drift in and out of consciousness at times - a definite improvement from when Mike first saw him. But the loss of blood finally took its toll as the spiraling plumes of Prince George's saw mills came into view.

While Mike was taking the last blood pressure before their descent into the Prince George airport, Tyler's limbs briefly jerked. His chest stopped rising and the color of his face turned dusky purple.

"Call 911 Chris, and come and help me as soon as you can! He's arrested!"

Tilda and Chester froze as they watched the doctor hastily retrieve the portable defibrillator from the wall mount and position the two paddles on Tyler's chest. There was a chaotic pattern on the monitor then a piercing alarm followed by a flashing READY light. Mike shouted, "Clear!" as the electrical charge was delivered to Tyler's chest, making his limbs jerk briefly again. Afterwards, the pattern on the monitor screen was no better. With a twist of the dial, the force of defibrillator's shock was increased.

The doctor again shouted, "Clear!" and the dusky body lifelessly lurched on the stretcher. This time, however, there was a rhythm on the screen with some semblance of regularity. "He's in sinus rhythm," the doctor called, removing the first oxygen mask and applying a thicker cushioned one with a soft latex bladder which he compressed regularly by hand. A pinker, though still very pale, color soon returned to Tyler's face. Every minute approximately, Mike paused to see if Tyler was breathing on his own, but he wasn't so he continued to squeeze the bag until his face dripped with sweat and the muscles in his forearms ached.

Nothing could have prepared Chester for this. He thought he was having a nightmare and couldn't wake up. Tears streamed down his face and he wept softly. Tilda put the stronger of her two arms around his shoulder trying to reassure and calm him. It helped. Her presence was the rock he needed to keep him from falling apart altogether.

The helicopter was on the ground now and Chris was able to bag Tyler so Mike could start another I.V and inject several medications into the new line. He hung the second bag of saline and squeezed it until the fluid ran in like a tap opened fully. Over the whine of gradually slowing rotors, the ominous wailing of two approaching ambulances grew louder. The flashing red and white lights and the crew of the first one seemed to come and go with Tyler within seconds. The second, just as efficient, quickly took its place alongside the Griffin.

The crew smoothly transferred Teddy, still unconscious, to their stretcher, and loaded him into the ambulance. Then Mike and Chris escorted Tilda and Chester up the steps into the back and helped them buckle for the ride to the hospital.

"Hope everything goes well for you people," called Chris and Mike, waving as the ambulance crew slowly closed the rear doors, giving them a minute longer to say good-bye.

"Thanks for everything," said Chester.

Tilda nodded her thanks, reaching out to touch the hands of the men who had saved Tyler's life. They smiled at her and Mike winked. Through the back windows, she and Chester watched as their helicopter quickly ascended to the clouds. She knew she would never see them again. Saying a silent prayer for their safety on all their future flights of mercy was her way of thanking them.

## CHAPTER SEVENTEEN

# JUMPING THE RIVER

Fatigue was taking its toll in Kluskus. After she thanked Teresa and her friends for their hospitality, Tonya and the others started for home in Bill's pick-up. She cried all the way back to the Blazer. The last images of Tyler in the helicopter; dried blood in his tangled hair, his ghostly white face, bloodstained jeans and socks, couldn't be erased from her mind. Despite Bill's countless stories with miraculous outcomes, she wouldn't be consoled. She refused to listen to anything Margarite had to say. In Tonya's opinion, Margarite was to blame for the whole mess.

Rick was silently dealing with his own issues. He couldn't forgive himself for not checking the safety on the gun. It was such a stupid oversight; as routine in police work as brushing your teeth before bed. But in the heat of the moment, when they first found the kids, *their* safety was all he could think of – getting them to Kluskus as fast as possible, where they would be fed and sheltered from the cold.

Exhaustive written and verbal reports would have to be given. Official inquiries. Investigations. Press. He would face that when he got home. For now, his focus had to turned to the urgent matter of bringing the Blazer (half the police fleet of Nazko), with a temporary patch on it's empty gas tank, stranded half way out on the Kluskus Trail, back to the police garage.

"Do you think you can tow me back Bill?"

"I can tow you, but unless you steer, it won't follow very well. It'll just go from one ditch to the other. And there will be no heat without the engine. You're going to freeze sitting in that thing. You sure you don't want to come back later with a tow truck, after we've dropped the girls off?"

"No, let's just get it back to town as soon as we can. You take the girls with you…"

"No, Daddy. I want to come with you," Tonya said pointing to Margarite with a sideways glance. "I don't care how cold it is. I've been walking all night in the cold. I was okay, wasn't I?"

"Okay, Tonnie. Wait in Bill's truck until we hook the cable to the Blazer."

In a few minutes, they were belted into the Blazer's bucket seats. Sliding from one side of the road to the other, trying to stay behind Bill's old beater, was quite entertaining. At first, they joked about its rust-riddled box that had holes big enough to let a dog could fall through. Then they pretended to be tubing down a logging road, like they did sometimes on the weekends, when the logging trucks were usually off the road.

Margarite leaned against her door. Her eyelids strained to stay open. She wanted to sleep but she was nervous about Bill's driving. He had proven several times in the past twelve hours that he was a remarkable driver. In her opinion however, he was over-driving for road conditions, particularly with a vehicle in tow. One near-fatal motor-vehicle accident per day was pretty much her quota.

She kept silent for as long as she could but when the Blazer clipped a ditch and spun sideways, she couldn't help herself. "Bill, will you please slow down. If you don't we'll all end up in the ditch?"

"You worry too much. And what if we do go into the ditch? It's full of snow – nobody's going to get hurt. Sometimes I spend as much time driving in the ditch as I do on the road. This old girl could go places a mountain goat would be scared of."

What she really feared, was how they were going to tow the Blazer across the Baezaeko, a few miles ahead. Again, she kept silent. She didn't know how to bring it up without offending him.

"Something on your mind Margarite? If there is just come right out and say it. Is it that you don't trust me or my driving?"

His perception of her feelings surprised her. She straightened in her seat, swallowed and stared straight ahead, avoiding his sideways gaze. She hadn't been consciously distrusting him, not really.

Finally, the words came out, "Have you thought about how Rick and Tonya are going to get across the Baezaeko River?"

"I've given it quite a bit of thought, you might be surprised to know," he replied, flabbergasted by the insinuation that, *he*, one of the most respected off-road drivers in the region, didn't know how to tow a pick-up with inflated tires, across a measly little creek. Was she serious? Did she have to have input on everything?

"Well I thought I would drag them to the edge, drive a quarter mile back and take a run at them."

She burst out laughing. "You're crazy, you know that?"

"I know." He laughed too.

But she didn't really trust him. Even though he had acknowledged her concern, she was still suspicious that he might be crazy enough to try to jump the river and Rick crazy enough to let him. Bill knew what she was thinking.

Without a word, he pulled to the side of the road, got out and walked to the Blazer. After a brief chat with Rick through his window he came back and started driving again. "You'd better tighten your seatbelt," he said – his eyes forward. Now she was positive he was planning to jump the river just so he could scare her to death.

"Bill, if you're planning to do something stupid, stop this truck right now and let me out!"

"Okay, have it you're way." He said rolling to a stop. "Don't let us out of your sight though. There are lots of hungry bears and wolves around here this time of the year."

"There are not! You're just trying to scare me."

"Look over there in the ditch," he pointed. "Grizzly tracks all over the place. And on your way out - would you mind shutting the door please, then stepping back?"

Dumbfounded, she collected her purse, pulled on her toque and gloves, then jumped out and slammed the door. "The nerve of him, blowing me off like that. Who does he think he is anyway?"

Leaving her in a fog of fine snow, he sped away. "I'll show her. Who does she think she is?" Rick and Tonya waved and giggled as they flew by her. She looked like she'd been dusted with a thick coating of icing sugar.

As the sound of the engines faded around the bend, she suddenly felt foolish for second-guessing him. The last of the afternoon rays were casting long eerie shadows through the snow-covered trees up the banks on both sides of the road and there was, indeed, a multitude of tracks.

Hastily, she marched towards the river studying as many as she could. Most were cloven; deer and moose she guessed. She wasn't truly worried, until she nearly stomped through a steaming pile of tarry bear scat. Crisp eight-inch wide paw prints trailed away from the scat. A couple branches snapped in the bush behind her, dropping their snow and startling her. She panicked. It had to be a grizzly.

She ran until her lungs hurt and she had to stop. When she turned to look for the predator, there wasn't one. There was, however, a magnificent January sunset; radiant emerald evergreens, partially covered with pastel orange and pink snow, framed by a steel grey sky. For a second, she forgot she had been abandoned. Surely, they weren't going to let her walk the whole way back to town. It would be dark in half an hour.

She began to run again, hoping to reach the river before they left. Her winter parka and heeled boots felt like they had been weighted with lead. Then she started to sweat and feel light-headed. Her legs buckled and she stumbled to the ground. Off in the distance she could hear motors revving and her heart sunk.

How had she offended these people? She was only doing her job, trying to be helpful, making suggestions, some of which, she thought, were pretty darned good. Like the 4X4 thing with Rick's pick-up in the morning. They practically couldn't have survived without her.

She stood on her wobbly legs, dusted the snow from her slacks and started walking. The revving quickly faded with the daylight. They had indeed left her to fend for herself.

In the dark, the rushing of the river seemed louder. She couldn't tell how close it was. Then she heard that awful sound again – branches braking close by. Something was stalking her. The hairs on the back of her neck stood up. Her heart raced. Against everything she'd been taught about surviving a wild animal attack, she ran. Her legs felt like rubber. This was *the* nightmare.

She dare not turn around. Then the ground beneath her feet vanished and she tumbled down the bank. Knees, elbows, shins and cheeks, were poked by sharp rocks and twigs. "God," she shrieked, "Help me! Somebody, please help me!"

When she finally stopped, she was straddling a log. She was sure every bone in her body was broken, particularly the ones she was sitting on. Blood trickled between her eyes, tainting her saliva with an iron taste.

Rolling off the log, she lay on her side, shivering and wincing from the pain. Tears welled up in her eyes as she strained to focus in the dark for the beast about to pounce on her. The haunting huffing and puffing was gone in the roar of the river. If she could only put the river between them, she would be safe.

She thought she heard laughter behind her. She turned, but no one was there. Oh, how she wished it were Bill. Who was she kidding? No knight in shining armor was coming to save her. No one ever had or ever would. She had crossed all the rivers of her life by herself. What was different about this one?

Damp and shaken she stiffly rose to her feet. Amazingly, everything worked. She would step into the river and cross it, one rock at a time. To assist with balance, she would use a pole. Fortunately, she found the perfect five footer laying by itself on the shore near the heap of washed up brush that had bruised a great deal more than her pride.

The moon rose high enough to faintly outline a course across the river. Icy boulders and logs seemed to emerge approximately three feet apart. With her pole, she made a dozen little hops. When she reached the middle, she had difficulty spotting the next rock. The current boiled around her feet soaking her boots. Then she saw her next step, a gleaming round stone six feet in front of her. It was a bit too far, especially with her boots. The only way to it was to jump over or jump in – neither was going to be pleasant.

She lowered her pole into the river to determine the depth but the current quickly tore it from her grip. Now she was on her own to balance. She tried to estimate the energy it would take to jump from a standing position. High school track and field had never been her strength. She flexed her knees and practiced a mock take-off. Just as she was setting up for the launch, a gruff masculine voice bellowed, "Are you trying to kill yourself? Just stay right there!" It was Bill. Rick and Tonya were beside him.

He scampered down the bank with a ten-foot pole he'd found and leapt between a half dozen stones to the boulder where Margarite would land. "Did you seriously think you could make it across this by yourself? Nobody can. You have to be pulled over. Grab the stick and I'll give you a little demonstration."

I'll just bet, she thought. You probably can't wait to let go and watch me float to the Pacific. "Are you sure about this?"

"I'm sure. You'll just have to trust me. It'll be good practice for you to trust somebody."

What was that supposed to mean? What he was asking her to do was way out of her comfort zone, but she had run out of options and she could barely stand so she grabbed the pole.

"Hold on tight! I mean *tight* because I'm going to pull hard. Just before you land here," he said pointing to the massive half-submerged boulder where he was standing, "I have to jump over there. Don't look at me. Focus on where *you* have to land, otherwise you'll loose your balance. Are you ready?"

"I guess…"

"On the count of three – One, Two….Three!"

The force of his tug took her by surprise. Before she realized it, the stick slid threw her hands knocking her off balance. Briefly, she teetered then fell backwards into the water. The mind-numbing cold was unlike anything she'd ever experienced before. Every ounce of air and strength was sucked out of her. When she bobbed to the surface, she gulped unsuccessfully for a breath and made an equally feeble attempt to cling to the rock where she had been standing.

She glanced up and Bill was kneeling down extending his bare hand to her. "Grab my hand Margarite!"

"I don't know if I can. I can't feel my hands or my feet."

"You can't be that cold yet. You just fell in. Take my hand!"

Her chest felt like there was an elephant sitting on it. The roar of the river and Bill's yelling quickly faded and she slipped beneath the surface.

"Rick! I need your help. She's gone under."

Bill thrust his arm into the frigid current and managed to grab her collar but the weight was too much and she slipped from his grasp. He peeled off his coat and leapt in after her. The cold was worse than any pain he had ever known. Instantly, he was out of breath. They ached excruciatingly but he willed his arms and his legs to swim, battling the current.

She drifted unconsciously; fortunately face up. A few yards farther, the branch of a half-submerged tree snagged her hood, slowing her down. That gave Bill a chance to catch up. When he reached her, she looked lifeless. In the moonlight, her face and lips were pale blue.

"Margarite!" he shouted, shaking her. "Wake up! Wake up you silly woman."

"She's still he alive but I don't think she's breathing," he yelled to Rick, who was on the shore waiting to see how to assist.

"Bill, I'll throw you a rope. Grab it and I'll pull you both in!"

While he waited for Rick to hook the yellow nylon rope from the survival kit to the Blazer's winch, Bill supported her flaccid head on his left arm and started mouth-to-mouth. After several breaths, her eyelids flickered and she moaned.

When the winch was ready, Rick tossed the looped line so it would land on the water just above Bill and drift into his hand. He looped it under their arms, held on tight and gave the wave to go. Rick flipped the switch for the rescue.

A few minutes later, they were at the shore where Rick and Tonya met them with blankets warmed in Bill's truck. The men carried her up the bank and gently laid her on the ground, and checked her for a pulse and respirations. The pulse was faint. When he didn't see her chest moving, Bill positioned himself beside her and prepared to start mouth-to-mouth resuscitation again. As his lips touched hers, she suddenly took a deep breath and her eyes opened.

"What are you doing?" she gasped.

At first, he didn't answer because he couldn't read the expression on her face. He wasn't sure if she was frightened or angry or simply in a state of shock.

"You were drowning. I jumped in."

"You both nearly drowned," added Rick. "We had to winch the two of you out of the river."

"It's true," Tonya nodded.

Tears filled her eyes. "Bill, I'm sor..."

"Sshh... It's me that needs to apologize."

"Thank you for saving my life," she cried softly, staring tenderly into his tired eyes.

"You're welcome," he replied.

CHAPTER EIGHTEEN

# PRINCE GEORGE HOSPITAL

"Code Blue Emergency! Code Blue Emergency! Code Blue Emergency!" dinned the alarming announcement. Seconds later a dozen uniform-clad young men and women scurried from behind desks and curtains towards a small glass room near the entrance of the Prince George Regional Hospital emergency department. A red cart, pushed almost recklessly, by a puffing greying man in a white lab coat, soon followed through the over-crowded waiting room to the trauma unit.

Superficial chitchat about the weather and complaining about the long wait suddenly stopped. Everyone's eyes, including Tilda's and Chester's, were riveted upon this room. Once the glass door was slid across and the curtains drawn, the audience was only permitted to observe jostling pastel-colored pant legs from the knees down and hear a muffled buzz. The masculine shout to, "Clear," the couple seconds of silence followed by a buzz of unrecognizable chatter was a cycle repeated at least a dozen times.

Rumors soon surfaced in the waiting room about the identity of the poor soul whose life hung precariously in the hands of the adrenaline-charged pack. Some assumed it was the victim of a heart attack. Others talked about the bad acci-

195

dent they had heard about on the morning's news, where a loaded logging truck had lost control on the icy highway west of the city and crashed over a steep embankment. Tilda and Chester were sure Tyler was in the room. They hadn't heard anything about him since he had been taken away in the first ambulance an hour and a half earlier.

Teddy was still lying on the ambulance stretcher in the main corridor, attended by the crew that brought him, where he, like three others, waited to be seen by the frazzled triage nurse. It was her job to assess each new arrival and determine who needed to be seen by the ER doctor first and who could wait. Now she, like all the other experienced staff, was tied up in the trauma room. The only staff left in the department appeared to be nursing students and the ward clerk sitting behind the window of the nursing station.

The longer the ordeal in the glass room went on the more agitated Chester became. He fidgeted constantly in his chair, his sweaty hands squeezing the arms of it. Finally, when he couldn't stand it any longer, he leapt to his feet and announced to Tilda with a husky whisper, "I'm going to ask the lady behind the window where Tyler is."

"No Chester! Don't bother dem now. Dey too busy. Just wait till dey come out of dare. Den we can ask em."

"This is driving me crazy Atsoo! I can't wait anymore!"

In three strides, he was standing in front of the glass-enclosed rose-colored counter, staring down at the ward clerk, who hadn't raised her head since they first arrived. Gold crescent shaped reading glasses balanced on the bridge of her nose and a telephone head set crowned her copper up-swept hair. As she mumbled into the tiny receiver positioned at the side of her mouth, staring into the bright blue screen, one hand danced across the computer keyboard while the other redirected in-coming phone calls. Sheets of green, yellow and white paper, stapled together were neatly stacked beside the computer. This was the hub alright. If anyone knew anything, it was her. He just needed a second of her time.

He stood there politely waiting his turn for what felt like a half hour. According to the clock behind her, it was the longest ten minutes of his life. Then a tall balding man wearing an expensive-looking grey pullover sweater stepped up to the counter. She immediately switched her gaze to his face, smiled and pointed in the direction of the main hallway. After he left, Chester patiently waited again for her to at least make eye contact.

Several minutes past and a distraught middle-aged woman, an older teenage girl and a boy, who Chester figured was his age, crowded the counter, inadvertently shoving him to the side. This time she removed her headset, walked around the counter and led the people to a tiny but tastefully decorated room not far from the desk. When she returned, her attention was again focused on her computer screen and answering the phone.

How had she not seen him for over thirty minutes? Did she have a problem with her eyes that she couldn't see people under a certain height or age? He couldn't imagine she was deliberately shunning him. Then she turned her back to him and softly whispered into the mouthpiece, "I wish this Indian kid would take a hint and get away from the counter. Geese, they're just like flies - once they start coming, you can't get rid of them."

Stunned and hurt, he returned to his seat. He had heard of the mistreatment of the First Nations people from some of his relatives but had never actually experienced it. He was angry and wanted to yell at her – instead he slouched in the uncomfortable hard plastic seat, holding his throbbing arm and sulked. It was all he could do to keep from crying.

"What's the matter Chester?" asked Tilda.

"That old bag wouldn't talk to me. She helped the other people, but not me. I overheard her tell somebody on the phone, that Indians are like flies – once they start coming, they never go away."

"She probably tired, over-worked, maybe a bad day, Chester. We got to wait until dey not so busy."

Almost two hours after the red cart and the staff had stormed the trauma room they began to trickle out. The glum exhausted expression on their faces told the whole story. Behind the curtain, a couple nurses appeared to be tidying the room and the patient. Paper rustled. Blunt objects were tossed into metal garbage cans. Bloodied linen was picked off the floor.

The few people left in the waiting room held their breath and tried not to stare as the man in the white jacket, the ER doctor Chester guessed, shuffled towards the room with the anxious family. Following close behind him was the triage nurse. Shortly after the door closed, there was an explosion of weeping and wailing and the lamenting cries of, "Oh God, oh God! Why?" Chester empathized with them but he was relieved that it wasn't Tyler.

Grief seemed to paralyze the department. The staff clustered in groups of three or four in the hallway and the nursing station, quietly discussing the tragedy and the resuscitation attempts. Patients in cubicles softly shared their concerns about the man's family, as did those in the waiting room. The telephone even stopped ringing for five minutes.

Then, from one of the hallway stretchers, there came a loud irreverent fart. Instantly, giggles followed by outbursts of laughter erupted from the huddles.

"Hey, where is everybody? I gotta take a whiz!" Leaning on one elbow, Teddy's upper body was swaying over the raised stretcher railing.

"Where do you think you're going?" called the man of the male/female ambulance crew as they sprinted towards the stretcher.

"I...*gotta*...*take a*......*whiz*! Don't you get it, man?"

"Hold on, buddy. We'll bring you a bottle…"

"NO! I'm going to the can and you can't stop me!" he slurred.

He would have crawled over the rail but they grabbed his arms and legs. Wilding flailing his arms in an attempt to release their grip, he narrowly missed the nose of the female attendant and she panicked.

"Call a Code White!" she cried. "Call a Code White!"

A few seconds later, "CODE WHITE EMERGENCY! CODE WHITE EMERGENCY! CODE WHITE EMERGENCY!" boomed over the intercom.

This time a dozen able-bodied male and female staff - nurses, housekeepers, maintenance and administrative workers swiftly responded to the page, flooding the hallway and creating a formidable presence around Teddy's stretcher. He continued to complain and curse but did so much quieter. It wasn't long however, until he was again adamant about going to a bathroom. Certain that his need for privacy was fuelling the show of hostility, the ER charge nurse, identified by his nametag, stepped to the front of the group and reasoned with him, "After we assist you to the bathroom, will you return to the stretcher and lay quietly until the doctor sees you?"

Teddy nodded his head. Then, while the ambulance team lowered the railing and steadied his feet to the floor, he jerked free and hollered, "Let go of me!" and he bolted towards the emergency entrance.

He might have made it but his fallen trousers tripped him. Instantly, the posse was hauling him back, one to two persons per limb, turning him face down on the stretcher. Someone exposed a buttock, hoping to humiliate him into submission. Then, as though he was hurling a dart, the head nurse fired a syringe into the muscular caramel buttock while a female voice soothed, "There now, have a little sleep. We'll get all of this straightened out and you'll be on your way before you know it."

Chester was impressed with the caring words until he realized it had come from the woman behind the desk who ignored him. When she returned to her seat she arrogantly confided to nurse beside her, "I think we get all the drunk Indians in the country."

"Did you hear what she said," Chester blurted, leaning against his grandmother's blanket covered shoulders. "They hate us!"

"Dey don't hate us."

"What would you call it?"

"Dey have bad manners"

"That's putting it mildly. I'd call it mean and plain old rude."

"We have to forgive dem, Ches. Someday God will reward dem for dare bad behavior."

"I'd like to reward her right now."

Chester's disgust with the woman was no match for his exhaustion. The next time he awoke, it wasn't to her phony polite telephone etiquette it was to the light tapping on his shoulder by a nurse telling them to follow her. He uncoiled from the seat, stretched and blinked in disbelief at the clock in the nurses' station. It was six thirty. He had been sleeping for nearly two hours.

The triage nurse they had been waiting to see for seven hours never did return after she came out of the family room. Everyone assumed she had a connection to the victim. Nobody knew for sure. Unfortunately, there was a flu going around and a staff shortage. No one to replace her, somebody said. Worse than waiting all day to be examined by the incredibly over-worked ER doctor, was not hearing anything about Tyler.

It was dark outside. Whenever a car drove past the emergency entrance snow could be seen swirling in the headlights. A trail of muddied slush gleamed in the corridor. The waiting room was again overcrowded with a fresh crop of pale, overdressed distressed-looking people, howling babies and coughing toddlers.

His hunger pangs hurt far worse than the throbbing in his arm. With the exception of a few mouthfuls of fountain water, nothing had passed his lips since Kluskus. They had no money for food - Tilda's purse was still on her dresser. Chester's wallet, though penniless, was in his other pair of jeans, on his bedroom floor. The hospital cafeteria had closed at six p.m., according to the sign near the entrance.

Too shy to come right out and say it; Chester sheepishly mumbled that if there were any leftovers from supper, could they please have them. The nurse, apparently lost in her own world, didn't respond. As she hurried ahead of them, she muttered something about vitals and getting their history before the doctor could see them. When they reached an open cubicle with a freshly made stretcher, she coldly took Tilda's arm and marched her onto a footstool and up onto the bed then told him to sit on the chair beside her.

He wasn't sure she had heard him in the rush so he risked her annoyance and politely repeated his request. As she efficiently wrapped the blood pressure cuff on Tilda's arm, shoving it this way and that way, she glared at him over her shoulder and snapped, "Will you wait a minute!"

When she was finished with the rest of Tilda's brief head-to-toe assessment it was his turn. Then she started in on the paperwork – a multi-layered questionnaire with green, yellow and white pages. Without lifting her eyes, she fired off what he thought were the most ridiculous and private questions he had ever heard:

Did you live in a house?

Do you own your own home?

Who all lives with you?

Are you allergic to anything?

How much alcohol do you drink?

Do use recreational drugs?

Are you sexually active?

When did you last have a bowel movement? After that, he decided she wasn't getting more information out of him.

But then she asked them, "What brought you to the hospital today? He was speechless. He didn't know where to begin. He glanced at Tilda and she gave him the nod to speak for both of them.

"How long do I have?"

"I'm off duty in fifteen minutes. Until then, I'm all yours."

"My brother Tyler, who's very badly hurt and somewhere in this hospital, Tonya, our friend, and I, were taking our grandmother to Kluskus because she had a stroke and we didn't want the social workers to find out. Otherwise, they might take us away from her. They have been taking a lot of kids away from their parents. It was going okay at first."

"Then we had a few little problems; I fell on a rock in the river and hurt my arm. Tyler lost all of his food and soaked the matches when he dove in the river after the toboggan with our atsoo on it. I got attacked by some wolves, but they didn't hurt me because Tyler scared them away. After we crashed the toboggan into a beaver house at the bottom of a steep hill, Teddy showed up. He was drunk and he chased us with his gun."

The nurse pulled up a stool from outside the curtain and sat down beside him. She was spellbound.

"Then Tonya's dad and old Bill showed up with the social worker. We were so mad. We didn't treat her very nice. Then Teddy passed out and Tonya's dad fell asleep behind the wheel of Teddy's truck. It rolled over in a ditch and Tyler got shot."

"Wait a minute, wait a minute! Why was Tonya's dad driving Teddy's truck?"

"You sure you got time for all this?"

"I'll make time."

Chester retold the whole story, including the parts about the doctor on the helicopter who stabbed Teddy in the butt with a needle and the women with the weird glasses at the nurse's station who ignored him. At the end he summed it up by saying, "No one has told us a thing about my brother since we came here seven hours ago and we haven't eaten since five o'clock this morning."

It was quarter to eight, fifteen minutes past the end of the nurse's shift. "You wait right here and I'll see if I can round up some food and information about your brother," she said. Then she tore off. When she returned ten minutes later, she had a tray stacked with an assortment of muffins, a half-pint of milk for Chester, and a Styrofoam cup with tea for Tilda.

Following her into the cubicle was an attractive petite middle-aged woman with a sassy blonde ponytail swinging about her shoulders, wearing navy Lycra ski pants and a matching turtleneck sweater. She leaned towards them, shook their hands and introduced herself.

"I'm Dr. Michelle Cook, the on-call ER doctor tonight. The nurse told me you haven't heard anything about Tyler. I apologize for the oversight. For some reason we thought he didn't have any relatives with him. Had we known, you could have signed the surgical consent. One lung was so badly damaged it was removed. He's in critical but stable condition in ICU now."

"Can we see him?" asked Tilda shaken.

"He's heavily sedated and a respirator is breathing for him. He's lost a lot of blood, which we've attempted to replace, but he's still very pale. When he's strong enough to breath on his own, we'll wake him up. I must warn you, he doesn't look that good yet and there's a mountain of equipment supporting him. There's a nurse with him around the clock. After I've checked the two of you over and you've had a chance to eat, one of the hospital volunteers will take you to see him."

By the time they had eaten, had their blood drawn, Chester's arm x-rayed and a fiberglass cast applied, it was eleven o'clock. An elderly gentleman in a red jacket appeared at the cast room with a wheelchair for Tilda, and then he escorted them through a maze of hallways and up the elevator to Tyler's room in ICU.

Through the partially curtained closed glass door, they watched as Tyler's pale chest heaved rhythmically. Crowding his bed was a machine large enough to be a washing machine which Chester assumed was the respirator they had been told about. On either side of it were various monitors with blue screens displaying various pressures and rates.

Farther from the bedside were small cabinets and tables cluttered with an assortment of chart paper, syringes, towels, tape, and stainless steel kidney basins. Three IV machines, each with two clear bags of fluid, dangled near the head of his bed. Two drainage bags hung under the bed, one with urine in it and the other with blood. There was a tube in every orifice it seemed. Yards of the stuff were woven around the legs of everything in the room.

They tapped on the door and waited. In a moment, they were greeted by a tall thin bouncy girl in her early twenties with spiked black hair and glasses that matched her fuchsia color panted uniform. She led them to the bedside where the pasty color of his skin was exaggerated by dimmed florescent ceiling lights. A white sheet was all that covered his naked body.

A thick rigid blue tube, attached to the respirator line, was secured in his throat and to his face by pink waterproof tape. Every two to three seconds, a soft rush of wind would resonate through the long narrow passage and make Tyler's chest rise and fall.

He looked peaceful – just the occasional flicker of his eyelids and outward twist of an ankle. Seeing that he was comfortable and the nurse attending him was alert, dutiful and caring, made them feel better. She encouraged them to stand near his head and tell him that they were there - perhaps a little about their day and when they would be back.

Tilda bent down and kissed his forehead and Chester stroked the back of his hand. It was pale but warm. Earlier that morning, when he was being loaded into the helicopter, and Chester had tucked his hand under the blanket, it had been cool and sweaty.

Assured that he was in good hands, Chester led Tilda out of the room and wheeled her back to the hospital lobby in the wheel chair left outside ICU for her. It was midnight and half the lights had been shut off. A janitor dressed in grey coveralls swept a small mound of sand ahead of his push broom into a larger pile to the side of the hall. Then he disappeared into the public washrooms with a rag in one hand and several rolls of toilet paper in the other. Before he came out, Chester went in.

"Long night for you people?" he said benevolently.

"Yeah." When he was finished doing what he came for Chester timidly asked, "You wouldn't know where we could get something to eat or lie down would you?"

"You folks from out of town?"

"Yes sir. From Nazko."

"Oh, there."

He wondered if that was another racial jibe.

"Is there something wrong with being from Nazko?" he asked respectfully.

"No son, don't take it the wrong way. By *there*, I meant, that's a long way from a hospital. Another person came from there today. A young teenage boy – in pretty bad shape they said."

"My brother, Tyler."

"You don't know anybody in Prince George?"

"No, and we don't have any money with us either."

The short frail seventy-plus gentlemen leaned on the handle of his broom and wiped his perspiring forehead with the cloth he had used in the bathrooms. "Hmm," he said, pausing for a few seconds. "I think I know where I can put you for the night. Follow me."

They followed him through a maze of corridors, different than the way they took to ICU, got into an elevator and rode it to the top floor. The doors opened to a darkened hallway, free of clutter, unlike the others in the hospital. Its glossy white linoleum floor vividly reflected the red exit sign at the end. Down the hall they walked, past a dozen closed doors with windows. When he reached one with a brass nameplate that read, CNC, he unlocked it, turned on the fluorescent lights and ushered them inside.

Both sides of the spacious rectangular room had four beds, each tidily made with crisp white sheets and a pastel-colored bedspread like those on the stretchers in the emergency department. Equipment for blood pressure, pulse and temperature like what was used in Emergency was mounted on the wall between the beds. In the center of the room were three long glossy wooden tables with matching chairs. At the right end was a small bathroom with a single toilet and sink. Next to the bathroom a bank of shelves was neatly stacked with bedding, sterile supplies and odds and ends like safety pins and tongue depressors. A counter with a sink and an older style rounded white refrigerator, not much different from the one at home, was stationed at the opposite end - this stuff he recognized. His biggest fear was that there wasn't any food in the fridge.

"You should be comfortable here," the janitor said. "Nobody will be coming in the morning. They take Fridays off."

That was a rather strange thing to say about a hospital, Chester thought.

"Don't touch anything on the shelves. You're welcome to use the washroom and if there's anything in the fridge that isn't green," he chuckled, "you're welcome to it. They're always leaving their lunches behind. Beautiful stuff, too – perfectly good apples, cookies. I'll come back in the morning just before I'm off at seven o'clock and show you back to the lobby. Hope that helps you out a bit. I'll see you folks in the morning." Then he disappeared down the hall, humming until the ding of the elevator took him away.

The only sounds left were the muted drone of traffic outside and the ticking of the clock by the door which read ten to one. Tilda hobbled to one of four enormous curtained windows and stared at the whitened parking lot and street six floors below. She was astonished how many cars were still driving around, their taillights blinking bright crimson when they slowed or stopped. Some of them turned into the hospital parking lot. A few people were strolling on the slick sidewalks, one with an excited black lab yanking on its leash.

Beneath the street lamps, flurries of tiny flakes floated and twirled in the soft yellow light. In the distance, perhaps towards Nazko, plumes of white smoke rose in two columns into the charcoal sky. Shades of soft pink from the city lights, tinted the canopy of light grey snow clouds. It was a delightful sight she thought, - but nothing compared to the flickering orange glow from her wood stove on the shiny log walls of her kitchen.

In the mean time, Chester was exploring the refrigerator. On the top shelf, in a stainless steel tray that resembled a cake pan, were possibly a dozen labeled pint-sized clear plastic bags containing, what he figured were body parts. The finger was certainly easy enough to identify. So was the ear. He wanted to read the labels to see if people's names were on them but the print was too small without getting uncomfortably close. It gave him a shiver. It was like a person was in here, all apart. It was just too weird.

On the shelf below, were much better prospects for a snack - a couple of scrunched brown paper bags. But they were tucked behind three white plastic containers with clear lids, also labeled with writing too tiny to read. The substances inside them appeared to be bubbling. The last thing he wanted to do was to knock a lid off and catapult who knows what all over the fridge.

Gingerly, he reached for the biggest brown bag at the back of the shelf trying not to disturb anything. Despite his caution however, one container tipped over another, sending a bulging twist-tied clear sandwich bag with an eyeball in it plummeting to the floor. The bag exploded on impact. By the time he noticed it, the eyeball was sailing past his feet under the refrigerator on a sea of preservative. It startled him so much he knocked over the container next to it, spreading the sawdust-like contents in every direction. The lid spun around between his feet and neatly came to rest writing side up.

It read – MAGGOT THERAPY.

Hundreds of white rice-sized worms began to wiggle on the shelves, climb up the sides towards the light and down inside the drawers. At first, they were dopey from the cold. But as soon as the room-air hit them, they sprung to life.

"Atsoo! Atsoo! Come quick! Help me catch them! They're all over the place."

"Chester Jimmy Chantyman, What did you do? Catch em, quick!"

"With what?"

"Your hands, stupid kid! Hurry up!"

"I can't touch them with my hands"

Tilda glanced around the room until she spotted a box of latex gloves. She hobbled to the box, retrieved a pair and brought them back.

"Here put deze on," she said handing him the gloves.

"There's an eye under the fridge too."

"Uh what?"

"An eyeball. It was in a plastic bag. I think this place is some kind of classroom."

Tilda pulled on some gloves too and together they corralled the worms in their hands then shoveled them back into their container and secured the lid.

After that, Chester got down on his belly in front of the refrigerator with his face plastered against the floor, straining to see the eyeball. When he spotted it he confidently said, "This'll be a piece of cake." Several attempts later and pushing it farther away, proved him wrong.

"I can't reach it. And it's too slippery. I need something to grab it with."

He remembered seeing a pair of metal forceps on the shelves at the other end of the room so he ran and brought them back. With his face glued to the floor again, he shoved his hand as far under the fridge as it would go. He couldn't see the eye but he was able to touch it with the forceps. He hoped to grasp it or tease it out the backside – which ever worked.

"There's only one thing left to do, Atsoo...."

"I don't like dat look on your face Chester Chantyman."

"I'm going to tip the fridge on its side and you grab the eye."

"How you going to do dat? You got a broken arm."

He hadn't thought of that. Actually, he hadn't noticed the pain in his arm since the cast was put on. His mind was a blank. Rarely was Chester Chantyman stumped for an angle or a solution. Then the light went on.

He grabbed the garbage can and began filling it with water when the classroom door opened.

"I was replacing a light bulb down the hall and noticed the lights were still on. Is everything alright?" asked the janitor.

Chester was speechless. He couldn't feel more guilt if he had stolen the eyeball or stepped on it.

"No, we're good," he stammered.

"What are you doing with the water, son?"

"Nothin'… Catch and release."

"You a fisherman then?"

"Yeah. Fishing. I'm a fisherman fishing."

"What are you doing with the water?"

"Oh, just cleaning the bucket. Kinda made a little mess. Just cleanin' it up now."

"Anything I can help you with?

"YES!" blurted Tilda.

"Atsoo!"

"The eyeball got out of the fridge," she said.

The janitor burst out laughing, in fact he howled until he cried. Taking the dust cloth from his back pocket, he dabbed his eyes and glasses.

"It's under the fridge isn't it?"

"How did you know?"

"That happens nearly every week around here," he chuckled. "I think the little devil's got legs. Help me move the fridge and we'll put it back in the fridge for you."

With Chester's help, the janitor rolled the fridge aside on its wheels, until the eyeball was centre stage. He picked it up, rinsed it off under running water, and put it into an empty container with enough formaldehyde to cover it, then snapped the lid on tightly and returned it to the fridge.

While he was in there, like a well-trained bloodhound, he tracked his way through the clutter and unearthed an unlikely looking white plastic Sears bag in one of the drawers. There were two juice boxes and a handful of homemade oatmeal raisin cookies inside. Chester and Tilda were amazed and starving. Everyone shared the cookies and Chester and his grandmother washed it down with juice. As they did, they fessed up to the maggot incident and they laughed hysterically again.

After the janitor left, Chester assisted his grandmother onto a stretcher. Covering her with a blanket and turning out the lights, he curled up on one himself. The wall clock read three thirty.

Tilda twisted incessantly. No position, on such a firm bed, was comfortable for her arthritic hips. The last time she glanced over her shoulder to check the time the clock read five thirty. A few seconds later it seemed, the janitor was hovering over them, gently shaking and calling, "Morning, you guys - time to rise and shine. Did you sleep well?"

"Not exactly," replied Chester.

Then he led them down the hall to the elevator, whistling and muttering to himself, yawning between sentences, "No, there's nothing like your own bed - can hardly wait to find mine."

When they reached the main lobby, he was still babbling about beds and sleep and staying awake on the way home. Oddly, at ten to seven in the morning, it was just as black outside as it was when they went upstairs. Snow was still swirling in the headlights as the cars pulled up in front of the emergency entrance.

The images of puddles in the hallway was more inviting this time, because of a silhouette, the silhouette of a man with a familiar gait. It was Bill. Chester ran to him and he embraced them both. Then he led them outside to the parking lot where his pick-up was running and warm. He was taking them home.

## CHAPTER NINETEEN

# GOING HOME

Snuggling into the rumbling pick-up, jabbering about the runaway eyeball, Tyler's tubes and the rude woman behind the desk, Chester suddenly remembered not seeing Teddy on his stretcher when they passed it. A heap of messed up sheets was all that remained.

"I wonder what happened to Teddy?" he interrupted. Bill and Tilda were too engaged in their discussion about Tyler to acknowledge him. For reasons beyond his juvenile understanding, he was worried about Teddy - the obnoxious drunk who had, only hours earlier, terrorized them.

"Bill! Bill!" he interrupted again. This time there was an urgency that couldn't be ignored.

"What is it?"

"Teddy wasn't on his stretcher! I think he might have run away from the hospital – in a night gown!"

"That sounds like Teddy. Well, if anybody can survive, he can."

"I don't think so. I think we should look for him. Maybe drive up and down a few streets near the hospital and see if we can find him. I've just got this funny feeling. I can't explain it."

"Okay, for you we'll look. Then I'm taking you two to Denny's for breakfast."

Starting at the parking lot, Bill made an ever-widening sweep through every street and alley in a four-block radius around the hospital. Heavy snowfall had covered all human or animal footprints, dashing any hope of sighting someone's trail and they soon found themselves at a gas station at an intersection on Highway 16, the main east/west highway through Prince George.

In the blue fluorescent daylight under the gas station awning, tire tracks and boot prints mashed into a slushy concoction around the pumps and in front of the cashier's booth. Just as they were driving past the men's bathroom, the door opened slightly and Chester saw something blue- what he imagined was a hospital gown.

"Pull over Bill. I think I see him."

"What are we going to do if we do see him? Do you think he's going to come with us?"

"I don't know. But we have to try."

Bill slammed on the brakes, throwing the truck into a skid, narrowly missing the side of the building. Clutching his cast, Chester bolted from the truck to the bathroom door. When he got there, it was locked. He waited a couple minutes then tapped on it, alerting the person inside that someone was waiting. If only Teddy would open the door and be decent enough to come without a fuss. Surely, he would recognize an opportunity to get back to Quesnel. Native hitchhikers were seldom picked up by the first or the twentieth car that went by.

"Chester! Chester! Wake up! Let's go have breakfast," called Bill as he reached over Tilda, to shake his arm.

When he opened his eyes, the lights of a chandelier twinkling through the restaurant window temporarily blinded him. He couldn't believe that he had been dreaming.

"Did we look for Teddy?"

"No son. We drove straight here. You asked about him then fell asleep."

"It seemed so real."

"After breakfast, when we go back to the hospital to see Tyler, we'll ask about Teddy at the information desk."

When they returned to the hospital parking lot, the sun was peering over the eastern horizon. Pink and orange sunlight reflected on the hospital windows. The last snowflakes of the evening's flurry were drifting down leaving a blanket of crystal feathers over the vehicles. Today, they hoped, would bring sunshine and the good news that Tyler could come home with them in a few days.

When they reached the information desk, an elderly couple was leaning on the counter. The snow on their black rubber boots was melting into growing puddles around their feet. Their ski jackets and mismatched ski pants looked as though they'd never been mended or properly cleaned. The sleeves had shrunk at least an inch above their wrists exposing skin that had a hot pink hue. After they shuffled to seats in the waiting room, it was Chester's turn, or so he hoped.

The phone rang repeatedly, tying up the matronly female attendant for what seemed an unreasonable amount of time. "Here we go again," he muttered under his breath. Then two steel-blue spectacle covered eyes stared at him, "What would you like?"

"Could you please tell me if Theodore Williams is still in hospital?"

In an instant, she had scanned through several monitor pages, "Would that be Ted Williams?"

"Yes, Ma'am."

"He signed himself out last night."

"He didn't have any of his own clothes with him. How could they let him go like that?"

"I don't know anything about it kid. Are you a relative?"

"Not exactly."

"I can't give you anymore information than that. Sorry. Who's next?"

He stepped back surprised, though not totally shocked by the indifference. Then he led Tilda, now being pushed in a wheelchair by Bill, along the corridors to the elevator which took them to ICU.

Tyler's room was crowded with medical personnel in white lab coats and green and blue scrubs. A middle-aged brunette nurse with a stethoscope slung around her neck, standing near the head of his bed, seemed to be fielding most of the questions asked by the pack. She glanced up, and spotted the spectators peering through the glass and kept talking. Ten minutes later, she was finally free to come to the door.

"Can I help you?" she asked coolly.

"I'm Tyler's grandma. How's he doing?" she slurred, the corner of her mouth drooping.

"When were you last here?

"Last night."

"There hasn't been a lot of change since then."

"How long, do you think, before he'll wake up?" asked Bill.

"The doctors and respiratory technicians are discussing a plan right now, to start weaning him off the respirator possibly tomorrow. The weaning process could take a day, two maybe longer. When he's able to breathe on his own, we will wake him up."

"So he likely won't be awake for a couple days?"

"At the earliest," she replied.

Turning to Tilda and Chester he said, "I think we should go home for a day or two, rest up and come back when he's awake."

"Could we come in and see him for a few minutes before we go?" asked Tilda.

"Certainly. As soon as they're finished, I'll let you in."

Five minutes later the starched procession glumly exited leaving the frail handsome bare-chested youth lying amidst coils of clear tubes. The regular swishing and sighing of the respirator was hypnotic. Cautiously, with the nurse's assistance, they navigated through the equipment to the bed, staring at Tyler, again in awe of his grave condition and the technology it took to keep him alive.

Eyes filled with tears, Tilda stretched out her healthy but shaky hand to stroke his cheek, his arm and finally his hand.

"Dear God," she whimpered, "Please take good care of him. I love him so much."

After a minute or two of silence, Bill prayed a similar prayer and Chester softly echoed, "Amen." Tears streamed down each of their faces. It was difficult to imagine him ever being well again.

As they turned to leave, three more people were waiting to come in. This time the faces were familiar and smiling. It was Tonya and her parents. Bolting to the door, Chester tripped on one of the long tangled drainage tubes, almost pulling it out. In an attempt to keep from falling, he reached for the nearest side rail with his broken arm and a poker hot pain shot from his head to his hand. The screech of pain had to be heard clear down to the emergency waiting room. His bellow, however, was no match for the nurse's. "What on earth are you doing?"

After she had reconnected the tubing to the drainage bag under of the bed, mopped the pool of blood with a towel and collected herself, she calmly stated, "I think you'd better go now before you hurt yourself." Her furrowed brow told him she had an unspoken message as well. He recognized that message. He had seen it many times before on his atsoo's face when he and Tyler were horsing around in the house and something got broken. His face and neck suddenly grew uncomfortably warm. If there was one thing he could count on when Tonya was around, it was making a fool of himself.

The disheveled nurse shuffled them out and questioned the new set of visitors.

"Are you family?"

"No," replied Tonya's father. "But very close friends."

"I'm sorry. Only family are allowed in ICU."

"But we've come so far," protested Tonya.

"Didn't you read the sign when you got off the elevator?"

I C U - VISITING HOURS – ANYTIME - FAMILY ONLY

Tonya hadn't considered the possibility that they wouldn't be allowed to visit Tyler. The nurse's lack of compassion took her by surprise. Tears clouded her eyes before she could stifle them.

"Have you people got no feelings at all?" snarled Chester. "They've just come from Nazko. Do you know how far that is?"

"Chester Chantyman! Watch you manners!" nipped Tilda. "You don't talk like dat to the lady."

The mean-spirited nurse was just closing the door when she stopped. Somehow the scolding seemed to soften her. With crossed arms, she stood in the doorway deciding.

"We're sorry lady," said Tilda. "Tonya been like my kid since Chester and Tyler came to live with me. She live next door to us and her dad the police in Nazko. Dey hep us a lot."

"We'll stay out here," said Tonya's mother. "But please let her visit Tyler. They've been best friends for a long time."

The remark stung Chester. He had suspected they were more than mere friends. Obviously, her feelings for Tyler weren't a secret at their house. He felt like he'd been kicked in the stomach.

"Okay," resigned the nurse. "But only for a minute. I really shouldn't be doing this," she grumbled as she led Tonya to the bedside. "Don't touch this thing or move that thing......"

The nagging went on and on. Eventually it faded completely as Tonya surveyed Tyler's lifeless-looking body from head to foot. It was as though the person in the bed was a perfect clone of him, but paler, wax-like. His chest rose predictably every three seconds and there was no movement in his arms or legs. The only sign of life was in his eyes. Beneath his closed eyelids, the eyes constantly rolled from side to side, like he was dreaming or trying to communicate with the outside world.

"Do you think he can hear us?" asked Tonya.

"They say unconscious people can hear at times. Some recall being spoken to when they come to. It might be good for him. Just talk to him like you would at home or at school. You never know – he might respond. Watch his eyes."

"Hey Tyler. It's Tonya. You're doing great. Everybody's here – your atsoo, Chester, Bill, my mom and dad. We're all pullin' for you."

The respirator's automatic sigh kicked in disturbing the regular breathing pattern. A huge gush of air bellowed through the tubing frightening her. She was sure Tyler had breathed his last breath.

"That's a sigh. It's programmed right into the respirator. It makes the breathing more natural. Lungs get tired and need a stretch sometimes so the brain tells them to sigh. Everybody sighs. We just don't notice it."

"Wow! That's so cool." Tears again flooded her eyes. "Do you really think he'll get better?" she whispered to the nurse. The nurse shrugged her shoulders.

She couldn't believe this was happening to Tyler, to her. Since they'd moved to Nazko four years ago, they had been in the same class. She couldn't imagine walking to and from school without him. Many a night, after supper, at her dining room table, they had done their homework together, giggled and drank hot chocolate. Chester, at home doing the dishes or watching videos, was often the brunt of their private jokes.

One of them would say something like, "I wonder how many he'll break tonight?" The other would come back with something equally rude, "It's amazing we have any dishes left" or "Soon, we'll be eating off the floor." And they would laugh until their sides hurt.

She loved how he made her feel safe. When they hiked unfamiliar trails, he would tease her if she got nervous, call her a girl, and insist on taking the lead. If they were in town, on a school field trip, and some loud mouth razzed her, he always seemed to show up at the right time and whisk her away.

They had an understanding, never verbalized, that they belonged together. She didn't really see herself marrying him, but she didn't see herself with anyone else either. They would simply stay Forever Friends. Now everything had changed. She felt sad, abandoned and lost.

The emotional guard that had held her feelings in check vanished. Waves of grief over-powered her and she began to sob uncontrollably. When the nurse heard her, she rushed to her and put an arm around her, assisting her to the door. From there her father and mother each took an arm and led her down the hall away from ICU. Chester followed them, then Bill with Tilda in the wheelchair.

"We'll be back in a couple days," comforted Bill. "You can come with us Tonya. I'm sure he'll be much better by then. Nobody is tougher than that kid, except maybe this one," he said, putting Chester into a neck hold and knuckling the top of his head. Chester laughed and so did the others.

When they reached the emergency entrance, the weather had drastically changed, as it often did in the Cariboo. Visibility to the other side of the parking was hampered by heavy snow. The traffic crept along the streets around the hospital.

"I don't like the looks of this," fretted Natalie.

"You're not alone," agreed Rick.

"I think it will stop in awhile. The sky has some blue patches over there," said Bill, nodding to the north. "Let's go to Tim Horton's for a coffee and take another look at it in an hour."

"Can Chester ride with us Dad?"

"I don't have a problem with that?"

At the restaurant, the happy din of clinking mugs, laughing hollering excited customers and the aroma of fresh coffee and donuts revived them. While the men joined the line of a dozen others anxious to place their order at the counter, Chester and the women elbowed their way through the clogged aisles to a table big enough for all of them. When the men returned with the spoils, they did not disappoint. Proudly, like flags of conquest, they carried two trays crammed with chocolate and butterscotch glazed, cream-filled donuts, steaming coffees and hot chocolates.

Chester and Tonya stuffed their faces until the whipped cream oozed out the corners of their mouths. Everyone forgot about the weather. Even concerns about Tyler didn't surface for a while. Some of the lighter hospital moments however, had to be shared. Like the worms, the eyeball, and Teddy's brush with the establishment while he waited on the stretcher in the emergency hallway.

Chester had them in stitches with his slightly exaggerated details of maggots in Tilda's hair as they scooped them off the refrigerator walls and the slimy eyeball that bounced on the floor and rolled under the refrigerator. Teddy's fart in the hallway though, and the staff's reaction to it, needed no embellishment. Every time he thought of it, it cracked him up.

It was the most fun they'd had in days. The challenges of the past four days and Tyler's grave condition seemed gentler in the restaurant's party atmosphere with family and friends around. Tonya, who had been most threatened by Teddy, fabricated all kinds of humorous possibilities for his whereabouts; the bottom of the laundry chute in a pile of dirty laundry, hitching a ride out of town on the back of a garbage truck, hiding out in the cubicle of a gas station restroom.

"Tonya, I dreamt that!" gasped Chester. "This morning - it was so real. I know he's an idiot, but I just have this feeling we need to find him. I'm sure he ran away from the hospital in a hospital gown."

"And hopefully a blanket," added Natalie.

"Bill thinks he can survive. What do you think, Mr. Clement?"

"He's a Kluskus Carrier. They're used to the cold," said Rick. "I'd say his chances are better than average."

"But he diabetic," said Tilda. "He need insulin or he die."

"My guess, if he's functioning at all," Bill interjected, pointing to his head, "is that he won't be far from someplace where he can get food, insulin and syringes."

"The hospital?" asked Tonya.

"Or a drug store," said Natalie. "Do you think he'll try to steal what he needs?"

"That would be my guess," said Rick. "Let's head back to the hospital."

"Could we take the highway? In my dream, there was a gas station on the corner of the highway and Fifteenth, the street the hospital is on. I saw someone dressed in blue in the bathroom when the door opened," implored Chester.

"What are we going to do if we do find him?" asked Tonya. "We can't take him with us. He's crazy. I thought he was going to rape me and kill us all yesterday. What makes you think he's going to be any different now?"

"She's right," Natalie agreed. "I don't want him riding with us."

"He can come with Tilda and me," offered Bill. "I think we can make him behave himself."

"We'll take the highway to the corner of Fifteenth and make a pass through the Petro-Can. Bill, you and Tilda sweep the streets on the north side of fifteenth. Then we'll meet in the hospital parking lot. Hopefully, something will turn up."

Visibility was only marginally improved. The red glow of bumper-to-bumper taillights was an ominous sign of poor road conditions. Falling too fast for snowplows to keep up, the snow was easily two inches deeper than when they left the hospital an hour earlier. Seasoned Prince George drivers were struggling to maintain control at the traffic lights. Highly polished tire tracks through the intersections warned drivers to feather their brakes.

When they reached the intersection of Fifteenth and the highway, a couple of RCMP cruisers had barricaded the road. Four officers in luminescent yellow vests were stopping the traffic, checking for seatbelts and inspecting tires. When it was Rick's turn he rolled down the window of their SUV and a policeman quickly scanned everyone for seatbelts.

"Where are you folks from?" he politely asked.

"Nakzo. The pick-up behind us is from there too. I work in Nazko. He unbuttoned the inside pocket of his parka, dug out his wallet, his professional ID and driver's license. The officer nodded in respect of his colleague.

"In case you're planning to return home today, the highway just north of Quesnel has been closed for two hours. A logging truck lost its load near the Cottonwood River Bridge. It could have been a bad one. Some of the logs narrowly missed a school bus full of kids. Are you heading down there today?"

"Yes, we are. Do you have any idea when it will reopen? And could you do me a special favor?

"Sure."

"We're looking for somebody who was in the Prince George hospital yesterday and may have eloped in a hospital gown?"

"Would that be Ted Williams?"

"You know of him?"

"Oh yeah. We've been looking for him since four o'clock this morning. We've been up and down these streets at least once an hour for the last seven hours. If he's out there in a hospital gown there's not too much chance he hasn't frozen to death."

"He's a diabetic and we think he may try to steal food or diabetic supplies from somewhere. He can be dangerous."

"We haven't had any calls like that. Let me check the highway status and you can be on your way." He left for a minute then returned. "They figure it will open in about two hours."

"Thanks. Keep your eyes open for our friend will you?"

Rick rolled up his window then stepped on the gas pedal. The wheels spun until they whined. "Woe, that's icy." When he glanced in his rear view mirror to see if Bill had been waved through, the officer was having a heck of a time standing up.

A hundred yards or so from the intersection Rick pulled to the side of the road and got out. Bill did the same. They discussed what the policeman had said about Teddy and the accident and they decided not to return to the hospital but rather head back to Quesnel.

Spun out cars littered the ditches. Tow trucks, snow-plows, chained semi-trucks and cautious drivers made the progress slow. Fifteen miles south of Prince George, at the congested Red Rock gas station and truck stop, Tonya asked if her dad would stop so she could use the bathroom. Chester, who had been sleeping, slumped against the opposite door from her, sat up. Rubbing his eyes, he watched Tonya disappear behind a door marked WOMEN.

For a couple seconds nothing about the picture seemed awry. Then his heart skipped a beat. Something blue had darted behind her just as the door was closing.

"It's him!" he screeched, grabbing for the handle and jumping out. "He's in there with Tonya!"

Rick shouldered his door open and bolted after him to the restroom door. Plowing it open, they found themselves in the midst of six younger and older women, all urgently waiting their turns for one of the two cubicles. The woman at the back of the line was wearing a powder blue ski jacket. Everyone shrieked then giggled in disbelief. Tonya gasped, "Dad! Chester! What are you doing in here?"

Faces on fire, they backed out of the crowded washroom. "Man, your face sure is red," said Rick.

"So is yours."

"Would you mind telling me what that was all about?" asked Rick.

"I don't know what's wrong with me Mr. Clement. I need to know where Teddy is and that he's okay. It just won't go away."

Tonya was climbing back into the SUV when she spotted something on the doorstep of a shed partially hidden by trees behind the gas station. "Look at that Dad," she said pointing to the shed. "Isn't that a blanket on the step over there? Doesn't it look like the one on Tyler's hospital bed?"

"You're right Tonnie. It does."

Bill noticed it about the same time and was also heading for the shed. When they reached the porch steps there were fresh bare-foot and shoe prints going up and down. Feeling like trespassers, they pushed opened the unlocked door. Inside, in a small heap, lie a blue hospital gown and a pair of matching pajama bottoms. Emptied packages of Glossett peanuts and raisins were strewn near by. Outside, on a clothesline strung between two pine trees, some articles of clothing seemed to be missing. Rick noticed it and made the educated guess the missing articles probably were men's clothing.

"I don't think he's far ahead of us," he said.

They fish-tailed off the gas station property only to run into the same bumper-to-bumper snail's paced line of vehicles. "I sure hope he found a coat somewhere," worried Bill.

"You don't worry bout Teddy. He going to be okay. Dat my sister's kid. Heez Carrier. Heez going to be alright," said Tilda.

The traffic crawled for half an hour when Natalie spotted a man shuffling along the road on the right shoulder. Rick lightly pumped his brakes to alert Bill to what they too had just noted. It was Teddy, walking with the traffic, his bare thumb stuck out indicating that he needed a ride. The half-inch of snow on his plaid work shirt stated the fact most simply, that he had been waiting for his Good Samaritan for quite some time.

Rick drove past him and parked on the narrow shoulder with his four-way flashers blinking. And Bill fenced him in from behind. His immediate response was to try to run and he bound over the three-foot ridge of plowed snow. Rick ran after him and tackled him from behind and they somer-saulted down the bank to the bottom of a ditch. Teddy started swinging but his punches were poorly controlled - his lack of co-ordination and strength, no doubt, the result of exposure to the cold.

"Ted, Ted, listen to me," yelled Rick, "Stop fighting us. We want to help you."

But he wouldn't stop.

Bill grabbed him from behind and pinned his arms to his side with a bear hug that would've suffocated him had he persisted. From up on the bank came a faint crackling voice, "Teddy, stop it, you stupid kid! Let'um hep you! Dey tryin' to hep you."

Like he'd been poked with an electrical prod, he stood to attention. He stopped resisting and let the Rick and Bill assist him up the bank into Bill's pick-up beside Tilda. He sat quietly next to her in respect.

Despite the poor visibility and slippery roads, the drive to Quesnel, albeit three times longer than usual, was quiet. Teddy, once warm, slept curled up leaning against the door – never once murmuring about being forced to go with them.

In the distance, the lights of Quesnel's mills twinkled and the vapor from their stacks spiraled up into the snowy night sky. Another hour maybe two and they would be in their beds. Teddy would spend the night on Bill's couch. Tomorrow would take care of itself.

Just past the turn off to Ten Mile Lake, approximately eight miles north of the city, Tilda moaned, shook then slumped towards the steering wheel. At first, Bill thought she had fallen asleep but when she moaned oddly again and gasped, he knew something was wrong.

He pulled to the side of the road hollering for Teddy to wake up. When Ted saw her, he sprung to life. "Aunt Tilda, wake up! Wake up!" he shouted. When there was no response, he felt her wrist then her neck for a pulse. There wasn't one.

"She needs C.P.R." he said. "I know how to do it. Lay her down and do what I say."

Bill put on his four-way flashers, got out of the pick-up, leaving his door open, and waited for instructions. Teddy opened Tilda's coat and began chest compressions counting, "One and two and three and four and five." When he reached ten, he blew into her mouth. Without breaking stride, he ordered Bill to straighten her neck, lift her chin, pinch her nose, seal his lips on hers and blow once when he reached five.

Bill fumbled her limp head and jaw into position, pinched her nose and was ready to blow when Teddy called, "Five." It went without a hitch. A minute later, they stopped to check for a pulse - when there wasn't one they kept going.

A few seconds later Rick and Natalie ran up to Bill's truck.

"I knew I should've brought my cell phone today," Rick ranted. "How stupid could I have been? We were backing out of the driveway this morning and something said, "Go back and get it." But I ignored it, telling myself that nothing is going to go wrong. Idiot!"

"Don't beat yourself up," comforted Natalie. "We've all done it. Maybe we can flag someone down. There're lots of people going by. Surely, somebody's got a cell phone."

"We don't have time to wait," said Teddy. "We'll have to take her ourselves. Natalie, do you think you can take over for Bill so he can drive?"

"I don't know. Where am I supposed to sit or kneel."

"Kneel on the floor, as tight to the gear shift as you can. I'll kneel right beside you. On the count of three, I'll stop compressions and we'll drag her down the seat so Bill can get behind the wheel, then Bill drive like ...like everybody says you can."

Natalie ran around to the passenger side, opened the door and scrunched under the dash, until her lower body was next to the gearshift and her chest and arms were above the seat, free to work with Tilda's face and mouth. Contorting his arms, to continue with the compressions, Teddy positioned himself beside Natalie. "On the count of three, we move her, one, two, three, PULL!"

They dragged her down the seat, buckling her knees against the passenger door. Then Bill jumped in and floored it – the wrong thing to do. He knew better. The tires spun wildly, clamoring for traction. Traffic had glazed the highway from shoulder to shoulder. A more delicate approach was definitely required. Despite repeated attempts however, he carved a rut he couldn't climb out of.

He couldn't understand why the four-wheel drive hadn't helped. Rick could see the problem but rather than wasting the time to jump out and push himself, he opted to nudge him out with his vehicle. He flashed his lights to get Bill's attention then gently rolled in behind him to line up their bumpers.

Rick made sure he was in low range four-wheel drive. In second gear, he slipped the clutch, certain the winter tires would grab, but he was wrong – they spun, just like Bill's. Going forward was impossible.

Bill rolled down his window and waved for Rick to stop, then he jumped out and ran back to him. "I'm going to try to back out," he panted. "There's better traction in reverse. If you can back up and block the road I'll give it a try."

Rick backed onto the road, stopped and put on his four way flashers. Then Bill, in low range also backed onto the highway. A silver BMW sports coupe had stopped behind Rick. The driver, a well-dressed businessman in his mid-thirties, hollered out his window,

"What's the problem?"

"We have a medical emergency."

"Is there anything I can do?"

"Do you have a cell phone?"

"Yes. Would you like me to call for help?"

"I don't think there's time for that. Call the operator and tell her to phone the hospital in Quesnel. Get her to relay the message that we've been doing CPR on an elderly woman for about ten minutes and we'll be there in five minutes."

Bill's taillights were barely visible by the time Rick finished talking to man. He raced to catch up, sliding into the corners. Tonya and Chester squeezed each other's hands in the back seat.

Chester bit his lip repeatedly whimpering softly. He tried to focus on one thought, any thought, but he couldn't. The events of the last two days blurred together in an ever-playing kaleidoscope. He would have screamed had it not been for Tonya. Her hand was the only thing that kept his heart from exploding. He wouldn't let his mind go near the thought of loosing his grandmother. When he hedged on it, panic sucked the air out of his lungs. She and Tyler were going to be alright – he willed it.

When they drove into the hospital parking lot, in front of the emergency doors, an ambulance crew of two men and a couple of female nurses were standing by with a stretcher. The pavement had been recently shoveled but there were frozen lumps of snow. Pushing a stretcher with someone on it required all four people.

Tilda was wheeled into a glassed room next to the entrance, not unlike the one in the Prince George hospital. Chester and the others were escorted by a nurse into the adjacent twelve-seat waiting room. A minute later, a graying middle-aged man wearing blue jeans, a white T-shirt and cowboy boots dashed through the emergency entrance and joined the rest of the team in the trauma room.

A white curtain was drawn past the end of Tilda's stretcher and the glass door closed, blocking sight and sound. The process was remarkably similar to what Chester had witnessed in Prince George. The outcome, he prayed would be different.

230

With hearts pounding, Bill had them join hands and bow in prayer. "Heavenly Father, we don't know what the outcome will be tonight, but we know that you love Tilda and you love us. You know what's best for us. If it's your will for her to get better, do it quickly. If it's her time, be merciful. Don't let her suffer. Help the doctors and nurses to give her the best care possible. Give us, especially Chester, your peace. We ask these things in Jesus name. Amen." They held hands, hesitantly waiting for the doctor to pull aside the curtain, walk towards them and deliver very good or very bad news.

The next ten minutes were an eternity. Muffled in the distance, there were repeated shouts of "Clear!" and excited jabbering. Suddenly it was quiet. When the curtain swept back and the blue jeans and cowboy boots strode into the waiting room, Chester couldn't lift his eyes to the man's face. In his heart, he knew.

Everyone but Chester stood as the doctor approached.

"I'm so sorry for your loss."

That was all Chester could process before he collapsed on the floor wailing and sobbing. Tonya and Natalie knelt beside him, clutching him, weeping and rocking with him on their knees. Bill, Rick and Teddy sat down, sniffled and listened to the doctor's suspicions for the cause of death – the strongest being a stroke, owing to the mottled dark discoloration of her skin on the back of her head and neck. He asked for permission to do an autopsy to determine the true cause of death but they refused saying his professional opinion was good enough. They explained her other grandson was critically ill in the Prince George hospital and they wanted to do what was easiest for Chester and his brother. The doctor left them and they wept.

## CHAPTER TWENTY

# APPREHENDED

They spent the night at the Fountain Motel, across the street from the hospital. Chester, Bill and Teddy shared a room. Tonya and her parents shared another. Before they could return home to Nazko, the transport of Tilda's body would have to be arranged, the standard death paperwork obtained from the government building and plans for a traditional Carrier funeral outlined. Because Tilda had been a First Nations Canadian citizen and the legal guardian of Tyler and Chester, Rick knew additional protocols would have to be followed and he didn't have a clue where to begin.

For help he turned to Nazko's chief, Dorothy Boyd, Tilda's niece. He found her office, the band office, in a tidy post-war white sided bungalow on a quiet side street on Quesnel's predominantly First Nations and East Indian Westside. Equally fluent in English and Dene, the official Carrier language, Dorothy calmly fielded phone calls, answered the questions of staff coming through her open office door while signing the document needed by a young mother with three chubby rosy-cheeked toddlers.

When she was finished, the young woman herded her youngsters out the door and Rick was invited to sit down on one of three plastic chairs in front of her somewhat disheveled mahogany desk. Removing his toque and leather gloves, he shook her hand then explained the reason for his visit.

He told her about the kids' ordeal on the Trail – how the boys, along with his own daughter, had tried to outrun a social worker after their grandmother had had a stroke. And now Tyler was fighting for his life in the Prince George hospital. Then they discussed the crisis in Quesnel's Family Services Office and how it was affecting many other Carrier families as well.

Deeply moved by the tragedy, Dorothy said she would have her staff contact relatives and friends and book the newly constructed First Nations elementary/high school in Nazko for the funeral. She would also act as Tilda's executor and personally oversee the transfer of the boy's guardianship and her estate. At the end she added, "Just take care of Chester and give him a big hug for me."

On their way back to Nazko, they stopped for lunch at the Pizza Hut in town. From the phone booth behind the restaurant, Bill phoned the Prince George hospital for an update on Tyler. The ICU nurse gave him a glowing report.

"We are weaning him off the respirator as we speak," she said. "He's still not out of the woods. But if all goes well, he should be awake tomorrow and possibly ready for transfer to the Quesnel hospital the day after. He's such a cute little guy."

Bill didn't know what to say. He hadn't anticipated having to deal with Tyler before the funeral. Caught off guard he exclaimed, "His grandmother died last night. Don't let him find out! She was his legal guardian. Please make it clear to everyone that we want to be with him when he finds out. No one is to tell him about her death, understood?"

He returned to the restaurant with a puzzled look on his face. Rick wasn't sure how to read it. "Everything alright, Bill?"

"Everything's great," he replied with a trace of sarcasm. "Tyler's being weaned off the respirator today and if all goes well he could be transferred to the Quesnel hospital the day after tomorrow."

"That's amazing," cheered Tonya.

"Just amazing," Chester echoed flatly, tears of grief filling his eyes.

"It sure would be nice to have the funeral out of the way before he comes back," said Natalie. "He's going to need a lot of attention for awhile. Did you reach the boys' mother yet Rick?"

"No. Dorothy assured me she would contact everyone. Once the date of the funeral is decided, she will fan out the news."

"How are we going to put together a funeral in two days?" asked Natalie. "And what about the people who have to travel any distance? Some of her closest relatives live in Kluskus. If they heard today they couldn't be here in time."

Teddy had little to offer to the conversation. His stolen plaid shirt and blue jeans were clean but wrinkled from drying on the clothesline. He had showered in the motel and his hair hung down past his shoulders, still dripping. Razor stubble made his slightly jaundiced face look thin and profoundly depressed. He shuffled his untied, also stolen, worn out running shoes, underneath his seat. He planned to bolt - that was clear by his turned away stare.

Wanting to curb his increasing restlessness Rick mentioned casually, "So, Ted, where did you learn to do CPR like that?"

"Kluskus," he mumbled, still not making eye contact. "I watched it on a video at Theresa's place one night."

"Have you practiced or performed it on anyone since then?"

"Plenty of times - in my mind. I wanted to be able to save my kids if they needed it," he answered.

235

"You did an amazing job," said Bill. "Thank you for what you did to save Tilda."

It was obvious he wasn't comfortable in the lime light. His face went bright red, he fidgeted in his seat and his gaze turned from the window to the floor. His low self-esteem couldn't handle a compliment.

— — — — — — — — — — — — — — — — — — — —

It was a perfect cloudless winter day - ice crystals glittered on the WELCOME TO NAZKO sign at the entrance to the rustic village. Sparkling eddies twirled across the polished frozen road between the four-wheel drive pick-ups as they streamed into the parking lot of the Nazko First Nations School. The potlatch funeral, scheduled to start at one, was running a half hour behind waiting for the latecomers. There was a saying here, "When you're in the Cariboo, you're on Cariboo time."

Two hours earlier, at approximately eleven a.m. Saturday, February 1st, Tilda Marie Chantyman had been laid to rest in the tiny picket-fenced First Nations cemetery. At a brief graveside ceremony, a much-loved pastor and an old friend of Tilda and Bill's read scripture, prayed and reminded them that she was with the Lord now, gloriously healthy and happy. While the frigid north wind tugged on their clothes and stung their faces, Chester's mother, her Caucasian companion, Tilda's sister from Kluskus, Teddy, his wife and kids, Tonya, her brother and their parents, Bill and Chester, huddled together and wept.

Inside the gymnasium, against the far wall, a table covered by crisp white linen tablecloths spanned the room. In the centre of the table was a spectacular two by four foot floral arrangement of red and white roses, vibrant green ferns, baby's breath and cream and gold bows. Around it were steaming roasts of sliced moose and deer meat, bear

jerky, foil wrapped baked stuffed salmon, mashed potatoes, raw and cooked vegetables, bannock, buns and casse-
roles – enough to feed the two hundred people filing in and
being seated in the wooden chairs lining the perimeter of the
room.

When everyone had finished eating and the paper plates
were gathered into plastic bags, Dorothy Boyd stood in front
of the banquet table. Draped in a traditional ornately beaded
creamy white cape and matching moccasins, the attractive
middle-aged Nazko chief squinted in the sunlight reflecting
on the glassy hardwood floor. The atmosphere was electric
with anticipation but respectful. Chatty wiggly toddlers were
swept into their parents' arms and hushed.

"We have gathered together today to pay our last respects
to our beloved mother, grandmother, sister, aunt and friend,
Tilda Marie Chantyman."

After the highlights of her life had been read, Bill was
invited to come and give a special tribute to her. "Tilda
Chantyman was my best friend. Five years ago, when I first
came here, I was a broken man. I had been in jail, had little
money and nobody wanted to hire me. Feeling lonely and
having nothing better to do, I wandered into the old church
one Sunday afternoon. I sat in the back row so I wouldn't
be noticed but she spotted me and smiled. I tried to put on
a happy face and I smiled back but she saw right through
me."

"After the service, she invited me to her house for tea
and cookies. Like I said, she saw right through me – to the
pain in my soul. She told me God loved me and that there
wasn't a thing I had done in my life that he couldn't forgive.
She said He loved people so much that He sent his son Jesus
to die for their sins. And if I asked Jesus to forgive my sin
that he would and I could start a new life. So I prayed for
forgiveness that day, and invited Jesus to be the Lord of my

life. I've never been the same since. Even on sad days, like today, I have a joy and peace that doesn't go away."

"Tilda's faith gave her the great love she had for her people, particularly her grandsons, Tyler and Chester. Oh, she would get frustrated with them at times. We've all heard her call them, "Stupid kids!" Bill chuckled, "but she loved them dearly." Off to the side of the room, sitting with Tonya's parents, Chester and Tonya looked at one another. They also chuckled.

"And we've all been touched by her selfless acts of kindness. She was often seen in the hospital at the bedside of a sick baby, a teenager, a dying man or woman, many of whom she never knew personally."

"But she was best known for her love of children. She was always babysitting. If someone was too sick to look after her kids, she would call Tilda. Or if a couple needed to get away for the weekend, she was the one they asked. She was a great mother, grandmother and friend and she will be greatly missed by us all."

When he sat down, there wasn't a dry eye in the room. Tilda had clearly left her mark.

In a few minutes, Dorothy took the floor again. "Last night, at the deliberation of the elders and council, it was decided that Tyler and Chester should return to the care of their mother, if she's willing. Otherwise, somebody else may offer to be their legal guardian. Tilda's house will be sold, hopefully today, and the money kept in trust, by the band, for them until they are old enough to claim it and I'm sorry, I've forgotten at what age that is."

"It's twenty-five, I believe," called a quiet feminine voice from the back of the room, near the main entrance. Everyone turned around and craned their necks to see who had spoken. Bill didn't have to look. He knew who it was, Margarite. She was the last person he expected to see today.

When he looked at her, their eyes met. She smiled sweetly, like a shy teenage girl catching the attention of the most popular boy in school. He wasn't sure what he felt - flattery, curiosity, distrust. How could she not know that her motives and presence here today wouldn't be questioned by those who knew she was a social worker? She had to know. Her risk stirred something inside him, something he liked.

"We're going to break for dessert now," announced Dorothy. "Jenna and Rosie will bring out the pies and cakes in a few minutes. After you eat, go outside and enjoy the sunshine. We'll continue with business in about an hour."

Bill waded towards her through the crowd lining up for dessert. She looked amazing. Had she cut her silken chestnut hair or restyled it? It glistened, accentuating her ivory heart-shaped face and twinkling grey eyes. When she uncrossed her legs and stood up to greet him, his heart skipped a beat. Black leather knee-high boots made her legs appear long and shapely. Her caramel suede knee-length suit clung to her petite waist like a glove. Had she lost weight or did the outfit only make it look that way? Her delicate perfume took his breath away.

Did she have any idea what she was doing to him? Was she oblivious to their age difference or the color of his skin? He felt like he like a love struck teenager about to make a fool out of himself.

"Are you flirting with me?"

"You could say that," she replied fluttering her eyes.

"Well it's working. Let's go outside so we can talk."

He helped her slip on a full-length double-breasted black leather coat and matching gloves then they discretely exited the main doors, strolling down the sidewalk in front of the building.

"What brings you here?"

"A few reasons. I liked Tilda. In the short time I knew her, I discovered she had something I needed – faith, love. I could see why Tyler and Chester loved her so much and why they were willing to risk their lives for her. She was a great mother to them."

"Weren't you a little afraid some people would misunderstand your appearance at the funeral?"

"I considered that."

"But there were other reasons for coming today."

"A memo came across my desk yesterday, about Tyler. It said he was being transferred back to Quesnel today and that he hadn't been informed of his grandmother's death yet, that he wasn't to be told until his family and friends were present. Is that true, he hasn't been told?"

"He probably hasn't been awake long enough to even realize he's in the Prince George hospital."

"That's taking quite a chance, isn't it – that somebody won't spill the beans before you get there."

"We had no other choice. We wanted to get Chester through the funeral, figure out where the boys will live and what will happen to Tilda's house before we dealt with Tyler. He's going to need a lot of support and we wanted to be able to give it to him without the disruption of a big funeral. We had hoped Prince George would give us one more day. They've given us four – we're thankful for that".

"From the government's position where do Chester and Tyler stand?" asked Bill.

"Because they're First Nations, the band is able to appoint guardians from amongst your own people. Their care will be monitored by a government worker, namely me. If there are any problems, the government has the power to intervene - that includes financial resources for special needs."

"Would you consider being their guardian, Bill?"

"I love those boys, don't get me wrong, but being the single parent of two teenage boys is not a job for a green horn. I had trouble housebreaking my dog. Their mother should take them."

"She looked pretty cozy in there snuggled up to Romeo, don't you think?" said Margarite.

"Someone said he's a truck driver – probably gone all the time. She couldn't handle them when they were young, with Tilda's help." said Bill. "How's she going to cope by herself with two teenagers fresh off the reserve?"

"Maybe Rick and Natalie would take them if she can't."

"We'll just have to see how the meeting goes," said Bill.

"What about the house Bill?"

"The house will likely be sold to someone on the reserve, for cheap. The members of the band will vote on the offer then the Ministry of Indian Affairs will give its stamp of approval. A few months later, the transfer of ownership will be complete."

"What about you, Bill? Are you interested in buying it?"

"I wish I could. I barely scrape by in my trailer on my Status cheques," he answered sadly. "We'd better get back to the meeting."

As they returned to the gym, all eyes were focused on them. Bill escorted her to her seat by the door then he took his place near Chester and the Clements. Tonya and Chester's glare burned a hole in the side of his blushing face.

"I'd like to discuss Tyler and Chester's guardianship now," Dorothy said. "It seems most appropriate to ask Lizzie if she wants to resume the care of her sons. Will you accept this responsibility, Lizzie?"

There wasn't a word. The only sound in the place was the furnace cutting in and the wind rushing along the countless yards of cavernous heat ducts. Nobody lifted their heads. They stared at their laps and empty dessert dishes for what felt like ten minutes. Finally, a chair scraped across the wooden floor and the young woman stood and cleared her throat.

In her early thirties, Lizzie was an attractive petite woman, like her mother, with generous breasts and well sculpted cheekbones and thick shiny chin-length raven hair. Her make-up and clothing had evolved to what most would consider, trendy and out-of-place for a First Nations daughter. Her ivory waist-length leather jacket and tight blue jeans emphasized her nicely rounded hips. Matching ivory boots with three-inch wooden heels, burgundy lipstick and nail polish completed the diva look. She'd come a long way from the jogging pants and ski jackets she wore when she lived on the reserve.

Her companion, close to her age, whom everybody assumed was her common-law partner was in anybody's opinion a hunk; six foot, shaggy salon coiffed blonde hair, muscular upper body, firm fit thighs. His clothing style was more western, as Cariboo truck driver's often were – blue jeans, matching jacket, cowboy boots. They looked very happy together.

Lizzie held his hand and stared at him then gradually released her grip and turned to Dorothy. "As you know I haven't looked after my boys for five years. I have a new life now. Steve and I are planning to get married in a year or two. I'm taking courses at the college. I don't know how I can look after them. Tyler can stay with us for a while until he's able to go home, but it wouldn't be long term. I'm sorry."

With that, she started to cry, sat down beside the young man and buried her face in his embrace. The crowd grew uncomfortable with the display of emotion and chairs started to shuffle, people coughed and murmured. It was obvious how they felt about the apparent lack of maternal warmth.

Then Dorothy asked the crowd, "Is there any family here who would like to assume the responsibility of caring for these two wonderful boys for the next three to five years. Tyler will be fifteen next month and Chester will be fourteen in April. They are well-mannered, doing well in school, and no doubt trained to do chores. Tilda has done a great job with these boys."

Chester felt like the prize bull at an auction.

Rick and Natalie looked at one another then Rick stood up. "We would love to take Chester but I just received news yesterday that I've been transferred to the Quesnel detachment. We'll be moving to town in a month. I don't think moving him to an over crowded, racially-insensitive high school would be very helpful for him right now."

Tonya was shocked – this was the first she had heard of her father's transfer. Chester, too, was stunned by the news. He was loosing his grandmother, his brother and the love of his life. Nothing else could be taken away.

The room was still and tense as the minutes passed and no one offered to take Chester. It hurt him that Bill hadn't offered or at least explained why not. Bill was also amazed but he felt strongly that he shouldn't. He had peace that it was best for Chester.

Then a chair grunted sideways and a man stood in the middle of the congestion of people. He coughed a couple times and straightened his jeans, looking bashfully around the room before turning his eyes towards Bill then Dorothy. "Bill, I've been sitting here, thinking a lot about what you said about God forgiving us and giving us a new life. I would like that, a lot. I've been a drunk, abused my wife and kids and I would like to be a better husband and father."

He paused for a couple minutes, trying to collect himself, but he couldn't. He broke down and wept out loud before regaining control. His wife handed him a Kleenex from her purse and he wiped his eyes. Everyone was unnerved. Chairs moved. People coughed.

Then he continued, "Bill, will you help me find my way?" He broke down again and a couple more minutes passed before his composure returned.

"And Chester, if you and Tyler will have me, I would like to be your dad."

Bill couldn't believe his ears. Teddy?

"I PROTEST!" shouted Margarite. "This man is a degenerate. He can't even look after himself let alone a family, his or anybody else's. Madam Chief, you don't honestly believe this man could turn his life around just like that and become a responsible adult and a father, do you? A week ago, he was a raving lunatic, behaving more like an animal than a human because of his alcohol abuse. I implore you not to buy into this façade of emotion and let me have custody of Chester and Tyler. I will see to it that they get placed in a good home."

"What is your name, Ms?"

"Ms. Phillips, Margarite Phillips. I'm Chester and Tyler's government caseworker. The government has given me power to protect children from people like him."

Bill was disappointed but not shocked by her outburst. He had hoped what he felt for her had been mutual. But he knew all along that her career would come first in her life.

"The government has given us power too, over people like *you*," retorted Dorothy. "We have been given the right to appoint our own people as guardians of our children. Welcome to the twenty-first century, madam. Now sit down and keep quiet."

She grumbled and fumed but she held her peace and sat down.

"You're from the Kluskus band aren't you?" Dorothy questioned Teddy. "Are you planning to have Tyler and Chester live with you in Kluskus and complete their education by correspondence?"

"No, Madam Chief. I would like to buy Tilda's house and move my family to Nazko so they can continue to go to their own school."

"You realize it will take time to register with our band and have the sale of Tilda's house approved by the Office of Indian Affairs in Prince George. It could take months."

"I realize that."

"Do you also realize that your problem with alcohol will need time and counseling to overcome. It will take time to win the trust of your new family and this community. Their well-being is far more important to us than your good will, Ted."

"I realize that and I understand your reluctance to trust me. But I will do my best to win your confidence. Chester, I will do my best to be a father you can be proud of."

"And I will help you," stood Bill.

"Anyone here think Ted *shouldn't* be given an opportunity to prove that he can be a good father?" asked Dorothy grimacing at Margarite.

Nobody moved.

Embarrassed, Margarite shrunk down in her seat and pretended to look under the table for a dropped napkin.

"In the meantime," the chief continued, "is anyone willing to take care of the boys until their new family moves to Nazko?"

Rick, Natalie and Tonya, rose to their feet. Others soon followed. The roar of chairs sliding sideways became deafening. People began to shout, "We'll take them! They can come to our house."

When the commotion died down nobody was sitting. Everybody in Nazko wanted Chester and Tyler to live with them.

The End

*Take away our children and you take away our spirits.*
Roberta Headrick, Aboriginal Family Support Worker, Quesnel.

Printed in the United States
96090LV00002B/121-501/A

9 781604 771183